A GIFT OF LIFE

A GIFT OF LIFE

by
S. Rickly Christian

Here's Life Publishers

Published by
HERE'S LIFE PUBLISHERS, INC.
P. O. Box 1576
San Bernardino, CA 92402

Library of Congress Cataloging-in-Publication Data
Christian, S. Rickly (Scott Rickly)
A gift of life.
1. Krainert, Dan — Fiction. 2. Chambers, Lloyd —
Fiction. I. Title.
PS3553.H7284G5   1986   813'.54   86-9879
ISBN 0-89840-094-5

HLP Product No. 951053

FOR MORE INFORMATION, WRITE:

L.I.F.E. — P.O. Box A399, Sydney South 2000, Australia
Campus Crusade for Christ of Canada — Box 300, Vancouver, B.C. V6C 2X3, Canada
Campus Crusade for Christ — 103 Friar Street, Reading RG1 1EP, Berkshire, England
Lay Institute for Evangelism — P.O. Box 8786, Auckland 3, New Zealand
Great Commission Movement of Nigeria — P.O. Box 500, Jos, Plateau State Nigeria, West Africa
Life Ministry — P.O. Box/Bus 91015, Auckland Park 2006, Republic of South Africa
Campus Crusade for Christ International — Arrowhead Springs, San Bernardino, CA 92414, U.S.A.

To Stanford University's team of cardiopulmonary
specialists for its wholehearted indivisible
commitment to humanity,
and
to Dan for his faith and courageous spirit,
and
to Lloyd Paul Chambers* for his gift of life.

*Lloyd's name, home town, and relevant incidents in his life have been changed to protect the privacy of his family.

TABLE OF CONTENTS

I will give you a new heart and put a new
spirit in you; I will remove from you your
heart of stone and give you a heart of flesh.
Ezekiel 36:26, New International Version

Chapter One — DAN

THE INITIATION

A champagne mist, fragile as fine lace, drapes the sprawling, voluptuous hills which parallel a great unfenced park, otherwise known as Napa Valley. The lace-fog shields the morning sun as its first hesitant rays trickle down over the hillsides, flow into tributaries and rush at express speed to flood the valley with pools of amethyst light. A scattering of live oak, cinnamon-red manzanita and harvest-orange madrona trees stand knee-deep in shadows as thick and moist as a mountain lagoon. As the depths of light and darkness mingle, four high schoolers crammed together in the front seat of a dilapidated Chevy sedan rattle along the sleepy two-laner, racing the dawn for Dan Krainert's house in the valley.

It would have been easier for everybody had two of the youths merely jumped into the back seat. But there is no place to jump. The back seat is heaped with the detritus of teenage life — discarded fast food packaging, ripened gym clothes, props for the upcoming school play, crumpled magazines, candy wrappers and a bruised banana peel.

Charlie Hughes, tall and thin with an ax-blade beard, crouches forward, his hands taut on the steering wheel. He wears a conehead hat, a pair of Mickey Mouse ears flapping at the top. Like his three passengers, Charlie is clad in spark-

orange overalls emblazoned across the back with the name of Vintage High's exclusive drama fraternity: JOLLY ORANGE COMPANY.

Charlie peers out the windshield of his Chevy, watching the early morning shadows evaporate with the mist, while the lupine and poppy covered earth turns first plum blue, then pink and finally a hue as vivid and golden as a vintage Chardonnay. "Awesome morning," Charlie says, relaxing.

"Haven't been up this early since I was born," answers Mark Troedson, a tousle-haired six-footer who rides shotgun in his friend's rattletrap Chevy. "You sure Dan doesn't suspect anything?"

"No way." Charlie wiggles his Mickey Mouse ears.

Cranking down the window of the car, Mark eases his head outside but quickly draws back when the ears of his rabbit-head hat pummel his face. "You viciouth wabbit!" he snaps in his best Elmer Fudd imitation. Removing the hat, he slaps the fuzzy animal face with the back of his palm, then tucks the hat safely between his legs before he again sticks his head into the cutting wind. He stares back at the trunk, its mouth yawning wide around a giant empty crate, labeled *SPECIAL ORDER* and addressed to *VINTAGE HIGH SCHOOL LIBRARY*." Perched precariously, the box threatens to dislodge with every rut and bump as the car rumbles along. "Slow down, Charlie, or we'll lose our load," Mark warns.

Charlie Hughes shrugs at the speedometer, then glances into the rearview mirror — not to check the box, but to adjust his flight goggles. "Only doing 60," he says.

"In a 35 zone," Mark notes, struggling to crank the window back up. "But it's your insurance premium, not mine. I just care about the stupid box."

"Me, I just care about my hair," says Dee Dee Tate, a honey-blonde with full, bee-stung lips. She sits between the two young men and on the lap of Nicole Jotter, a curly brunette whose face is hidden behind a Ronald Reagan mask.

"Yeah, Mark, roll up the window," Nicole begs, shifting beneath her friend's weight. "And as for you, Dee Dee, scoot up a bit. You're squashing me."

"That any better?" Dee Dee asks, leaning forward, her tone nasal from her hooded Porky the Pig snout.

"Now you're grinding."

"How's this?"

"Forget it," Nicole grimaces. "We're almost there. And, Mark, roll up that stupid window."

"Careful of the window handle, Mark. It's loose," Charlie says.

"This whole junker's loose," Mark responds. "Everything in this heap's either busted or rusted."

"As long as it gets us to Dan Krainert's house."

"Mark, I'm freezing."

Mark slowly faces Nicole, flashing a leering grin. "I thought you were Charlie's girl, but . . . well, slide a little closer and — "

"The window, Sicko," Nicole says. "Raise it."

"Can't."

"Come on, crank, Mark."

"The handle won't turn."

They ride in silence for a few minutes, Charlie's foot heavy on the gas pedal. Bounding the road on either side of the Chevy are long rows of perfume-scented eucalyptus trees. The trees grow tall and twisted, their leaves dusted with a bluish fairy-powder, their shell-pink blossoms like delicate frost-stars, their trunks scarved with long trailing petticoats of bark. Beneath these fairy queen trees, mustard flowers are scattered like Hansel and Gretel crumbs catching the morning dew. The spring air blooms with the scent of growing things — a heavy bouquet of gardens and orchards, wine and roses. In the stirring breeze of dawn there is another aroma, the faint earthy smell of Herefords and Angus which feed beyond the manicured vineyards in this leisure valley where Robert Louis Stevenson lived and wrote, and across the hills from where Mark London found his Valley of the Moon. And along this same road, the four Vintage High drama students plan their strategy.

"How much farther to Dan's house?" Dee Dee asks.

"We're almost there. Hang on." Charlie makes a sudden turn into the residential area.

"Mark, get your randy paws off me!" Dee Dee barks.

"But Charlie said to hang on."

"Not to me, Idiot," she snaps, prying his arms loose from around her waist.

"Left!" Mark suddenly yells, looking up. "You missed the turn. Back up and hook a left back there. That's Dan's street."

"Idlewild? You sure?" asks Nicole.

"I'll whip a U."

"Dan will die when he finds what he's in for," Mark says. "And I'll die if it all goes according to plan."

"Dan's got it tame compared to my drama club initiation," declares Charlie. "On my first night out with the Orangies, they tied me to a chair on the back of a flatbed truck. Except I was only wearing a diaper, this little skimpy thing they made out of an old sheet."

The girls giggle.

"Stop laughing," Charlie says. "It was no joke."

"What happened, Charlie?" Mark urges.

"They pulled up to the Swensen's Ice Cream Factory across town, strung me up to a couple of poles — still in my diaper — and then these four guys ran me around inside Swensen's with that gong thing banging, siren wailing, and causing a royal racket." He grinned, savoring the memory. "That was bad enough, but then they crammed me in a huge box and dumped me off in the middle of the mall and then ditched me. When I crawled out, this security guy didn't know what to do, whether to arrest me or what. So I ducked out before he had time to make up his mind. I had to walk home wearing only a diaper. *That's* what you call an initiation."

"No," says Nicole, "that's what you call stoo-pid."

"OK, everybody. Shut up," Charlie hushes, nodding out the window. His eyes gleam. "That's Dan's place. That's his car parked out front. This will be one for the history books," he laughs, pulling to the curb fronting the gray tract home. "OK, grab the bag, the sheets and the rope. Also the M&Ms, just in case."

"What are the M&Ms for?" Nicole asks.

"Dan's dog."

"He's got a dog?" she asks anxiously.

"Yeah. An old fleabag — eats anything."

"People?" Dee Dee asks.

"M&Ms, I hope."

Dee Dee drags behind. "What time is it, Charlie?"

"Six-thirty."

Nicole frowns. "The house is still dark. I thought you cleared this with Dan's parents last week."

"Maybe they got the day mixed up. Or I might have said Thursday."

"What a ree-tard."

"Never mind. Let's get this over with," Charlie says, hopping out of the Chevy. The others trail him up the front drive to the porch. He grasps the knob of the screen door and gives it a gentle twist. The door is locked.

"Stoo-pid."

"Plan B, here we go." Charlie adjusts his tilting conehead hat, then proceeds quickly to the side gate where he is greeted by a barking, football-size black dog. The animal glowers, tail between its legs as it prepares to protect home turf. "Quick, Mark, lay out some M&Ms," Charlie orders.

Mark fumbles in his pockets for the packet, spills a handful of candy under the gate, and when the barking stops, the four Jolly Orangers promptly scale the fence and hurry to the back garage door.

Charlie tries the handle, but finding it locked reaches up through the doggy flap and springs the door from the inside. "OK," Charlie says quietly, "girls in the lead."

"We could come back tomorrow," suggests Nicole.

"Yeah, at least his parents will be expecting us then," Dee Dee whispers.

"Keep walking," Charlie says, prodding the girls into the garage and up the steps leading to the kitchen. Nicole reaches for the doorknob, her hand shaking.

Suddenly the dog bursts through the flap behind them. The animal wags its tail hesitantly. But then it goes limp and tucks beneath its compact body. Its lip curls. Charlie turns quickly and drops to his knees. The dog growls. Charlie approaches the animal on all fours. The dog's eyes glow hot as briquettes. Charlie's eyes bulge and his lip twitches menacingly. Suddenly he slaps his palm on the cold cement. "BOO!" he explodes. The dog springs into the air with a high-pitched whelp, spins 180 degrees, and bolts back through the doggy flap with a whimper. Laughing hard, Charlie rolls to his side on the garage floor.

"Shut up, Charlie!" Nicole hisses.

The dog is at the flap again. It loosens a machine-gun blast of barks. Mark quickly steps over and empties the remainder of the M&Ms outside. The mutt goes silent.

Nicole stands quietly, her ear against the kitchen door. She gives a thumbs-up and reaches for the knob. The handle turns, but the door cracks with a grating squeak.

"Hold it," Charlie says, turning away to rummage atop the garage workbench. He spots a familiar blue and yellow can on a nearby shelf, and hurries back with it to Nicole's side. "WD-40," he whispers, spraying the door hinges liberally. With a brimming smile, he hands the can to Nicole, plants a kiss on her masked lips and steps past her into the house. The door glides quietly open. He beckons the others to follow.

Inside the house, the four Orangers — clad respectively in a conehead topped with Mickey Mouse ears, Ronald Reagan mask, rabbit head and Porky the Pig snout — tiptoe single file through the kitchen, down the hallway and, without knocking, straight into Dan's bedroom.

Dan Krainert, 17, a junior at Vintage High, bolts upright in bed. A shock of sandy hair cascades over his forehead. He fumbles blindly for his wire-framed glasses and shoves them to the bridge of his nose.

"Grab him," Charlie orders.

Mark takes a flying leap, slams against the solid 170-pound Krainert, and sends him sprawling back onto his pillow. Dan grapples, clawing like a bear. His breaths are short, stunted; his thick neck pulsates. With a sudden jerk, Mark pins Dan's arms behind him and quickly wraps his wrists with duct tape.

Mark tosses the tape to Nicole and Dee Dee; they lunge against Dan's sturdy, kicking legs. Gritting their teeth, they finally succeed in binding his ankles. Charlie pulls something from the dresser drawer. Just as Dan prepares to scream, Charlie stuffs a gym sock into his open mouth.

Dan twists his head futilely back and forth, his glasses slipping down his nose. Charlie grins, grabs a comb and runs it carelessly through Dan's hair, parting it in the middle. He does a quick comb-through on the sparse sideburns growing wild to the tips of Dan's ears. He starts on the drooping mustache that hugs Dan's upper lip, but thinks better of it. Then Charlie courteously helps Dan with his glasses, pushing them back in place, steps aside and takes a deep bow.

"With humble regards and all due respect," he begins, "I Charlie Hughes, thespian at heart and member-in-good-standing of the often famous, though sometimes infamous Jolly Orange Company, would like to extend our corporate greeting on this bright April morning, and offer you the unparalleled opportunity this spring day to establish your calling, advertise your manhood, thoroughly embarrass yourself and otherwise join us as a fellow Orangie."

Dan squeezes his hazel eyes shut, moaning loudly.

"I take that to be your assent that we should proceed with your initiation," Charlie says, taking another low bow. With a graceful sweep of his hand, he extends his open palm at his side, "Ladies, the Magic Markers, please."

Nicole extracts three indelible pens from a crumpled brown bag and places them in Charlie's hand. With a muffled cough, Dan writhes in bed, kicking his taped legs furiously. Charlie nods to his companions. In a moment, Dan is pinned to his mattress. With a flourish, Charlie removes the caps from the pens. He glances at his watch, winces, and with quick determination, begins to tattoo Dan's arms, chest and face with green, black and blue indelible ink. Fifteen minutes later he steps back to admire his artwork.

"Let me do an angel," Nicole says. "I can do angels good."

"There's no place left," Charlie observes.

"His back."

Charlie hands her the marker, and she quickly pens a cherubic face with bright blue eyes, green wings and flowing black hair across Dan's back. Then Mark does his arm pits in green. Finally, Dee Dee takes a turn.

"The boy is like the Tin Man. He needs a heart," she says. Mark and Nicole hand over the markers. She shakes her head. "A heart has to be red." Reaching into her purse, she extracts a flat of lipstick. She pops the plastic lid and, with tiny lip brush, draws a bulbous red heart in the center of Dan's chest. Dan coughs again, his eyes bulging. His chest heaves, as if he's fighting for breath. He looks frightened, and his nostrils flare. Dee Dee asks for the black marker. Brandishing the pen like a rapier, she then pierces the lipstick heart with a long inked arrow.

"OK, girls, turn your heads," Charlie commands. Nicole and Dee Dee step into a corner, their backs to the bed. "Mark, keep his arms pinned; I'll take care of things south of the border." Charlie whips Dan's pajama bottoms down to his taped ankles, yanks the covers off the bed, and folds the top sheet in quarters. He then tucks the quartered sheet between Dan's legs, draws the corners up around his hips and ties the ends with two gigantic knots.

Suddenly the bedroom door bursts open. Dan's mother, Elizabeth Krainert, stands in the doorway in her bathrobe, her eyes wide. She takes one comprehending look and her mouth drops. Her hand flies to her mouth and she steps slowly backward, shaking sleep-tangled hair from her face.

"Let's go," Charlie snaps. "I'll take his feet, Mark'll get his head and arms, Dee Dee'll catch the doors, and Nicole, you make sure that stupid dog stays away."

"Say goodbye to your mother, Dan," Mark says, bracing himself to lift. Dan's comments, filtered by the sock in his mouth, are unintelligible. "That means he loves you," Mark says, winking over his shoulder at Mrs. Krainert as he and Charlie lug her son out of the bedroom, down the hallway and through the front door.

Outside, the sun sits atop the trees. The earlier mist has receded. At the curb Dee Dee opens the front door; Charlie and Mark temporarily lay Dan in the front seat. Then Charlie opens his trunk, pulls out the large crate and removes the lid.

Pausing to wipe a growing pool of sweat from beneath his tapered conehead, Charlie waves Mark over. "Got the hammer and nails?" he asks. Mark nods. Together they return to the front of the car, pull Dan out and carry him to the side of the pine crate. He writhes hard, but to no avail.

"From here on out, Dan," says Charlie, "the key is cooperation. You fight us on this next step and we'll have to hurt you. Or maybe your ugly dog."

Dan nods. Charlie motions to Nicole, who suddenly appears at Dan's side with a pair of scissors. She cuts the tape from his ankles and wrists. Dan promptly pulls the sock from his mouth. Charlie motions him into the box. Rolling his eyes, Dan takes a deep breath, exhales heavily and then steps inside. He eases himself down and curls like a cinnamon roll. A minute later, the lid is nailed shut and loaded back into the trunk of the car.

Mark and the girls scramble for the front seat. Charlie lags behind, instructing Dan in a low voice through an air hole in the top of the container. He reinforces the message one final time. "Remember," he says, "follow what I've said to the letter if you want to be an Orangie. And absolutely no noise upon delivery. The show starts once *they* open the lid. That's your cue, the opening curtain."

"You can't be serious!" Dan exclaims, his words punctuated by a light cough.

"Like I said, think of it as an opportunity."

"An opportunity to get kicked out of school?"

Charlie grunts.

"My reputation!" Dan pleads.

"This will establish it," says Charlie calmly. He steps around the car, slips into the front seat and eases into gear. Then he stomps the gas, laying a long trail of rubber down the road.

Mark checks out the window to see if Dan is still with them. The crate lists to one side. "What are you doing?" he brays, flashing Charlie the eye.

"Just giving Dan a day to remember. Something to tell his kids about someday."

At seven, the car rolls to the curb fronting Vintage High School. In a half hour, the now-deserted campus and parking lot will be like Disneyland on Labor Day. Charlie and Mark quickly lug the crate up the walkway and set it down in front of the administration office.

"Half hour 'til show time, Dan," says Charlie, knocking lightly on the box.

"Break a leg, Krainert," says Mark. And then the two of them move to a safe vantage point across the courtyard to await the arrival of Frank Silva, the school principal.

When Mr. Silva finally saunters up, he summons the janitor to haul the crate to the school library, which is occupied by twenty-five students who begin their school day by passing notes, reading teen magazines and catching up on their sleep.

"Let's keep it down," Mark Doroshenko, the librarian, snaps at two girls giggling in the corner. He's a Mr. Magoo look-alike with heavy jowls, squinty eyes and a long, bulbous nose. He wags a bony finger at a couple holding hands and whispering intently at a far table. "Uh, this is *not* the Love Boat. No public displays of affection in here," he says. His pronouncement is greeted with a chorus of hisses.

But the moment Mr. Doroshenko turns his attention back to the crate, where the janitor stands with a crowbar, the couple quickly embrace and share a kiss. The other students clap. Mr. Doroshenko spins around. His bat-wing eyebrows twitch as he flashes a squint-eyed warning from table to table. Every head bows. The only sound is that of yawns and turning pages. A dozen yellow Ticonderoga pencils scribble intently in notebooks.

Mr. Doroshenko nods to the janitor. He works the lid free and lifts it off without looking inside. The puzzled librarian steps closer, then gasps.

Dan gives him an embarrassed smile before popping out of the box in his bed-sheet diaper. Everybody is laughing now, and the librarian tries to shush the noise. Nobody listens. Mr. Doroshenko scolds Dan with his finger and starts to say something, but the words die in his throat.

Dan is standing on the counter now, flexing his muscles. He raises his hand for silence, then turns to face a homely girl sitting alone at the table nearest the counter, and drops to one knee. "How do I love thee?" he asks the girl. She looks down at the table. "Let me count the ways," Dan continues. "I love thee . . ."

When he is finished, he stands and bows, sweeping his hands before himself with a flourish. And then he jumps off the counter, and steps to the girl's side. He gets down on both knees and plants his lips on the girl's scuffed shoe. "Yes," he coos softly, "I love thee. . ." When he looks up, everybody but the girl is on their feet clapping. She remains seated, crying.

Dan shrugs at the girl and then glances toward the doorway where a huddle of Jolly Orangers whistle and caw. "More! More!" the Orangies shout. He turns back to the seated girl but finds another girl beside her — a knockout brunette, with dewy skin, a serious, sensitive face, high sculpted cheekbones and fiery dark eyes burnished like a fine piece of mahogany. She looks familiar to him. He remembers that radiant 100-watt dimple on her right cheek. History? English? She's in one of his classes, but he's not sure which.

The brunette hands a Kleenex to the girl at the table, and elbows Dan aside. "Just ignore him," she says, bending down to console the girl. "This school is full of jerks like him. Everything they do or say is at somebody else's expense. They don't have the mentality of a slug. So please, please don't cry. Don't take it personally. This creep and all his Orangie friends are . . . well, they're just a bunch of creeps. Please don't cry," she says, handing the girl another tissue. The brunette rises to face Dan, her eyes hot as coals. "You should be ashamed," she snaps.

Dan meets her burning gaze, his face puzzled. "I think I know you from somewhere," he offers.

Suddenly the librarian steps over. He squints hard at Dan. "If you would confine your thespian activities to the drama department stage, and kindly refrain from disrupting this library further, we'd all be obliged," he says.

Dan nods and moves quickly toward the door. Standing on the threshold, surrounded by the Jolly Orange troupe, he glances back over his shoulder at the girl he recognized. She looks up, her eyes still flashing fire. "We're in a class together or something," he shouts, and then disappears down the hall.

Later in the day, during lunch, Charlie Hughes leads the Jolly Orangers, with Dan in tow, into the school cafeteria. Dan protests at the entry by bracing his 5' 10" frame in the doorway but he concedes to peer pressure when Mark Troedson gives him a swift boot from behind.

"OK," Charlie commands the others, "let's round 'em up!"

They quickly gather eight empty chairs from the lunch tables and form them in a line. Each of the Orangies takes a seat and rolls up his sleeves. Charlie prods Dan in the ribs with a fork. Dan, who now wears his diaper as a toga, mounts one of the tables and, clanging two plates together like cymbals, beckons for quiet. The cafeteria is still. Two hundred heads turn to face him.

"LADIES AND GERMS!" he bellows across the crowded lunch room. "I'd like to WELcome you to the VINtage High CREWWW Classic. We pick up this athLETic telecast in MID-course, due to UNforeshadowed TECHnical difficulties. But in LANE ONE, as you can see, the VINtage High Crushers have a FIVE-boat lead over their CLOsest rivals!" he shouts. And with that, Dan jumps down, grabs a chair, and assumes the role of coxswain.

"Stroke!" Dan barks, clapping the plates against the sides of his lead chair. The other seven Orangies strain their backs, dipping imaginary oars, and scooting their chairs backward three feet. "Stroke!" he bellows. Students gather closer to see what the commotion is all about. "Stroke!" he yells again and again. Oars dip and chairs scoot as the rowers begin weaving between tables. "UP TWO!" he brays, urging for a higher stroke count. "Let's take it up! Come on, UP TWO!" Now the crewmen are really rowing. The chairs slide faster. "Let's go, sissies. The other boats are gaining! UP TWO MORE!" Students are now standing on tables. "Fifty yards!" Dan screams at the top of his lungs. "We're almost to the finish! DIG DEEP! UP TWO! EVERYTHING YOU GOT!" Students scramble to get out of the way. Dan bangs the plates louder and louder. "YOU'RE

ALMOST HOME FREE! DON'T QUIT NOW! FASTER! UP
TWO! WE'RE GOING FOR RECORD TIME! TAKE IT UP!
UNBELIEVABLE! KEEP IT UP! THE FINISH IS — "
    Suddenly, a flood of cold water hits Dan in the face. He
sputters to a stop, coughing hard. His toga is sopping. A large
puddle gathers at the base of his chair. He wipes the water
from his face and forces his eyes open. Everything is a blur.
His chest heaves with each forced breath. He blinks hard. And
then he sees her. Standing on a table above him with an empty
pitcher in her hand is the same girl who confronted him earlier
in the library, the brunette with the lone-star dimple.
    "You lose!" she cracks. There is a hint of a smile on her
lips as she steps slowly off the table. She sets the pitcher down
and turns toward the door.
    Dan jumps to his feet as she walks away. "Who *are* you?"
he yells. "I know you, I know I do! We're in a class or
something!"
    She ignores him.
    He grabs her shoulder and turns her around. "Who are
you?" he demands again. "And what's your problem? Why are
you so stinking uptight?"
    The girl pushes him away. When he reaches for her again,
she slaps him hard across the face and spins on her heels. Dan
stops in his tracks, momentarily stunned. He reaches to massage
his stinging cheek, struck with a growing sense of mystery,
more than indignity or disgrace. Shaking the water from his
hair, Dan watches her exit, straining his neck to catch a fleeting
glimpse as she disappears into the milling crowd outside. He
turns back to his laughing crew.
    "Nice legs," he says. He shrugs, forcing a smile, and
heads for his physical education class — an hour of calisthenics,
jogging and a three-inning softball slugout.
    The afternoon sun is blistering as Dan takes the easy
half-mile jog. Normally he runs near the front of the pack, but
today he forces each stride. The gravel field shimmers beneath
the mid-day heat. He slows his pace, letting others pass. Each
ray burns into his back like a shard of glass, and a knot of
pain pulses up his neck. He squeezes his eyes shut, but the

throbbing ache creeps higher. It swells into the base of his head, pounding as hard as his shoes on the gravel. He wipes the perspiration from his face with the back of his hand and peels off his drenched gym shirt. Some of the felt-tip tattoos on his body are running, and blood-red tributaries flow from the lipstick heart which is melting on his chest. Only the jet-black arrow which pierces the heart remains indelible.

"Hey, Tattoo Man!" huffs a friend, pulling alongside Dan and slapping him on the shoulder. "Great show in the library this morning. And heard all about the circus in the cafeteria," he laughs.

Dan looks over and nods as the friend breezes past. His mind fills with thoughts of the mystery girl with the deep radiant eyes. He tries again to place her, but his throbbing headache beats the thoughts away.

"You're bleeding, man!" another friend yells, taking a jab at Dan's red-stained ribs as he darts by.

Dan swabs the rivulets of lipstick clean with his T-shirt, smearing the heart into a big, red blob. And then he tries to pick up his pace, but his feet are leaden. Dan slows to a walk, his lungs heaving. He takes a few steps, but is doubled by a cough with roots deep in his chest.

"Three more laps!" the coach yells from the infield.

"Coach, I can't," Dan huffs, walking off the track. "My head, it's killing me. And this cough — the running only makes it worse."

"Want my suggestion? Quit smoking."

"Don't smoke."

"Sure."

"Got me a chest cold or something. Or maybe the air's bad. This heat is — "

"Second time this week, Krainert."

"Sorry, Coach, but — "

"Save the excuses, Krainert," he says. "I'll let you off again today, but this is it. Go hit the showers and scrub those cartoons off your body, hear?"

"Thanks, Coach. I don't know what — "

"One more thing, Krainert. If these headaches and hacking of yours continue, I want a note from a doctor. Else I'll have to drop your grade, hear? Can't have you skipping class every day."

Dan nods.

"Now get out of here — double time!" the coach barks as Dan lumbers away at a slow jog toward the locker room.

After showering, Dan changes into a pair of old sneakers and Levi 501s, purloined from the gym's lost-and-found closet, and a letterman's jacket borrowed from a friend. He knows his interpersonal communications teacher, who lost her sense of humor sometime back around the Vietnam War, would no sooner allow him into class wearing a toga than she would if he wore nothing at all. He checks his watch, and picks up his pace.

Heading down a crowded corridor, Dan high-hands his way through a group of friends, then stops momentarily when he hears his name being called. He spins around to face five Jolly Orangers who are sitting on a low wall with their shoes off, banging Coke cans together.

"Yo, Dan!" Charlie yells. "Took a vote at lunch, and you're in."

"Hey, great!" beams Dan.

"Got a couple extra cans here," Charlie says. "Come on over and help make music. Nobody's paying attention. They're all going to class."

"Sorry, but I'm one of them," Dan shouts. "And I'm late." With an apologetic wave, he ducks into the locker hall to pick up his books. Slamming his locker door, he sprints fifty yards toward the next building, whips around the corner and promptly smashes into another student. When he looks up, he shudders. It's her. The *mystery* girl. She is flat on her back, surrounded by books.

"Wouldn't you know it," she breathes, glaring up at Dan with scorching eyes.

He steps quickly to her side to offer his hand. She pushes it away and gets up without his help. Dan shrugs.

"You know, roller derby practice doesn't start for another two weeks," he says, bending down to pick up her books.

"I can get them," she says brusquely.

"We really must stop meeting like this," he says, gathering the last of her scattered texts. "It's becoming dangerous to one's health."

She holds her arms out for the books, but he does not return them. She shakes her head, walking away empty handed.

"Hey, what have I done to get you so riled?" he asks, falling into step beside her.

"Can I have my books?"

"What did I do?"

"You're rude. And inconsiderate. That girl — this morning in the library — she was crying because of you."

"That was just a silly — "

"To *you*, maybe. But to her it was like — "

"OK, OK. Calm down or you'll need CPR. So I'm occasionally rude and inconsiderate. A slob on my off days. But most of the time I'm all right. Really — you can ask my mom."

"Can I have my books?" she repeats, stopping at her locker. He hands them over one at a time, peering over her shoulder at other texts in her locker.

"I see you've got interpersonal communications. Who's your teacher — Old Hippie?"

She rolls her eyes, but remains silent.

"What period?"

"I'm in your class, jerk."

"Right now?" says Dan, bursting into a deep round of laughter. "This period? You know, this is wild! I *thought* you looked familiar. You sit toward the back, right?"

"Welcome back from your coma."

"Sure, sure now I remember. And your name starts with an S. It's all coming back. Susan? Sarah?" He pauses to think. "Sylvester? Scott? Help me out . . ."

"Whether you know my name is not — "

"Come on, be a sport. Shannon?"

"Shirley."

"Well, tell you what, Shirley," he says. "If it won't give you a heart attack, I'll walk you to class."

She slams her locker and heads down the hall to the right.

"No, this way — it's quicker. Less cross traffic."

She turns to follow him, a half-amused smile on her face.

"You know, I usually don't wear togas and diapers to class. I can see why you might think — *mistakenly* think — I'm rude . . . and inconsiderate . . . and impossible . . . a little strange, perhaps . . . maybe slightly demented . . ."

"Keep going. You're on a roll."

"Well, maybe I am some of these things some of the time, but not all of these things all of the time. And if . . ." he says, darting her a sideways glance. "And if — "

"If what?"

"If . . . well, I mean, if there'd be a chance you wouldn't mind going out sometime, I could prove that my mom isn't half wrong in her estimation of me."

"Forget it."

"Try me," he says. "There's a good pizza this weekend, and maybe we could grab a movie afterward."

"What?" Shirley asks.

Dan looks at her puzzled expression. "I mean, a good movie and afterward a pizza."

Shirley shakes her head no.

"Come on, at least give me a chance. Wait, I know. You don't like pizza?"

"No."

"You don't like movies?"

"No."

"Why then?"

"I don't like *you*."

"Come on, you haven't even talked to my mom," Dan protests as he dodges oncoming students. "At least give me a chance. A chance to prove I'm a regular Joe and all-around good guy. And if you won't give me that, at least give me your phone number."

Shirley shakes her head.

"You don't have to go out. Just answer the stupid phone if I call. We probably have a lot in common."

Shirley smiles, but again shakes her head.

"You have to give me the number quickly — we're almost to class."

"I'm sorry, but — "

"Please? I can be very persistent. If you don't give it to me, I can always just look it up."

"Good luck. It's unlisted."

"I know you want to give it to me. I can see it in your eyes. You may say no, but your eyes say yes, yes."

Shirley stops at the classroom. "This is a mistake, I know. I'll regret it in five minutes. But you can have it, Ben Hur, if you can remember it." He fumbles for a pen in his borrowed jacket, but to no avail. She dictates the number once.

"Thanks," Dan smiles, riveting the seven digits to his brain. He follows her toward the room, but stops just outside the doorway. "Just a second. Was that 4-1-6-7 or 6-1-4-7?" he asks.

Shirley smiles without answering, and steps quickly into the room.

"Feisty," Dan mumbles to himself, "but unbelievable legs." And then he turns around and walks smack into the wall.

Inside the classroom, the chairs are in a circle. Dan slips into a chair across from Shirley. The teacher, a holdover from the '60s, launches into a rambling discourse about her usual — the value of open communication. Students pass notes and whisper. All eyes are on the clock. A half-hour drags past, second by second. And then the teacher stops. She pauses for dramatic effect, but there has been no drama and everybody thinks somebody else is in trouble. Heads follow the teacher as she takes a step forward.

"The basis of interpersonal communication," she begins again, "is sharing. Sharing with each other one's failures, one's dreams, one's values. Being transparent enough to open up and talk about things that matter. Not necessarily the little everyday things, although don't get me wrong, those things are an important part of communication as well. But I'm talking now about sharing those things that matter. I mean, really matter."

Dan squeezes his eyes shut and battles a yawn.

And then the teacher turns to one student and, out of the blue, asks, "What's the most important thing in your life?" The student looks down at his feet.

"Please be honest," the teacher says.

The student looks out the window. Then he looks plaintively around at his other classmates.

"Honesty counts ten points," the teacher prods.

The student flashes a sheepish grin. "OK. Getting it on," he blurts.

The class erupts in laughter.

"How about you?" the teacher asks, turning to the girl next to him. "What's the most important thing in your life?"

"To get married and have a family."

The teacher moves around the circle with the same question. The students shoot back rapid-fire answers.

"Athletics."

"Cocaine."

"Friends."

"Friday night."

It's Dan's turn. "Glowworms," he says, drawing laughs.

"Playboy."

"Penthouse."

"My car."

"Graduating from this class."

The teacher turns to Shirley. She looks her square in the eye. "Jesus," she says.

Dan glances up suddenly. And then he buries his head in his hands.

"What's wrong?" asks the student next to him.

"Jesus!" he moans.

"Are you all right?"

Dan shakes his head.

"What's the matter?"

"Her," he says, nodding toward Shirley.

"Shirley Simpson? What's wrong with her?"

"The girl of my dreams," Dan sighs. "And it turns out she's some kind of religious fanatic."

Chapter Two — LLOYD

WANTED:
A FUTURE

Half a continent from Napa, California in the Ma-and-Pa prairie town of Stillwater, Oklahoma, the afternoon's last gasp of wind whips a tattered page of obituaries down the street. Like most small Midwestern towns, this nickel-and-dimer has seen a procession of years marked by corn blight and locusts and blizzards and dust storms and drought — a history as scuffed as Stillwater's clapboard homes which have dared to stand before the jawbone west wind. Elsewhere they may call the wind Mariah. Here they use much more earthy terms.

The piece of dry newsprint, torn from the local *Stillwater Journal* (a.k.a. the *Stillwater Urinal*), contains the death notice of a local, good-ol'-boy feedstore clerk and would-be renowned artist who, to some people's surprise and most people's horror, opened a vein and painted a self portrait from the puddle of his own blood. The AP wire gave the story a paragraph and a San Francisco gallery bid for the painting. But Mr. McGee, the dead clerk's old man, early one morning after his first smoke, resolutely splashed the canvas with tractor oil, tossed it into the incinerator and then slowly backed away, tears welling in his eyes for the first time in 25 years as his son's only claim to fame curled into the bleached sky in a gray haze of smoke and ash. And now, the clerk's pavement-pocked obit disappears in a cloud of exhaust and dust beneath the tires of his own low-gear funeral cortege. Headlights glow and tiny black flags wave solemn goodbyes from radio antennas as the procession moves down Main Street.

Suddenly a cry splits the stillness.

"Hey-o!" shouts Lloyd Chambers as the motorcade drags by. Chambers, a wiry 18-year-old with a mop of red hair, sits at the stoplight, gunning his Kawasaki, eager to sprint with the green.

"Hey-o," he yells again.

Somber, soft-spoken country folk turn their scorning gaze on this neighborhood kid with the lofty pipedreams — dreams that hit the dust as often as his motorcycle slams over the dusty backroads of Stillwater. Lloyd glares back at them with eyes as blue as the Oklahoma sky. He chomps his gum, lifts his defiant, freckled face to the sun and laughs cockily.

The light changes but Lloyd doesn't budge. The funeral cortege has right of way. As he waits his turn a wasp takes a droning pass at his tangle of red hair and a grasshopper on the curb springs straight into the air. Lloyd hunches low over his Kawasaki 400, catching the reflection of his "Ski Oklahoma" T-shirt in the cycle's hand-chromed gas tank. The waning sun glints off the silvery surface and flashes in the hollow of Lloyd's chiseled jaw. He combs his fingers through his fiery hair and eyes the traffic light. Unhelmeted, he wears on his head only a pair of made-in-Korea sunglasses, found in the parking lot of Moon-Lite Bowl the preceding week when he'd quit his job as a pin machine assistant.

Lloyd, of course, hadn't intended to quit. He merely wanted to discuss a private financial matter with his boss. But their conversation deteriorated from bad to worse almost as soon as it had begun.

"Hey-o, Mr. W!" Lloyd had said to his boss late that day near the end of his shift. "We need to talk."

Hal Weisberger, a ruddy six-footer with beady rooster eyes, flappy jowls and perpetually sore feet, hobbled across an empty lane and peered at Lloyd from behind low-slung hornrims. "You got that look in your eye again, kid. The answer's no."

"How's the family, Mr. W?"

"The answer's no."

"How's your feet — still hurting?"

"Goldarn these hangnails!" Weisberger groused, shifting painfully on his feet. "Kid, the answer's no. Period. Kapoot. Final. No. No. No. Now, get back to work. The pins are jamming on seven. Get yourself some oil and loosen up them gears."

"Mr. W, please just listen to me. Just give me a minute."

"I don't got a minute. Now, get."

"I need more money. Not much. Maybe just a quarter an hour."

Weisberger squinted hard. "You lost your friggin' mind, kid? You on drugs or something?"

"I ought to at least be getting minimum, I think."

"You *think*? What you be thinking ain't no concern of mine. I got a business to run."

"And I've got a life to live. And I can't live it on two seventy-five an hour. Come on Mr. W, have a heart. I been slaving here going on four months now. And slaving hard . . . below scale. I ain't asking for a promotion or insurance or free bowling or food or nothing. Just to be brought up to minimum. I'm only talking about a lousy quarter more per hour. After all . . . I mean, it's the law."

"Don't hark unto me 'bout the law, kid," Weisberger huffed, scowling at Lloyd. "Goldarn these feet! And goldarn you. Now I said to get back to your job. So, get. Otherwise you won't have yourself no job."

"But minimum — "

"Minimum cinnamon! What do you think this is, Tulsa or something? Kid, you're living in Stillwater, Oklahoma. And I ain't running no bank."

Lloyd glared at his reflection in the man's glasses. "The law's the law, here or there."

"Goldarn, kid, ain't you been reading the newspaper?"

"If I could afford it, maybe I would."

"Well, there's a recession going on. A borderline depression. And people are hungry for work — any work they can get their friggin' hands on. Goldarn, but the President's own son can't even find a job."

"My sincere sympathy," Lloyd droned, placing his hand over his heart. "We ought to send the poor little bimbo a card."

"Don't be badmouthing — "

"I'm serious. Or write his old man," Lloyd snapped, suddenly kicking a rack of pins. His ears burned and his eyes went wild. "Better yet, get on the phone and call the President. Call him collect. And tell him if it's work his kid wants, there's an opening here!" Grabbing his windbreaker, he stalked for the door.

"Don't quit on me now, kid. We got tourney tonight!"

"What the hay, stack the pins yourself," Lloyd yelled over his shoulder from the open doorway. By now, every lane was quiet. Every bowler's head was turned.

"I'm gonna have to fire you then!"

"Fire me?" Lloyd brayed. "That's a good one, 'cause I've already quit!"

"You're fired!" Weisberger barked. And then a throaty growl rose from a depth somewhere near his toes, and he bellowed like the best of the big-league umps calling a close one at home plate, "You're outa here!" He then spun around on his sore toes, spread his legs wide, hunched low, jabbed the air with his clenched fist and bellowed again and again at the top of his lungs, "You're outa here! You're outa here! You're outa here! You're outa here!"

Lloyd had never seen anything like it. He stood and stared for a long moment, then disappeared out the door. With a disgusted shake of his head, he crossed the shimmering parking lot and hopped on his motorcycle. Revving his bike into the power band, he slammed into gear and blasted into the street. His first stop: The 21st Amendment, where he invested his remaining cash in a case of Stroh's. And then he sped out of the lot and around the corner to Tastee Doughnuts where Marilyn Sparks, his high school sweetheart since the 10th grade, was getting off work.

"What are you doing here now?" Marilyn asked when he strode through the door. She leaned down on the counter, smiling.

"Never mind. Just punch out and let's split this rat hole."

Marilyn brushed powdered sugar from her hands. "Something's wrong, isn't it?"

Lloyd glanced away. "Come on. We'll talk later."

She tucked her coffee-splotched apron beneath the counter, and then walked toward the time clock. She studied her card for a moment, adding the hours in her head. Money was tight, and this would be a short week. Nevertheless, she resolutely inserted her card into the slot and punched out. "See ya later, Maggie," she called to the fat girl working the far end of the counter.

"Yeah," she nodded. "Be good."

"You, too." Marilyn winked at Lloyd and slipped her hand through the crook of his arm. "Where to?"

They stepped outside. Even in the early evening of early spring it was hot. "I don't know," Lloyd said. "Anywhere there's not people. Anywhere but around here."

"Want to take my car?"

"No, the bike."

Riding tandem, they headed for an outlying grove of blue spruce beyond the fairgrounds. She wrapped her arms tight around his waist. Through his jacket he could feel the comforting closeness of her body. The night was quiet and still. Lloyd pulled off the road, cut down a dirt trail and parked behind the largest of the trees. A jackrabbit darted from a nearby stand of bushes and cut a zig-zag path as if dodging its own moonlit shadow.

"Let's get drunk," Lloyd said. "I want to get totally blitzed. To forget. . ."

"Forget what?"

"Everything. To just go blanko. To wake up and not remember anything." He carried the case of beer behind a large granite boulder and slumped in a soft patch of grass.

"So tell me what's wrong," she said, easing down beside him. She reached over and ran her fingers through his red hair.

Lloyd said nothing. With his nail he picked a scab of lichen off the face of the rock.

"You got in a fight?"

"No."

"No?" she challenged.

"Well sort of."

"At work?"

"Yeah."

"You lost your job."

"I quit. Mr. W, the guy acts like Howard Hughes or something. As if a lousy quarter an hour is going to bankrupt him."

"And what about us?"

"Huh?"

"What about *us*? You know. How are we going to get married if you don't even have a job?"

"Before we get mental, let's get numb."

"No, Lloyd. Not again. You've got to think of us."

"OK, *us*. I'll think of *us*. Scientists are seeking a cure for thirst. And we're the guinea pigs," he said, popping a can.

A full-bodied chorus of crickets rose in the husky air as the moon perched atop the grandstands. The spring night hung heavy with the scent of little things growing as a litter of aluminum cans quickly grew. In the distance, the whistle of a train rose and fell. Lloyd turned to Marilyn. His eyes were heavy and slow to focus.

"You shoulda hurr the ol' man," slurred Lloyd after his eighth beer. "You wunna believe it — rye out inna open, gol-darning his feet ann me, ann sayn, 'Wheredee thinn this iss, Tulsa or summinn?' "

Lloyd flung his empty can at a battered spruce and reached for a another.

"Please, Lloyd," Marilyn said, placing her hand in his. "I get frightened when you drink this much."

"You shoulda seen the faces," he continued, ignoring her and popping another can. "People stopped doon whatever they were doon ann just stared like he was some loontic," he said, growing more agitated. "The ol' swine!" he grunted. "Well, goldarn yerseff, Misser W!" he bellowed at the bowling ball moon.

"Shhh!"

"Heeza biggess pig inna whole worl!" Lloyd yelled again. The crickets went silent.

"Shhh! You're braying so loud you'll get us arrested," Marilyn said, removing the can from his hand. "Let's think about something else. Let's think maybe about getting married," she purred, leaning her head on Lloyd's shoulder. She reached across, took his hand and kissed his fingers.

"Mmmm," Lloyd breathed. "You haff sugar everwhere." He stared at her unblemished white skin. Then he inched closer.

"It comes with the job," she said, brushing a bit of white powder from the neckline of her Tastee Doughnut uniform.

Lloyd kissed her neck. Her long brown hair, pinned atop her head like a cinnamon roll, was full of the aroma of crullers and cream puffs.

"You smell lie a doughnuh," he said, inhaling deeply. His fingers traced the smooth sweep of her collarbone and tickled the downy hollow behind her ear.

"Do I taste like a doughnut, too?" she giggled. He nuzzled her ear. Taking her chin in hand, he eased her face up into the moonlight and kissed her full on the lips. "Well?"

"You tase lie a chocluh eglair."

Marilyn smiled as he stroked her cheek and kissed the base of her throat. His fingers dropped lower and fumbled with her top button. She looked at him. He said nothing. His hands grew sweaty. He wiped his hands on his pants and tried again. But the button slipped in his fingers. His face was pressed against her hair, and he could smell nothing but doughnuts. He grabbed hold of the button. He was ready to pull it off. The evasive button again wriggled free. Lloyd could not understand what was happening.

"What's wrong?"

"You haff sweaty buttons."

Marilyn giggled. "Who ever heard of that?" And then she really started laughing.

"I canna undo it. Iss all wet," he grimaced.

"You poor drunk boy."

Lloyd looked up into her eyes with a crooked grin. And then he redoubled his efforts with increased determination. He stared hard at the button, which was now beginning to move. He blinked his eyes and reached for it. "Iss not only wet, but iss moving," he complained.

She locked her fingers around his neck and drew him close. "Forget the button," she said. Her warmth rose as Lloyd eased her back into the damp grass.

And then suddenly she went stiff. She screamed and pushed him away. Lloyd rolled to her side.

"I dinna mean a hurr you," he apologized, trying to focus his eyes. "Really. I dinna mean — "

She screamed again.

"Whassa matter?"

"Ants!" she wailed. "They're all over me!" She jumped to her feet, wildly brushing little red ants off her body. Lloyd laughed loud and hard.

"It's not funny!" Marilyn yelped. "And don't just sit there. Help me!"

Lloyd struggled to his knees, but toppled over. He lay in the grass, shaking and holding his side. "They thinn yerr a doughnuh," he snorted, breaking into a new round of laughter. "You shuh see yerrseff!"

She slapped her back as if it were aflame.

Lloyd rose slowly to his feet and stumbled over, still holding his side. "I doan thinn the anns ate mush," he said, bending closer to inspect her. With his palm he gave her a playful swipe. "There! Killt the sonnagun."

"Some help you are," Marilyn huffed. She batted Lloyd's head and turned around, examining herself for any stray ants that had survived the onslaught.

Lloyd took a hesitant step closer. He reached around from behind, embracing her waist. "I'll help eat what the anns leff behind," he offered.

"Don't!" Marilyn snapped, trying to pry his hands away. He held her tighter, pulling her close. "Stop!"

"I know advertisin wenn I see it," he said, planting warm kisses on her cheek. His breath was hot against her neck.

"You stink like beer."

"Shhh!" he said. "I'm busy."

"Come on, Lloyd, stop fooling around. I don't like this anymore. You're drunk, and I'm just a body to you."

"Shhh. You gotta wonnerful body." He pressed his lips hard against her own, and gently fingered the soft lines of her neck. "Mose wonnerful body at that." With his other hand he stroked the long expanse of her back. Marilyn squirmed, and whispered something Lloyd didn't quite hear. His fingers traced down her spine.

"Answer my question," Marilyn whispered.

"I dinna hear the queshun."

"I asked if you want to get married?"

"Yerr assing *me?*" Lloyd said, stopping cold.

"Well?"

"Well? Well. . .thassa verr good queshun. Serious, you really wann get married?"

Marilyn nodded.

"Jussa seconn," he said. He stepped over to the scarred old tree and rummaged amidst his pile of empty beer cans.

"Please, Lloyd. Don't drink any more."

"Ouch!" he yelled.

"What's wrong?"

"Cut my finner onna can."

"Don't bother with the cans," Marilyn whispered across the darkness. "Bother with me."

"I was juss genn you a rinn," he said, snatching a glinting tab of silver off the ground. And then he walked back to her side, lifted her hand to his lips and kissed it.

"A what?"

"If you wann be my wife, you need a rinn," he said, slipping the discarded pop top around her ring finger. "In sinness ann health, in good times ann bad, in . . . um, help me out. What comes ness?"

"Good times and bad — "

"Alreddy said that."

"For better and worse — "

"Yes, ferr bedder ann worse, till death do we. . ."

"Part."

"Right." Lloyd slipped his hand under the yawning gap of her uniform.

"No you don't!" Marilyn said, lifting his hand free.

"First we get married. With a real diamond."

Lloyd tried again.

"Uh uh. First a ring."

"Maybe you still haff anns in yerr panns," he cooed in her ear. "I'm juss tryinn help catch them."

"Bedder anns in my panns," she mimicked, "than hanns in my panns."

"I canna buy a dimonn withow a job," he tried to explain.

"If you want to get married, you've got to find a job. You've got to make something of your life, Lloyd. Enough of these two-bit jobs and part-time hours. And enough of these Friday nights at the fairgrounds. A real job, Lloyd. You need to get a real job."

"Can yerr old man help me fine sumthinn?"

"My *father*? You two haven't talked in months."

"Thass 'cause he dunna like me. I'm juss a high school dropout to him."

"It's not you he doesn't like. It's your drinking and everything."

"What the hay," he said shaking his head. "Gettin' blotto dunna hurt nuthinn. If you wanna know the truth, it *helps*."

"Helps what?"

"Clear the spider webs. Ann helps loosen yerr brain so you can juss haffa lil fun. Come on, drinn a few ann you'll see."

"Getting drunk isn't fun, Lloyd. It's just some temporary escape you're always running off to. But tomorrow you'll wake up with train whistles blowing in your head, and your life won't be any different. You'll have the same hassles, the same spider webs. . .and a hangover, too."

"Now yerr starn sounn lie my mother."

"Lloyd, you're just eighteen with your whole life ahead of you. And you've got so much potential. So much to give. But you've got this . . . this bug somewhere deep inside that keeps you — "

"If I got bugs, then why you wann marry me?"

"Because, you stupid fool," she said taking his head between her hands, "because I love you. And because I believe you can do something with your life."

"But I dunna know what that *sumthinn* iss. I juss dunna know. All I know iss two thinns. The firss," he said, pausing to lick his lips, "the firss iss that I dunna haff a job. Anna seconn is — " he said, squeezing his eyes shut and pursing his lips.

"Yes?"

"Anna seconn is that I sunnly feel verr verr. . .sick a my stomach."

Pausing now behind the Stillwater funeral motorcade, Lloyd grimaces at the memory of the inauspicious ending to his evening with Marilyn the week before: how she helped wipe his face off, walked to a nearby gas station and called for a taxi to take her home, and how he awoke the following morning, like always, with locomotives in his head. He vowed then never again to get drunk. Yet it wasn't that long ago that he'd vowed never to quit another job, and within a year he'd walked away from three: as a fry cook, parking lot attendant and, most recently, pin machine assistant at Moon-Lite Bowl.

Leaning low over his Kawasaki, Lloyd's left foot dances on the shift pedal, anticipating the green light. When it comes, he cracks the throttle, whips around the corner onto El Dorado Boulevard, and guns his gleaming motorcycle to 50 m.p.h. Wearing a pair of Levis and his sun-bleached T-shirt, he is soon hot on the tail of the McGee procession. Horns try to honk him away as they might a lazy dog nosing too close to traffic, but Lloyd simply beeps back as he weaves closer to the head of the funeral train.

Pulling even with the hearse, Lloyd motions to the attendant riding shotgun. The man's jaw twitches and his face goes red. But his piercing squint eyes remain fixed on some dusty point in the straight-ahead distance. Behind the hearse, slumped in the back seat of the limousine, the McGee sisters try to ignore the disturbance. But their old man glares out the window at Lloyd, and shakes his fist at him. Lloyd glares back at the

geezer, and then turns his attention back to the attendant in
the hearse.

"Hey-o, Padre! Roll down the window!" he shouts, drawing
no audible response. Lloyd pulls the clutch and snaps the
throttle. His throbbing engine screams, rattling the little plastic
Jesus on the dashboard of the hearse. The attendant's lip curls
like a snarling coyote's. "Hey-o, open the window! It's me!"
The man mumbles an apology to his companion, then turns
his cold-steel squinty eyes on Lloyd. His nose, tattooed with
a web of ruptured capillaries, wrinkles into a sneer as he cracks
the window an inch. Lloyd eases his bike closer.

"Hey-o, Dad! How's it going?" Lloyd shouts against the
wind. His father mouths silent curses through the pane. Angry
veins rise like earthworms from the temple of his balding head.
"I'll be home late for dinner tonight. Finally got me some job
interviews!" he yells. "Wanted you to be the first to know."

With that Lloyd darts around the hearse and races down
the dusty two-laner that fronts eroded brick buildings and
sag-faced shops. Standing on the corner with his expansion-band
wristwatch hiked to his elbow, Stillwater's one-armed barber
sweeps the day's accumulation of clippings from his shop.
Across the street sits the Marathon Service Station, fenced with
long rows of discarded tires. Lloyd whips a left at the church,
and careens past the cinder-block Wal-Mart, plastered with
day-glo green "SPECIAL OF THE WEEK" signs for electric
bug zappers that flash like Instamatics when struck by moths
and horseflies. Beyond the adjacent empty lot, a shaggy mongrel
sniffs a dandelion growing through a crack in the pavement,
and then gives a hind-leg salute to a hydrant.

Dusty clouds putter across the sky as Lloyd jerks his
wheel and slows to a stop in front of a low weatherbeaten
building, its stucco facade crumbling on the sidewalk. Shards
of sunlight glint off its double glass doors, lettered with extra
bold type: JOINT RECRUITING OFFICE. He swallows hard,
tugs up his faded denims and tries to smooth a wrinkle from
his "Ski Oklahoma" T-shirt. He paces back and forth close to
his cycle, then cramming his sunglasses in his back pocket,
he combs his hair with his fingers. "You know who loves ya,

Baby," he says to himself, and spits in the street for luck.

Inside the building, he is greeted by a picture of Ronald Reagan, smiling down from the wall fronting an American flag. A small-framed woman with a menopausal mustache sits at the front desk filing her nails to dagger points.

"May I help you?" she asks, with a toothy smile. On her desk is a litter of nail polish and cuticle picks and a photocopied placard reading: *I've been beaten, kicked, lied to, cursed at, swindled, taken advantage of and laughed at. But the only reason I hang around this crazy place is to see what happens next.*

"I'm not sure," Lloyd grunts, glancing around the reception area.

"Do you have an appointment with one of the recruiters?"

"Appointment?" he smiles nervously. "No, not really. I mean . . . I didn't know I needed one. I just wanted to talk with somebody on a kind of casual basis about the different programs and offers. I saw . . . you know, one of your commercials on TV the other night, and sort of thought — well, I was in the neighborhood and decided to stop by. The commercial mentioned some sort of cash bonus," he says, shifting on his feet as his voice trails off.

"Your recruiter will have the details," the woman says. "Which branch of the armed forces are you interested in?"

"The . . . uh, refresh my memory."

"Army, Navy, Air Force, Marines."

"Anything but the Army. I saw 'Private Benjamin. '"

The woman smiles. "That's Hollywood for you." She fingers a mole on her cheek and smiles again, looking as winsome as Bruce Springsteen in drag.

"So what happens now? Do I need to set up appointments or what? Maybe I could just take some brochures home with me — you know, some PR stuff about the different branches and special bonuses."

"Well, things are rather quiet today," she says, glancing at the clock. "Each of the four recruiters has an office down the hallway to the right. In fact, feel free to wander back and talk with all of them if you'd like."

"What time do you close?"

"About an hour."

"Thanks," Lloyd says halfheartedly, stepping around a large wicker basket sprouting a four-foot rubber plant. He reaches out to touch it.

"It's fake," the woman grunts without looking up.

Lloyd nods. And then, with hands buried in his pockets, he turns down the hall as the woman resumes work on her nails.

Lloyd stares at the first door on his right. Before he can knock, a John Wayne baritone beckons him in. He reaches for the knob, but the door swings wide and Lloyd stumbles across the threshold into a white panelled office.

"Hey-o," Lloyd says, forcing a polite smile.

The man eyes him, and then extends his hand. "Hey-o," he says. "Sergeant Eckle's the name."

"I think I'd, uh . . ."

"You want facts," the man says with a nod. "The straight scoop, the hard data about the Navy. That's why I'm here — to provide that information for you."

"So give it to me straight," Lloyd says. "What's the Swabs going to give me if I sign up. I'm possibly considering it, but first want to know what's in it for me."

"OK, sure. No bull. Everything out front. I can tell you're a bottom liner," the sergeant says, slapping Lloyd on the back. "We'll get along just fine."

"Well?"

"Relax. Sit down," he says, guiding Lloyd to a white naugahyde couch. Lloyd fingers a small hole in the armrest and looks up.

"Well, what's the bonus to join the Swabs?"

"A cup of International House Cafe Mocha for starters."

Handing Lloyd an insignia mug of coffee, the recruiter flashes a warm, understanding smile. "Young man, let me first explain that Navy life is not 'just a job.' It's an adventure. It's an exciting challenge — one that can take you around the world and show you new places. New people. And a new life.

"The best thing is that you'd be making good money. And keep in mind that we'd get you trained in a skill of your choosing, would take care of your meals, housing, medical and dental, and would even let you grow a mustache. Even the haircuts aren't too bad these days. We like to think of ourselves as the *Modern* Navy — nothing like the old war movies. Yet we still sound the same call to adventure that has brought sailors to the sea for generations," he says.

"That's what I was afraid of — the sea," Lloyd says. "You know, I've never been much good on boats," he explains. "I once even barfed on a paddleboat. And no telling what would happen to me on an aircraft carrier or submarine."

"We could get you shore duty anywhere in the world," the officer smiles, pointing out the wall posters of the ports of the world. "You name it — anywhere. From Pensacola to Guam, from Norfolk to the Philippines. With luck, even the Bahamas."

"Guam," Lloyd repeats politely. "Sounds great — for somebody else."

"Well, Club Med we're not, but — "

"Thanks anyway," Lloyd says, chugging his remaining coffee. He licks the rim of the cup, and then excuses himself, walks down the hallway and enters the domain of the Air Force.

The smiling, back-slapping recruiter, a clone of the first, guides Lloyd to a soft couch.

"Coffee?"

Lloyd shrugs.

"Cream and sugar?"

"Tequila if you've got it."

After several minutes of strained small talk, the Air Force officer launches straight into his pitch.

"Let's talk about potential," he says.

"Potential?" Lloyd asks.

"Potential in many people goes unrecognized, undeveloped and unused. And that's tragic," the man says. "Because when a person's potential is never developed, a terrible thing happens."

"What's that?" Lloyd stifles a yawn.

"Nothing. And that's just the point. *Nothing* happens. You see, the Air Force looks for potential. And we challenge people, people just like you, to explore and discover that potential in themselves," he says, flashing a gleaming smile. "Of course, we encourage young men like yourself to continue their education," he adds. "And then, with sheepskin in hand, to accept the challenges of modern technology, whether in fields such as aerospace avionics or electronic computer communications."

Lloyd rises to his feet, explaining to the smiling officer that he never graduated from high school and doesn't care to go back.

"As for avionics, I don't even know what you're talking about. And computers, I've never been into them — not even video games."

"Don't worry about that. We can — "

"Sorry, but I just don't think I'm smart enough for the Air Force," Lloyd says. "All I'm looking for is a bonus to sign up, and some sort of job — preferably one I can understand — so I can get married. The job you're talking about would take Einstein to figure."

"Please. Please, don't worry about that!" laughs the recruiter. "There is *another* Air Force, so to speak, for people like yourself — people with potential in other areas. But you know, computers think for you. Our jets these days practically fly themselves."

Lloyd waves him off, slips out the door and pokes his head inside the Army recruiting office.

"Coffee?" the recruiter chirps with a big smile.

"Uh, no thanks," says Lloyd. "I went to the movies and know all about the Army or the *New* Army — whatever you call it now. I just want to know where the restroom is."

Five minutes later, Lloyd quietly enters an open door, which is emblazoned across the front: *United States Marine Corps: The First to Fight.* Inside behind the desk sits the recruiting officer in dress blues, with the office receptionist in his lap. Neither acknowledges Lloyd's presence.

Lloyd coughs and knocks lightly on the door. Only then does the man look up. He pats the woman on the fanny as she rises slowly and leaves. "Give me five minutes," he says, smiling after her.

When she is gone, Lloyd shifts uneasily on his feet, and tries to break the silence. "Hey-o," he offers.

"Speak up," the man orders.

"How's it going?"

"Cut the crap, kid. What do you want?"

"I was just . . . well, thinking about maybe joining the military and was wondering what the Marines would give me to sign up."

"*Give* you?" the recruiter asks, struggling not to laugh. "Sit down," he snaps, without rising. Lloyd takes a seat in the metal folding chair in front of the desk, and immediately feels the glasses in his back pocket crack. "Young man, the Marines will give you nothing but free haircuts. You'll eat out of a can, hump a pack and sleep under the stars. Sure, you'll see the world — but from behind the sights of an M-16."

Lloyd swallows hard.

"That's giving it to you straight. Of course, the other recruiters up the hall make all sorts of promises to prospective recruits. And it's all a crock — the *Modern* Navy, the *New* Army, the *Other* Air Force. Son, your kid sister could join them and be promised the world in a champagne glass."

Lloyd takes a breath and sits up taller in the chair.

"My point is that *somebody* has to defend the country, and that's the job of the Corps. You'll get paid for doing that job, and be provided with basic amenities — the key word, of course, being *basic*. Also, keep in mind that not too many young men can cut it as Marines. Like the sign behind my desk says, we want only the few, the proud. Marines are tough bruisers. And if you're not a tough bruiser coming in, I'll personally guarantee you will be after eleven weeks of basic training." The officer pauses. He takes a cloth from his desk drawer and wipes a smudge from his brass buckle. "Any questions?"

"Well, I . . . yes, what time do you close?"

"Eighteen hundred hours — in fifteen minutes."

"I need some time to think," Lloyd says, reaching across the desk to shake the recruiter's bear paw. There's a knock on the door. Lloyd turns around. The receptionist pokes her head inside, and mouths something to the recruiter. He smiles, motioning her in.

"One more thing," the man says. "The Marines are in the business of turning boys into men. And the men of the Corps," he adds, winking at the woman, "know how to have fun."

The woman resumes her post in the officer's lap. Placing his arms around her, he darts a glance at Lloyd. "Anything else?"

Lloyd shakes his head.

"Then consider yourself dismissed," he commands.

Outside again, Lloyd paces in front of the double glass doors. Then he hops on his bike, revs the engine into the power band and darts down the street. He whips through traffic with one hand on the throttle, the other trying to fix his crushed sunglasses. Stopped at a light, he tosses the pieces to the street in disgust, whips a tire-burning U-turn in the face of oncoming traffic, and roars back toward 'he Marine recruiting office.

Chapter Three — DAN

MATTERS
OF HEART

Upon returning home from Vintage High, Dan Krainert retreats to his bedroom with a bag of Oreos and flops down on his bed beside the phone. The last four digits of Shirley Simpson's phone number, which she had given him earlier in the day, are a blur in his mind, and he can only hope that he has the four *right* digits. On a sheet of ruled paper, he lists all of the possible combinations: 4-1-6-7, 4-1-7-6, 4-6-1-7, 4-6-7-1 . . . . There are 24 possibilities. He picks up the receiver and begins dialing.

"Hi, is Shirley home?" he asks.

"Who?"

"Sorry. Wrong number."

After working the list for a half hour, Shirley answers. But it is the wrong Shirley. Finally, his mother kicks him off the phone. Later that evening after dinner he reaches the right Shirley.

"This is Ben Hur. Remember?"

"Ben who?"

"Hur. Also known as Dan Krainert."

"Oh, right. I figured you'd call."

"Yeah, well I just wanted to pick up where we left off."

"Where was that?"

"Where we were discussing my high standing on your list of jerks. I'd like to redeem myself."

"Once a jerk, always a jerk."

"Be serious, it was just a silly Jolly Orange initiation."

"Jolly Jerk initiation, if you ask me."

"That's not what I wanted to ask."

"No?"

"I'm calling because I wanted to ask . . . well, if you're not doing anything Friday, I'd — "

"I've got plans."

"Saturday?"

"Busy."

"How about Sunday?"

"Church."

"Right. After church then?"

"You can be persistent, can't you?"

"I'll make it easy. Just say yes this once, and if we don't fall madly in love, elope and start a family, I won't call again."

"Look, I don't want to hurt your feelings, but — "

"Don't sweat the feelings, 'cause I don't have any. Just say yes to Sunday night."

"I go to church twice. Morning and evening."

"OK, then after whatever you do there Sunday night. I'll pick you up wherever. Church. Your place. Name the place and time."

"What if I say no?"

"I know you want to say yes. I can hear it in your voice," Dan says.

An hour before his appointed departure on Sunday evening, Dan locks himself inside the bathroom and surveys the damage caused by a festering pimple that has erupted on the end of his nose.

"Rudolph, the red-nosed reindeer," he sings to himself in the mirror, "had a zit upon his nose. And all the other reindeer, laughed to see the pimple glow. . ." After camouflaging the damage with a tube of Clearasil, he stares hard in the mirror and, like an actor prepping for an important play, rehearses some lines he will use on Shirley later in the evening. But his reverie is suddenly interrupted by banging on the bathroom door.

"Open up," commands his older brother George. "Your face is beyond hope."

"I'll be out in a minute."

"That's what you said ten minutes ago."

"When you've got a date with the dream girl of Napa, it takes time to get things right," Dan says.

"What you need ain't time, but some 80-grit sandpaper and a quart of spackle for your nose. Or is this girl blind?"

"This girl loves me."

"With a honker like that, you'd better make sure it's real dark when you make your move. Or bring a grocery bag just in case."

Patting one final hair into place, Dan reluctantly unlocks the door. George barges in, takes one look at his brother's nose and bursts out laughing. "Do the girl a favor," he chides. "Take a bag."

"Fifteen minutes and I'll be sitting next to the girl of my dreams," Dan says, bumping George against the door frame on his way out. "You, on the other hand, would need a hamburger tied around your neck to even . . . get . . . a dog in the car." His words are suddenly forced, and Dan braces himself against the wall. "Everywhere I look, all I can see are white spots," he grimaces. "It's like it's snowing. And these headaches, they're killing me."

"What's wrong?" George asks, stepping to Dan's side as their father approaches from the end of the hallway.

"White spots everywhere. And pressure inside my head, like a vise squeezing my brain," Dan says, fumbling in the medicine cabinet for aspirin. He pops the container open and downs three capsules.

"You've been having a lot of these headaches lately," his father says. "Are you sick?"

"Just in love," says Dan. "There's a bug going around."

"You'd better get it checked out."

"There's no time in my schedule."

"I want you to make an appointment to see the doctor."
"Yeah? When? I've got school till 3. Drama rehearsals till 5:30. Grab a bite to eat, then off to work till 10. But let's talk about it later," says Dan, snatching his keys and darting for the door. "I'm already late to pick up Shirley."

Inside Lyons Restaurant on Napa's main drag, Dan eyes the waitress as she approaches the table with her pencil and pad.

"How's the chili tonight?" he asks, rubbing his head to help ease the lingering pressure. But as she begins to tell him, another item catches his eye. "I think, maybe, I'll order a BLT instead, with fries . . . except I always have that. What's the Chef's Special?" The woman eyes him coldly.

"Let me order," Shirley volunteers. "Fish and chips, please, with a root beer."

The waitress turns back to Dan. He surveys the menu a moment longer.

"Just make mine the same," he says.

When the waitress leaves, Dan glances at Shirley with a smile. She smiles back tentatively. Dan's eyes move toward the window. His fingers trace the rim of the empty cup. He looks down and turns it over.

"Cheap china," he says, without looking at Shirley. When he glances back up, her eyes catch his. Dan's fingers drum the table. He smiles again, trying to remember something to say. But when he finally opens his mouth, Shirley also begins to speak.

"Excuse me," he says.

"Go ahead," Shirley says.

"That's all right, you go ahead," he says. Forcing smiles, they both reach for their water glasses as if on cue.

"OK, let's cut it out and be normal," Shirley says.

"I rehearsed everything I was going to say for the first hour," Dan laughs. "But guess I've got opening night jitters."

"Yeah?"

He nods. "I had my doubts that you'd ever agree to go out."

"You caught me during a momentary lapse of good judgment."

"Well, I'm glad you lapsed. I guess I didn't want to live my entire life with you thinking I'm El Jerko. The toga and tattoo thing was really no big deal. And without the diaper, I'm just your regular high school junior."

Shirley raises her eyebrows.

"Really. I mean . . . I'm 17. I drive a Datsun. I've got a dumb little dog. I do mostly B's — some C's — in school. I'm not so hot in Spanish but always ace drama. In fact, I've got the lead in "Ten Little Indians' this spring. You've heard of bag ladies? Well, I'm a bagboy — at the grocery. I work evenings, and my boss is a tyrant. Oh yeah, and my shoe size is 9½."

"How about family?"

"I've got one. Mom, Dad and brother. The whole nine yards. Grandma, too. My brother, he's a typical big brother type. Works as a painter, but works pretty hard trying to bug me, too. As for my dad, he drives a truck for Colombo French bread. Mom, she works at Bank of America. And that's about it. Not exactly the Waltons, but we get along. How about you?"

"Just me and my mom. My sister moved out, and my dad died in a trucking accident when I was twelve." She seems suddenly fragile, vulnerable.

"I'm sorry," Dan says, fumbling with his spoon. "She remarry?"

"A couple of years later. But then the guy she married, he and my brother were both killed in an accident similar to my dad's."

Dan shakes his head.

"It got to the point that every few years I expected another tragedy, somebody else to die. I thought my mom or sister would be next, because they were all I had. But if it came to them, I asked God that it would be me instead. I would rather die than to go through it all again. You know, the phone call, funeral arrangements, all the food and hugs and visits from friends and relatives, who pretty much ignore you after the first week or so. And when that happens and you've cried yourself dry, then all you've got is this intense loneliness. And you just lay in bed, trying to stare down the ceiling and wondering who's going to be next." Her voice is calm, controlled, but her wide dark eyes register pain.

"I've never even been to a funeral."

"That probably explains why we're so different."

"What do you mean?"

"I mean death changes you. You can't live constantly in its shadow and not be different. Me, I'm more serious than anybody I know. Anybody. And that's probably why I have a hard time with the high school stuff — you know, the silliness, the games, the — "

"The togas?"

"That, too. You and your friends with those pumpkin overalls probably have a lot of fun, but sometimes your laughs are at others' expense. Like the other day. To you it was funny, but the poor girl in the library . . ."

"Look, I'm sorry about everything you've gone through, but you've dumped on me since we met, and I'm hoping you're going to taper off sometime soon."

"I'm serious!"

"You're too serious, and that's your problem. You've got to lighten up a little. And I wish you'd quit your barking about — " Dan looks up suddenly as the waitress arrives with the orders. He drums his fingers impatiently on the table until she disappears around the corner, and then turns his attention back to Shirley. "Like I was saying, please quit the barking about what happened the other day in the library. For the five hundredth time, nothing was meant by it."

"That doesn't excuse you," she says, looking Dan square in the eyes. "I may need to lighten up, yes. But you — you need to be more sensitive."

"You want sensitive? I'll be sensitive," he says, reaching across the table to gently grasp her hand. "How's this?"

Shirley quickly pulls her hand free.

"If you won't let me touch you, let's at least declare a truce."

An unexpectedly warm smile crosses her face. She takes a bite of the fish, and looks up at Dan. "I didn't come here tonight with the intention of saying all of this," she says. "In fact, I normally don't talk about my past. But you've got me a little wound up. And because of who I am and where I've been, it's hard for me not to take everything seriously."

"That's hazardous to your health."

"It's not that I can't and don't have fun. I do. But when you spend half your life looking out the window of a hearse . . . I mean, a view like that changes your outlook. You might say it's sobered me up. And drawn me closer to God."

"If you still trust God after all you've been through, I'd recommend that you frisk Him next time He shows up on your doorstep," Dan says, smiling. "Actually, I'm curious about something. Without getting into a sermon, why are you drawn *to* God? Isn't that kind of masochistic? Didn't you ever feel paranoid — that you were next on His hit list? Or wonder, 'Why me?' 'Why my family?' "

"Of course. For months I cried myself to sleep every night, thinking that if it weren't for God, the tragedy wouldn't have happened. I never doubted His existence, though. It was just a matter of whether He truly was good, or whether He was some celestial maniac running around saying, 'Well, I think I'll have some fun today: I'll smash up those two cars on the freeway . . . give that baby a cleft palate . . . make that kid flunk algebra . . . give this woman a tumor and that man a hernia.' But for me, thinking of God in that sense just seemed kind of ridiculous after a while. He doesn't maintain a hit list, nor does He chase people around with a stick, waiting for the opportune time to bash them on the head."

"You're probably right. A *club* would be more like it."

"No, Dan. God doesn't cause hurt. Nor is suffering a specific punishment by Him — an attempt to get even for some wrong committed. But a lot of people, they try to explain suffering just that way, in terms of cause and effect. That is, 'You must have done something to deserve this,' or 'None of this would have happened if you were just a little more Christian . . . or prayed a little more.' Or they think God doesn't really give a rip about pain — that He sort of sits idly by, working on His tan by the pool while everybody else is thrashing around trying to keep from drowning."

"That may be, but you haven't answered the question *why*. Why doesn't God jump into the pool more often and pull the drowning people to the edge, so to speak? In your case, why didn't He cut you some slack?"

"Dan, there's a lot about God we don't know. And trying to explain the kinds of things we want explained is like trying to present the theory of relativity to a garden slug. Maybe I'm a little like the slug, in that I don't understand a lot about the theory of relativity. But I've seen enough to know, to *really* know there's an "Einstein" out there; one worthy of worship.

"I'm convinced God takes our suffering personally. In the Bible, Christ's reaction was not much different from our own. When His best friend Lazarus died, He wept. When He met somebody in pain, He suffered with them. And when asked, He healed them. When He faced His own death, He shuddered. Three times He begged God for a way around it, and when He was finally hanging from the cross He cried out, 'My God, my God, why have You forsaken me?' *Forsaken*? Not really. The Bible says He could have called on a legion of angels to pull Him off the cross."

"You're really up on this," Dan says.

She nods. "His suffering was the cost of our forgiveness. There was a purpose for it. And I guess what I'm trying to say is that there is also a purpose in our human suffering, even if we don't understand it at the time. Pain is redemptive — it strengthens us."

"You sound like my coach. 'No pain, no gain.'"

"I hope I don't sound preachy." Shirley says, pausing to weigh her words. "I really don't want to."

"I thought you were warming up for an altar call," Dan says. "But don't worry about it. While I haven't experienced the kind of suffering you've faced and all the funerals and deaths, I have had my moments."

"What's that?"

Dan hesitates, then says, "I was born with heart disease — congestive cardiomyopathy with secondary mitral regurgitation — doctor's lingo for an incurable heart, with a leaky valve. They didn't give me even a year to live. I was taking strong drugs like Digitalis from birth on, and weighed only seventeen pounds on my first birthday. But I suddenly started gaining weight, and before long I was bigger than the other kids. It seemed like some kind of miracle. I mean, every game in Little League I slammed one over the fence. And by the time I was eleven, doctors decided they had misdiagnosed me as an infant. So they took me off the heart pills, and I haven't really had any problems since."

He pauses, wondering how much to say, then adds, "But I still sometimes wonder — about my heart . . . and, yeah OK, about God. I always kind of believed He had a purpose for my life — like playing major league ball. Acting, maybe. *Something*, but I've never been really sure what that something was. But even though I pretty much thought God was real, it never seemed that way in church. I still go with my parents and all, but the place pretty much seems empty, even when it's full, if you know what I mean. The priest, he always sounds like he's reciting from an encyclopedia or something. So going to church has always been like sitting in a boring history lecture. I don't know, maybe I keep going because they serve doughnuts afterward," he says, laughing.

"Why don't you come with me sometime?" Shirley asks.

"We'll see," Dan shrugs. He looks up at Shirley. "You know, you *are* different. But in a good way. Kind of . . . not feisty, but certainly . . . what's a good word?"

"Big-mouthed."

"No, frank. You feel a certain way about things, you believe certain things, and . . . you stick to your guns. I like that about you."

"Except when I stick to my guns and call you a jerk."

"Right. That's the exception."

Shirley smiles. "Come on, let's get out of here," she says. "Are you done with your plate?"

"I mean that. I like your honesty. I've never been able to talk about these kinds of things with anybody else."

"Come on, pay the bill," she says, gathering her jacket and purse.

Outside in the thick night air, Dan's uncooperative sandy hair becomes as unruly as a tumbleweed with the first gust of wind. Brushing it from his forehead, he and Shirley stroll quietly along the cobblestone walkway of the downtown Napa Plaza. A full moon hangs low in the sky, and a light mist drapes the banks of the nearby river. Taking the lead, Dan heads down toward the water, sidestepping a drunk old woman who burps with each staggering step and mumbles something about Harry Truman in between. Leaning over the railing of a footbridge, Dan watches their shimmering reflection in the water.

"You know, I'm glad you agreed to go out," he says. "I know you had your doubts about me."

"That's an understatement," she says, picking a sliver of wood on the handrail.

"I don't want to be presumptuous, but we could probably hit it off. And I was just thinking how great it would be if we. . .you know, saw more of each other. Maybe even started going together." He holds his breath expectantly, and then casually drapes his arm around her shoulder. "I really enjoy being with you."

But Shirley steps out from beneath his arm.

"We'd do OK as a couple. I know we would."

"This is our first time out," she laughs, "and you're suggesting we *go* together? On the basis of what? A $3.95 dinner and a talk about suffering? Be serious, Dan. I mean, if you like frankness, I'll be frank: Just a couple of days ago I slapped you, poured ice water over your head, and generally thought you were dirt."

"That was before we talked. Before we got to know each other. Before tonight."

"It will take more than tonight to change that."

"Just give me a chance, and I'll — " he tries again, but his efforts are interrupted by the old woman who stumbles up the bridge and retches over the railing across from them. "Oh gross," Dan scowls, leading Shirley away. "Let's get out of here."

"She needs help," Shirley says, turning back.

"Not ours."

"Nobody else is around."

"*Now* isn't the time to play Good Samaritan," Dan states. But Shirley ignores the comment and steps to the woman's side. She exchanges a few quiet words with the disheveled lady, links elbows, and then slowly ushers her past Dan.

"You can stay here if you want, but she needs help getting home. Says her husband beat her up."

"Smart move," Dan cracks sarcastically. "Take her back so he can pop her again."

"Like I said, you can stay or you can follow."

"*Just when I'm trying to make my move*," Dan mutters under his breath. He follows sluggishly. As they pass beneath a street lamp, the woman's matted hair glistens. Her overcoat is stained and from the ripped hem drags a spider web of thread. He shakes his head as Shirley leads the woman through the gate of a nearby apartment complex and up a rickety flight of stairs. "I'll wait here," he says, shoving his hands in his pockets and turning his back to a sudden gust of wind. "No sense in us all getting beat up."

Ten minutes later, Shirley reappears. Silently, they walk back toward the car.

"Was her old man home?" Dan finally asks as they head down the darkened street.

Shirley shakes her head.

"I would have come up if there was trouble."

"Of course."

"Really."

"You're bothered that I helped the woman, aren't you?" Shirley asks.

Dan shrugs. "Maybe not, but the timing could have been better. We were talking about pretty personal things."

Shirley rolls her eyes. "We simply look at life differently," she explains. "As far as I can tell, we're a world apart."

"You act like I'm E.T. or something," he says, trying again to put his arm around her.

"Sometimes I wonder," she says, peeling his hand off her shoulder. "I mean, you seem like some kind of alien being by the way you're coming on to me. And now . . . ." Her voice trails off. "I can't figure you out. I don't know, maybe if you go home and take a cold shower this mood of yours will pass."

"Highly unlikely."

"Dan, relationships simply take time to develop — if they
ever do. But you act like I'm instant rice or something, and
can be had in a minute. Tonight was simply a starting point.
Maybe there will be another time, maybe there won't. But
please don't throw yourself at me the first time we go out."

"At least think about it."

"There's nothing to think about."

"Please."

Shirley stops suddenly on the sidewalk, cocks her head
momentarily, then resumes her stride. "OK, I've thought about
it. The answer is no."

"Over the weekend, I mean."

"You're outrageous! Maybe you are from another planet
after all," she laughs.

The following week at school, Shirley catches up with
Dan in the locker hall and asks how his preparation for the
spring play is coming.

"The hardest part is the lines. Take this one, for example," he says, turning to face her. "Have you decided whether
you'll go with me?"

Shirley heaves a sigh.

"I'm going to keep asking until you give me a definite
answer. You could spare yourself the trouble by just saying yes
now, you know."

"Where are you headed?" she asks, trying to change the
subject.

"Drama. How about you?"

"Free period."

"Bring your books to the Little Theatre," he suggests.
"We'll be doing a few practice scenes later in the period, and
I can use the support."

"Sounds better than hanging out in the cafeteria," she
answers, trying to hide a grin as she falls into step beside him.

Inside the theater, half the stage lights are on. Dan points
Shirley toward the center bank of seats, and then disappears
behind the musty curtain.

"Yo, Dan," Charlie calls out. "Grab a script, find a chair and let's get rolling. Mr. Payne wants to go over the second part of scene one in twenty minutes."

Dan slumps down in an easy chair in the backstage shadows, rubbing his temples briskly as he reviews his lines. But suddenly the script drops to the floor and he breaks into a round of heavy coughing. Pulling a small bottle of Vicks from his jeans, he takes a quick swig when the class flirt wanders over and plops down in his lap.

"I know a better cure for that cough of yours," she breathes, draping her arms around his neck.

"What's that?" he winks playfully.

Teasing his neck with her fingers, she leans down and plants a passionate kiss on his lips. As she opens her eyes, Dan goes white. Her quizzical look turns somber as fear flashes across his face. He clenches his jaw and tries to massage away the pains that shoot down the underside of his arms and blaze across his chest.

"Please get off," he tells the girl. She jumps to her feet, yelling for the teacher.

"Try to stand up," Mr. Payne says, knocking two chairs over as he rushes to Dan's side. He motions the girl away. "You, go summon the school nurse." Standing over Dan, he kneads his gray, Solzhenitsyn beard that hangs from his chin like a clump of steel wool. His sad, gray eyes are glued to Dan's, watching for a glimmer, a sign that the pain has passed. "Try to stand up," he says again. "Or would you rather just sit? Maybe you'd better just stay where you are."

"Let me try to get up," Dan grunts, squeezing his eyes shut.

"Not by yourself. Let me help you," the teacher says, grasping him by the elbow. "Take even, steady breaths. Nice and steady. That's it, don't force it."

Dan rises, and takes a few hesitant steps toward the curtain. "The pain, it came out of nowhere. And then it alternates with stiffness. My arms feel like lead," Dan grimaces, massaging his right arm and kneading the muscles of his chest.

"Better?" Mr. Payne asks.

Dan nods, takes a few more steps, and parts the curtain.
He drapes it around his head, and forces a smile down at Shirley.
"What's all the commotion?" she asks, her eyes darting
back and forth like a scared bird's. "What's wrong? Something's
wrong, isn't it?"
"Nothing," he says. "Just part of the rehearsal." He lets
go of the curtain and turns back to the stage.
"Walk around a little," Mr. Payne says. "How's things
now?"
"I'm seeing white spots again." Dan drops back into the
chair, his neck taut. Veins rise in his neck. "No," he grimaces.
"No, no. The pressure . . . I've got to stand. It's all over my
chest." His fingers claw the upholstery of the armrest as he
struggles to his feet.
"My arm, Dan! Take my arm!" his teacher says. "That's
it, real slow. Up on your feet, that's right."
"Something's wrong," Dan says, squeezing the words out.
"Slow, even breaths. Keep them real slow and even."
"It's like somebody was sitting on my chest."
"Just stay on your feet then. Take a few steps."
"It's better now."
"Good. Breathe in, slow and deep. That's it, relax."
Dan releases his grip on Mr. Payne's arm and walks a
small tight circle around the chair. "Scared myself there for a
minute," Dan says. "Thought I was a goner." He glances up
at his teacher with a sheepish grin just as the backstage door
bursts open. A substitute school nurse, carrying a green-plaid
blanket, mounts the steps and huffs across the stage. Mr. Payne
nods at Dan. She rushes to his side and drapes the blanket
over his shoulders. "There, there," she says. "Where does it
hurt?"
"It doesn't anymore," Dan says, trying to wriggle from
beneath the blanket. "But I feel all stiff."
"Chest pains," Mr. Payne interjects, fingering his long,
wiry beard.
The nurse frowns.
"I'm fine," Dan says. "Really."

"You had chest pains?" she asks, her eyes darting back and forth between Dan and his teacher. Other students gather around in a circle.

"Break it up," Mr. Payne says, motioning them away. "This isn't a car wreck."

"Well?" the nurse asks.

"The pain's all gone now. It was just kind of a sudden thing. Hit and run, you know. But now that I'm on my feet I feel fine."

"Any kind of pain is a warning signal," she says. "Like a flashing yellow light. Sometimes the pains mean a real problem. You fall and break your leg; you get help fast. Other times, the pains are dull and sort of nonspecific, as with the flu or a bad cold. And then there are those times when you bend over the wrong way, and you get a zinger up your spine, like somebody hit you with a sledgehammer . . . ."

"Tell her about the white spots, Dan," his teacher says.

"I've been having these headaches," he shrugs. "But like I said, everything's OK now." He pulls the blanket off his shoulders and hands it back to the nurse.

"Just in case, young man, come down to the office, and we'll have a quick once-over."

Taking his arm, she leads him out the back door, down the steps and across the courtyard to the office. Inside, she listens to his heart, takes his temperature, and checks his ears and throat.

"This is silly," Dan says. "I really feel OK, now. I've got to get back to class."

"Young man, I don't think you should go back to class," she says.

"Why?" Dan asks. "What did you find?"

"Nothing. You didn't even have a temperature."

"Good. So I can go back to class then? My girl friend will be . . . actually she's not my girl friend quite yet, but she'll be wondering about me."

"Take these aspirin first," the nurse says, handing Dan two tablets and a small glass of water. "But I want you home right after school. There's been a lot of bugs in the air. So I want you to go straight home, hop into bed with a bowl of chicken soup, and *stay* in bed until Monday."

"Until Monday?" Dan objects. "But I — "

"You can't ignore these warning signals," she says, giving him a grandma pat on the shoulder. "Take my word, Dear. Rest is what you need most."

SEMPER FIDELIS

In the dining room of Lloyd Chamber's home in Stillwater, Oklahoma, the table is set for three, though only his parents are eating. A Coca-Cola lampshade with green tassels, purchased to enhance the atmosphere for Thursday night poker games, hangs low, tinting the meal with subtle shades of red and green until it resembles the molded plastic food found in department store refrigerators.

"That lousy kid," his father says, stuffing his mouth with meatloaf and jabbing his fork toward the empty place setting. "He busted up a funeral procession and darn near got me fired. And what for? Just to say he'd be late for dinner! I oughta clean his plow but good — kick his fanny right outa this house. Saints alive! He raced right up to the hearse on that cursed cycle of his and shouted to me through the window, if you can imagine."

"The poor family," his mother says, staring sadly out the window. "That dear, dear family."

"They all nearly croaked right there — each of 'em," Mr. Chambers continues. "You shoulda seen their faces and heard — pass the potatoes — shoulda heard 'em talk afterward, bad-mouthing the mortuary and all. And who's to blame 'em? If

it was my family in the box and something like that happened,
I'd be making me some evening news."

"He's really not a bad boy," his mother says. "Not in his
heart of hearts."

"Thing of it is, with a haircut and a decent suit the kid
could make a mediocre mortician himself. Not a great one,
mind you, because he don't know how to behave around civilized
people. But he could make a living at it, which is a far cry
from what he's doing now, which is nothing. Nothing but freeloading, that is. But he's throwing away a solid future, not to
mention wrecking mine, by blasting around town on that grease
bike of his."

"I imagine jaws are flapping all over town by now," Mrs.
Chambers says. "God knows what they're saying."

Her husband grunts loudly, and pops a beer. "*I* know what
they're saying. And I'm going to get in Big — capital B —
trouble if Mr. Hell's Angel doesn't shape up . . . or else ship
out of town to California or someplace. Someplace with a
bunch of freeloading weirdos where he'd fit right in. You know
what I mean?"

"I remember when he was a baby — how he'd crawl into
bed with us," Mrs. Chambers says, a far off look in her eyes.
"Remember how practically every morning he'd pull himself
up, and then hug us awake? He was such a happy, contented
baby. But now that he's not a baby, I'm afraid I really don't
understand — "

Suddenly Lloyd rounds the corner and strolls into the
kitchen. His mother looks up, covering her mouth.

"How long have you been standing there?" his father
demands.

Lloyd ignores the question and pulls a seat up to the
table. As he dishes up his plate, his mother tries to force
pleasantries.

"How did your day go, Dear?" she asks.

"Busted my sunglasses," Lloyd says, without looking up.

"See what I mean," his father retorts, glancing at his wife.

"Lloyd, your father and I were talking about how you
need to start thinking about your future."

"About getting a job, like everybody else's kid I know,"

his father corrects.

"You want me in the business," Lloyd comments dryly. "But we've talked about that a hundred times, and I haven't changed my mind."

"*Mind*? After today, I wonder if you've got a mind, let alone the ability to change it," his father snaps.

"The thought of embalming Okies the rest of my life spooks me good."

"Way I see it, you either get a job, or you're shipping outa here quick."

Lloyd looks up. "I got me a job."

"I'm talking about a real job."

"*And* I'm shipping out quick," he says, glancing over at his mom. "I joined the Marines."

"Lord o' mercy," his father chokes, spilling coffee in his lap. "You joined the *what*?"

The No Smoking sign flashes, and Lloyd cinches his seat belt tight as the United DC-10 jet screams to a landing at San Diego's Lindbergh International Airport. Lloyd checks his watch. One-twenty. He glances out the window, looking skyward. Everything is soot black. He searches for a moon, but finds none. Having been in the air just a bit more than two hours, it feels too soon to be in California. Oklahoma ought to be just over the horizon. Or closer. Maybe at the far end of the runway. He pulls the *Mainliner* magazine from the seatpocket and surveys the airline chart. He smiles. Oklahoma is 1,500 miles away. This is San Diego, not Stillwater. And that's just fine with Lloyd. He tries to think of the words to "California, Here I Come," but can't come up with the tune. And the song is not the same when sung to the music of "Yankee Doodle."

Marilyn flashes into his mind. He still sees her standing there by the plastic airport chairs in her best red dress, smiling and laughing, and then suddenly crying with the final boarding call. He thinks of her soft beauty, their kisses, the Friday nights at the fairgrounds and her sweaty buttons. The plane pulls to a stop at the terminal. Lloyd looks out the window again, quietly humming a Beach Boys' tune as the plane's engines shut off.

Waiting inside to meet Lloyd and dozens of other Midwestern enlistees are two women Marines, their dress uniforms pressed with razor-sharp creases. Lloyd signs a clipboard one of the women is carrying, and falls into file behind the others as they walk toward the baggage area, claim their luggage and board a Greyhound bus for the Marine Corps Recruit Training Depot in Point Loma.

The bus ride is silent. Lloyd stares out the window. San Diego passes silently by outside. Lloyd sits and watches. It feels too much like watching a travelogue on TV, with the sound turned off. He wonders for a moment how real it all is. But just for a moment, because the bus suddenly lurches around a corner and passes through the receiving gate to MCRD. The guards at the gate salute. The women Marines salute back. Waiting just inside the gate is another man in uniform. He looks more official than even the guards. The bus stops. The doors open. The women Marines get off. And then the man bursts aboard like the cutting edge of the North Wind.

"I'm your DI [Drill Instructor] and I've got some RULES," he blasts, as the doors close behind him. He looks around. His ears hug his head as if they have been stitched down. His face, lean and slim, looks like an anvil. "Rule number ONE. The FIRST word out your mouth be SIR. Rule number TWO. The last word out your mouth be SIR!" The bus moves ahead. "Not 'Sir,' but '*SIR!* '" His hawk eyes sweep from face to face, waiting for a response. The young men stare straight ahead. "Is that CLEAR?" he shouts. The young men nod. "Can't HEAR you," he grits. He is greeted by a chorus of mumbled acknowledgments. "Let me HEAR something! Blow it out!"

"Sir, yes, sir," the young men shout.

"LOUD, girls. With EMOTION!" "SIR! Yes, SIR!"

The bus pulls to a stop beside a set of 64 footprints, painted yellow on the pavement.

"You girls have 60 seconds to GIT you soft bodies OUT this bus onto the footprints!" he barks. "And 30 seconds have already passed! Now MOVE it! Let's GO!" The recruits stampede for the door. Lloyd slides open the window. He forces himself through the small opening, drops to the ground and then dashes to the footprints. He lines his feet up on the marks, and takes one long, very deep breath.

The DI steps slowly off the bus, and walks to the front of the group. He surveys the recruits for a long moment. He shakes his head and seems genuinely bothered. He begins moving through the ranks, his prowling eyes darting side to side. He stops to shove a pair of glasses higher onto the bridge of a recruit's nose.

"You're sweating, Spot," he says, stepping closer to examine a John-boy mole on the side of the recruit's face. "You're sweating like a girl, Spot," he repeats, "and we ain't EVEN started having FUN." The DI fingers the dime-sized mole, and shakes his head. His nose, unlike the rest of his pointed facial features, is thick and blunt, and is thrust into the young man's face like a boxing glove. Their heads are an inch apart. The recruit stares straight ahead. His glasses slide again, and the DI pushes them back up. "You like GAMES, Spot?" he asks. "That why you joined the Marines, for FUN and GAMES?"

"Sir?"

"I said, you like GAMES?"

"I guess," the recruit says.

"He *GUESSES!*" the DI laughs, turning around to face the others. "We're going to have some FUN and GAMES together. Eleven weeks of FUN and GAMES, girls. Going to give SPOT here something to SWEAT about. But FIRST we need to review some rules. You got a problem with RULES, Spot?"

"No, Sir."

"Review time, Spot. Rule number ONE. The FIRST word out your mouth be SIR! Rule number TWO. LAST word out be SIR! So let's back up, Spot. You got a problem with RULES?"

"No, Sir."

"FIRST word, Spot. *Salutations!*"

"Sir. No, Sir."

"Pump it UP, Spot."

"Sir! No, Sir!"

"*VOLUME!*"

"SIR! No, SIR!" the recruit screams. Lloyd darts a glance over. Even in the dark he can see the recruit's face shine red.

"Much better, Spot. I can tell we're going to have some FUN and GAMES, just the two of us."

"SIR! Yes, SIR!"

"Oooh, Spot! With a little practice you're a REAL polite girl," he smiles, pushing the recruit's glasses atop his nose before spinning around and walking to the front of the group.

"Welcome to the Marine Corps Recruit TRAINING Depot," he says, a smile returning to his lips. "It being 2 A.M., I know you girls are tired. But FIRST we're going to get your pretty hair cut, get you OUT of your dresses, issue you some RIFLES and other toys, and teach you some HOUSEkeeping." He paces back and forth like a wolf, his face poised between a snarl and a smile. "Maybe there will be time for some beauty rest before the FUN and GAMES start tomorrow. But maybe not. Any QUESTIONS?" He looks around. "NO? Then fall in behind this girl here," he says, jabbing his finger at Lloyd's chest. The DI pauses to fasten a missed button on Lloyd's shirt. "What's your name, girl?" he snaps.

"SIR! Lloyd Chambers, SIR!"

"Oooh lucky! Got a girl here's a QUICK learner. Well children, Miss Lloyd Chambers will be LINE leader. Now, you all GIT your faces in SINGLE file, and then we'll MARCH over to the beauty salon and GIT your little pony tails cut. *NOW! MOVE IT!*"

An hour and a half later, the newly-uniformed, bald-headed, rifle-toting group of recruits marches into their barracks for housekeeping instructions, followed by rigid bed-making lessons.

"Only TWO ways to make a bed," snaps the DI suddenly. "The WRONG way and the MARINE way!" He quickly demonstrates, and then gives the recruits 60 seconds to strip and remake their beds. Sheets and blankets whip the air like hurricanes. The DI strides quickly to Lloyd's bunk. Lloyd snaps to attention. The DI motions Lloyd away, and turns his attention to Lloyd's new bunkmate who is tangled within his bedsheets on the mattress. He is a gangling young man with a sharp, anteater nose and beady rooster eyes.

"You're not just SLOW, Private! You're also UGLY! And I don't like SLOW, UGLY recruits!" the DI bellows.

"What's your NAME, Private?"

"Sir! Harold Stankowitz, Sir!"

The DI thrusts his finger at Stankowitz's beaked nose. "What's that, STINKOwitz, a nose or a carrot? Anybody ever say you've got a vegetable face?"

"Of course not," he responds defensively, pushing the DI's finger away.

"Don't you TOUCH me, Boy! Don't you try HOLD my hand! What's your problem, you like boys? You a homo*SEX-UAL*?"

The recruit suddenly blanches. He glances around for support, but the other recruits are stone-faced.

"Answer me!"

"Don't be silly."

"*WHAT* you say?"

"Sir! No, Sir!"

"Is your MOMMA a whore, Stinko?"

"Sir! No, Sir!"

"Your DADDY got the clap?"

"Sir! No, Sir!"

"Then why you have VD of the BRAIN? I said you had 60 seconds to make your rack. Not 65. Not 62. But *60*! And it's VD brains like YOU that cause trouble for the whole platoon!" he yells, ripping the covers from Stankowitz's mattress. He orders 30 pushups from each recruit, and then commands them to again strip and remake their beds.

Bedsheets fly as the privates jump to action. When they finish, the DI walks to the doorway and waves. "Gotta go now, girls," he says. "Get your beauty rest, and I'll see you in the morning." He clicks the lights off and disappears outside as the black eastern sky begins to lighten.

"That's one mean bleep," says Bart Thompson, the recruit on the top bunk next to Lloyd. "He bleeping kept us up all night."

"What time is it?" Lloyd asks quietly.

"Almost five."

As dawn settles in, Lloyd hears muffled sobs coming from the bunk below.

"That you, Stinko?" Lloyd asks, but gets no response. "Hey, Stinko, you can't take the guy's guff seriously. Everything he says is just a head trip."

Stankowitz kicks the springs of Lloyd's mattress.

"Like water on a duck's back," Lloyd says. "Gotta shake it off."

Ten splendid minutes of sleep later, an amplified bugle blares reveille. The DI suddenly whips back through the barracks, banging the beds with a stick and blasting a whistle.

"Let's GO, girls! Everybody UP! Time for FUN and GAMES!" He strides up and down, blowing on his whistle. And then he stops near the foot of Lloyd's bunk and stares at an 8 x 10 mahogany picture frame propped atop the footlocker. He clears his throat loudly. "Oooh, lookie," he says, picking up the frame and pulling the family picture from beneath the glass. "The girls are homesick already!" Private Stankowitz eyes him nervously as he crawls out of bed. The DI looks up. Their eyes catch. The DI glances back and forth between the recruit and the picture. "Noses like that only run in ONE family," he says. "Let me guess, but this MUST belong to you, Stinko."

"Sir. Yes, Sir."

"Some fundaMENTAL etiquette!"

"Sir?" Stankowitz says, rubbing his eyes.

"Forgot to introduce me to your family." the DI says, smiling down at the picture. His smile withers to a frown. "And that hurts."

"Sir. Sorry, Sir."

"Being sorry does NOT take away the hurt, Stinko."

Stankowitz points down at the picture. "Sir. That's my father, mother, sister, and our two dogs."

"Can't tell which are the dogs, Stinko."

Stankowitz clenches his teeth. The side of his head pulses.

"Said I can't tell the DOGS!"

Stankowitz points at the two labradors in the foreground, and then tries to grab the picture.

"Where's your politeness, boy?" the DI asks calmly, holding the picture just beyond reach. He then folds the picture in half. Stankowitz looks away, his eyes glistening. When he looks back, his nostrils are flared. "Pictures of dogs," says the DI, folding the picture twice again, "belong in your wallet." He hands the folded glossy to Stankowitz, and turns his attention to the wall, where Lloyd has posted a snapshot of Marilyn, his Oklahoma girlfriend. Holding his nose, the DI removes the picture.

"Soo-ie! Soo-ie!" he calls. "Who's HOG is this?"

Lloyd steps forward. "Sir!" he says, snapping to attention. "That's my girl friend, Sir!"

"I asked whose *HOG* this is," snaps the DI. "With something THIS ugly, the flies must have to file a flight plan! Soo-ie, Private Chambers! This REALLY your hog?"

"Sir! Yes, Sir!" Lloyd says.

"She taking UGLY pills or what, boy?"

"Sir. Private don't know, Sir."

"Say what?"

"Sir! Private don't know, Sir!"

"She MUST be taking ugly pills. Or was she stinking BORN this way?"

"Sir! Private don't know, Sir!"

"You know what, boy? You're getting under my SKIN. Matter of FACT, I'm beginning to dislike you intensely. Get down there and give me 50 pushups!" the DI orders. Lloyd drops to the floor. With a pen, the DI writes across the top of the snapshot, HOG OF THE WEEK, and pins it on a bulletin board near the door. "Rule number THREE, children. All photos go here, or stay in your wallets. This is the United States Marine Corps, not summer camp!" He gives his whistle a long blast. "FUN and GAMES, in FIVE minutes. So GIT your fannies outside! On the DOUBLE!"

A chill westerly wind blows in off San Diego Bay and sweeps across the "Confidence Course," where the recruits gather at the base of a four-story tower, topped with a doughnut shaped platform. A commercial jetliner screams overhead, banks and heads out to sea.

"This is the 'Hell Hole, '" the DI says, standing against the wind. "That one over there, that's the 'Stairway to Heaven.' We'll start with HELL, and if your pants stay CLEAN we'll take a crack at HEAVEN." He looks from face to face. "We all jump," he says, "but which of you girls going FIRST?"

Lloyd looks skyward at the platform, jutting forty feet in the air. Everything is still and calm and quiet, except for the howling wind and a pair of raucous blackbirds which caw from atop the obstacle. A rope ladder dangles down. Lloyd eyes the DI. Their eyes catch. Lloyd's heart booms. "What's the object?" he asks, stepping forward.

"The object, Private Chambers, is to make MEN out of GIRLS. That process starts with FUN and GAMES. Hit the ladder, and you can demonstrate for the children. There's ropes up top — eleven-millimeter Goldline. All you do is STEP into the saddle, fasten the carabineers . . . and JUMP. Nothing more to do after that. Just enjoy the ride down."

"And to stop, Sir?"

"Hit the END of the rope."

"To slow?"

"Heh-heh. Hit the END of the rope. We've got a ONE speed operation here, Private. And like I SAID, all you have to WORRY about is making the JUMP. Everything else takes CARE of itself."

Lloyd purses his lips and moves toward the rope. He spits on his hands, rubbing them together. He looks up. Then he spits again, toes his shoe in the dirt, and reaches for the rope ladder. It is thick in his hands. He pulls himself up, stepping onto the first rung. The ladder swings out beneath him, and he is suddenly thrust backward. He takes the next rung. He tries to adjust his balance, but can't. He looks back. All the other recruits are laughing nervously. Lloyd ignores the heartbeat in his temples and climbs higher. Faster. Confidence comes as the others grow small behind him. The laughing has stopped and all eyes are on him. He nears the platform. The blackbirds take wing. His hand reaches through the opening and grabs the edge. His fingers lock around the heavy timber plank. Muscles strain, and he feels his arms begin to quiver. His elbows seem to have a life of their own, and turn to Jello. He takes one last deep breath, grits his teeth and pulls himself up. He lifts his knee over the edge, and on the count of three forces himself through the gaping opening. Lying atop the platform, his breaths are forced. He looks down and spits at the thirty upturned faces. Then he crawls away from the edge, and cautiously rises to his feet. He turns around and stops suddenly. Propped against the wall is a hulking black man with corn chips scattered at his feet. The man, clad in Marine sweats, flashes a gap-toothed smile.

"'Bout time, Honkey," the man says. "Ain't nuthin to do up here but feed the birds while I be waiting."

"Scared me," Lloyd says, forcing a laugh. And then his face turns serious. "Waiting for what?" he asks.

"DI sent me up befoe you turkeys got here," he volunteers. "My job be to give you li'l push jess case you doan jump. But iff'n I push you, you better say yo prayers cuz yo li'l white face be hamburger when you hit muther earth."

Lloyd peers over the edge, and then glances back at the man.

"So, Honkey. Step into this here saddle. Thass right, uh huh. You fast for a white boy! Thass right. Now hook youseff up with this li'l gadget. Thass right. Now the ress is easy. All you gotta do's say yo prayers'n jump.

"So the DI wasn't putting me on," Lloyd says. "I'm just supposed to bail out? Period?"

"You's gettin smarter by the minute."

Lloyd pulls against the carabineer, and leans against the anchor where the rope connects to the wall. Everything seems to be in order. At least it *seems* to be so. He hears a whistle from below.

"Thass yo signal, boy. Now you be jump'n quick like, else I haffa hep you down with a li'l push. Thass right, toes on the edge. Lean back, ann — "

Lloyd looks down one final time between his legs. His heart is in his throat. His toes feel like the Fourth of July. He squeezes his eyes shut. Three deep breaths. And then he steps into midair. His brain flashes death. But the next flash tells him the Marines wouldn't kill him off the first day during fun and games. The ground screams closer. The third flash tells him the Marines might. His body goes weightless. The thought of Jesus passes through his mind. It's been a good life. He closes his eyes. Suddenly his stomach is in his mouth. The rope jerks taut. He opens his eyes the instant before impact. But his fall has been slowed. His feet hit the ground, and he takes the hit in his knees. He falls to his side, rolls over once in the dirt, and then stands up and looks around. The other recruits smile nervously. Lloyd dusts off his hands, which are still shaking. He spits in the dirt.

"No sweat," he says, stepping out of the saddle. He unhooks the carabineer and hands it to the DI.

"NEXT!" the DI bellows, turning to Stankowitz. "Stinko, let's GO!"

Stankowitz hesitates. There is panic in his eyes. Lloyd crosses over to his side. "Nothing to it," he says. "Better than Disneyland."

"HIT the ropes, Stinko," the DI grunts.

Lloyd sits down in the dirt, watching his bunkmate negotiate his way up the ladder. Several times he almost falls. Lloyd jumps to his feet, cheerleading from below. The sun rises higher in the sky. An eternity later, Stankowitz is pulled through the platform hole by the black Marine. He is helped into the saddle, and the carabineer is hooked. Everybody waits. Lloyd's neck grows stiff watching. There is an uncomfortable silence. Stankowitz peers over the ledge, but steps back.

"JUMP, Stinko! JUMP!" the DI bellows from the ground. But Stankowitz refuses.

Lloyd pictures the black man's words to the private. He shudders. He counts slowly to ten, waiting for the push. Suddenly it comes. He hears a scream. Stankowitz falls through the hole backward, his arms flailing. The DI shades his eyes against the sun. A second later, the private hits the end of his line. He screams again. His face goes white, his pants darken. A puddle grows at his feet.

"Oooh lookie, children!" huffs the DI. "Stinko just lost his last THREE pounds of courage."

"The more you crack, the more he'll jerk with you," Lloyd warns Stankowitz that night in the barracks after lights were out. "Got to stay cool, Stinko. Remember — water off a duck's back."

Stankowitz kicks Lloyd's mattress, harder this time than before.

"Serious, Stinko, it's nothing. Got to calm down."

Bedcovers fly beneath Lloyd as Stankowitz jumps out of bed. He madly paces the floor, slamming his fist against the neighboring bunk. "*Nothing?*" he blurts, striking the bed. "You call today *nothing?*"

"Get your bleeping hands off my bed, else you're dead meat," Bart, in the next bed, shouts.

"*Dead* meat," Stankowitz says, pondering the words. "That's what you call funny." His voice suddenly goes shrill and he breaks into a high-pitched laugh. "*Dead* meat!" he brays, repeating the words again and again. "*Dead* meat, now that's funny."

"Shut the bleep up!" Bart warns.

"I've never met a more foul human being than this pompous DI," Stankowitz continues. "He's like a demon or something, something much worse. Something subhuman. An animal."

"It's a silly head trip, I'm telling you," Lloyd says.

"Well I don't know how much longer I can take his humiliation and his . . . his degradation. My *dogs*. Your *hogs*. Two *days* without sleep. And ridiculing me after I was pushed off the tower? You think I'm going to take eleven weeks of that dope?"

"Calm down, Stinko! It's a game. And you've got to play along."

"I won't," he sputters. "By God I won't!"

"Water off a duck's back," Lloyd says again, rolling over and pulling the blanket up over his head. He listens to Stankowitz pace the floor, back and forth. His feet patter like dripping rain, steady and soft, beckoning Lloyd into a deep sleep.

But somewhere in the middle of the night, he is awakened by screams. He bolts awake. He tries to focus, but his mind is a blur. For an instant he thinks he's still in Oklahoma. The screams jolt him back to the present. A recruit he doesn't know bursts through the barracks yelling.

"Stinko's dead in the head!"

"What the bleep's going on?" Bart shouts.

"Stinko! He's dead in the head!"

"He's a bleeping idiot all right," he says, rubbing his eyes.

"No, he's *dead*! He's done himself in — guzzled a bottle of Wisk detergent! He's in the head now, flopped over the johns!"

Lloyd jumps from his bunk and sprints for the stalls. Throwing open the door, he quickly checks Stankowitz for signs of life. His skin is already growing cold. Finding no breath or pulse, he launches into CPR. Within minutes, an ambulance skids up. Medics dash through the crowd of recruits and lift the limp private onto a gurney. Continuing CPR, they race back to the vehicle and the siren wails away.

An hour later, the DI steps into the center of the room. He glances at his watch and shakes his head. "Some THINGS I want you to know," he says abruptly. "FIRST. Thanks to the QUICK action of Private Lloyd Chambers, we've got some good news. You'll be happy to know, children, that Stinkowitz pulled through. He's in stable condition, and should get a FREE airplane ride home next week." He pauses before continuing. "SECOND. Don't want anybody to forget something. To reach graduation and become a Marine, you've got FIRST get by me. As your recruiters may have TOLD you, the Corps wants only the FEW, the PROUD. And I don't know how many of you GIRLS qualify. Stankowitz is the first to be thinned from our ranks. But there WILL be more, because only the MEN among you will stand to the end. Only the BEST, most COURAGEOUS among you will wear the Marine uniform. And that's how it SHOULD be, the only way it CAN be," he says. And then he turns and heads for the door. He pauses on the threshold, whips around and barks the Marine Corps motto. "*SEMPER FIDELIS!*" Always faithful.

"*Semper Fidelis!*" the platoon members shout as he shuts

off the lights and strides out of the barracks.

And when he is gone, Lloyd crawls back into bed, burying himself, his sorrow and his uncertainties beneath the covers. And then he waits for the dawn of a new, better day when he shall arise.

Chapter Five — DAN

R-O-L-A-I-D-S

There is a feeling you get on bright Sunday mornings in Napa when you are young and fresh out of church. It is as indistinct as the tickle of a far away sneeze, yet as real as the sweet smell of dawn. It is a sense that there is something worth smiling about, something worth believing in, something worth hoping for. With it comes the assurance that love is just around the corner, that yesterday's worries will dissipate with the morning mist, that the winds of the night will no longer howl and the rats of the mind will no longer gnaw. It is a feeling of expectation, of quiet satisfaction which accompanies the initial scent of a freshly mowed lawn, the first day of school, or the words "You've never looked better!" "Welcome home!" "The exam's been cancelled!" and "Keep the change!"

And so it is with Shirley Simpson who, departing church with her car windows down and her brunette hair flying in the breeze, U-turns on her way home and makes an impromptu stop by the grocery store where Dan works. She pulls the car into the nearest spot, jumps out and steps briskly inside the store. Her lips silently mouth a Sunday hymn as she scans the deserted checkouts, glances down the nearest aisles, and then bounces over to the courtesy booth. A short, fat man stands behind the counter, enveloped in a smog of cigar smoke. He wears a faded yellow and brown striped shirt, open at the collar. His dark hair is Vitalis slick.

"I'm looking for Dan Krainert," she says. "Do you know if he's working today?"

"Down there," the man grunts without looking up. He jabs his cigar toward aisle four. Shirley smiles her thanks and spins around. The man calls out after her. "You a friend?" he says to her back. She nods back over her shoulder. He works his cigar around in his mouth. "Then let me warn you, young lady," he grumbles, eyeing her over his low-slung glasses. "He's not paid to socialize."

"You must be the manager," Shirley says, her smile fading momentarily. "I've heard so much about you." She crosses her eyes at the man, and then scurries down the store aisle. She spots Dan at the far end, shouldering a large case of Del Monte grapefruit juice, and hurries toward him. Box blades and price stamps jut from the pocket of his green apron. He eases the box onto a lower shelf, then wipes a stream of sweat from his face.

"Hello, He-man," she says.

Dan glances up suddenly. "Shirley!" he says, unable to hide his surprise. "What are you — "

"Thought I'd stop by on my way home."

"From church?"

She nods.

"Well you look great," he smiles, rising to his feet. "I didn't even know you owned a dress." His eyes follow the smooth lines of her body, up and down. "It really looks good. The dress. You. Everything about you."

"It's my go-to-church dress," she says, returning his smile. Their eyes catch for a long moment. Shirley looks down, smoothing a wrinkle in her bodice. When she glances up again, Dan has moved a step closer. He has a funny look in his eyes.

"You really look good," he blusters again. His voice sounds squeaky.

"Did you make mass-and-doughnuts?" she asks, quickly changing the subject.

"No, Hitler Junior called me in at seven this morning.

Five hours of sleep, and the blasted phone rings."

"I just met him a second ago."

"The manager?"

"Yeah. Nice guy."

"The kind of guy only a mother could love."

"I asked him if you were working, and he basically told me to get lost."

"He never went to charm school."

"So I can't stay long. You might get fired."

"Don't worry about him."

"You look beat."

"Then I look about as good as I feel," Dan coughs. "And the Scrooge won't get the dolly fixed. The wheels have been busted for a month, so I've got to lug all of these cases from the dock to the shelves."

"Builds strong muscles."

Dan flexes. "I'll let you feel my biceps for a quarter."

"Can you make change for a buck?" Shirley says, reaching for her purse.

"Check with the manager," Dan laughs. "I'm sure he'd oblige."

"How's your head?" Shirley asks.

"Doing tricks again. The lifting doesn't help any. White spots, headaches, you name it."

"You should go to the doctor. Get a check-up."

"Yeah, maybe," Dan shrugs. "One of these days when things slow down."

"Soon!" she says, wagging a delicate finger. She glances nervously over her shoulder. "Before Mr. Congeniality comes looking for me, I wanted — "

"Stick around. He's all hot air."

"Anyway, I was wondering if you'd go to church with me next week?"

"Where do you go?"

"First Assembly of God. It's kind of in the sticks, out past the elementary school. But if you're not working — "

"This is really a coincidence," Dan says, shaking his head.

"What?"

"Well, I was wondering if *you'd* go with *me*."

"To mass-and-doughnuts?"

"No, *go* with me, he answers. "Period. We could hit it off big time, I know we could."

"Like your boss said, no socializing on the job," Shirley smiles. "But think about next Sunday. Seriously."

"Only if you'll go with me to the Giants game tonight. They're playing at Candlestick."

"Uh . . . football?"

"Baseball, Dumbo."

"Oh."

"Bob Knepper's starting, so it should be a good game."

"If I dare ask, starting what?"

"He's the pitcher," Dan says, shaking his head. "The starting pitcher."

"Oh."

"He's hot stuff."

Shirley nods.

"Nobody can hit him."

"I'm trying to get excited, but — " Shirley suddenly peers up the aisle and jumps. "Oops, gotta disappear," she whispers. "The cigar man cometh."

Dan hurriedly bends over the case of grapefruit juice and begins shelving the cans. "What about the game?" he asks out of the side of his mouth. Shirley doesn't answer. "The game," he hisses. "Do you want to go or not?" She still offers no reply. He darts a glance up, only to spot Shirley halfway down the aisle. He cringes as she stops the approaching manager.

"This store of yours needs a map," she says loudly. "I've been looking all over, but can't seem to find the Maxi-pads."

Dan's jaw drops. The store manager chews the end of his smoldering cigar, looking from her to Dan. Dan bites his tongue to stifle a laugh.

"The Maxi-pads," Shirley says impatiently.

The man removes his wet cigar and points. "Feminine hygiene's on thirteen," he grunts. "Other end of the store."

"*Stationery.* Maxi-pad *stationery.*"

The man blushes. Shirley waits. He mumbles something

about the mall. Shirley nods her thanks, and then disappears around the corner on her way to the door.

The following day as Dan strolls across campus amidst a pack of Jolly Orangers, he spots Shirley in the courtyard. She is sitting on a bench beneath a fragrant eucalyptus tree. Budding pink petals sprinkle the branches like handfuls of confetti.

"I'll catch up with you," he tells his friends. "I've got to detour for the girl of my dreams."

"Don't be late," Charlie warns. "Mr. Payne's uptight about Friday night."

"What does he have to sweat? It's my reputation that's on the line."

"What reputation?"

"Funny."

"Just don't say I didn't warn you, Romeo."

Dan runs across the courtyard to Shirley's side. When he draws beside her, he is huffing.

"Tried to call last night about the game," he says, straddling the bench. "But your mom said you were out."

"Church," she says.

"Oh, that's right. Twice on Sunday."

"Did that pitcher of yours, the guy you mentioned — "

"Bob Knepper."

"Did he win?"

"It was terrible. They hit him like crazy. At least that's what the papers said. I didn't go to the game."

"So you just stayed home?"

"All by my lonesome. But the whole night I wanted to be with you."

Shirley smiles.

"After you left the store, I couldn't think of anything else. I really wanted to go out with you last night. To be alone together."

"So what did you end up doing?"

"Stayed home and got saved," he says.

Shirley searches his eyes. "What?"

"I got saved."

Her face is puzzled. "Don't joke with me, Dan. Sometimes I can't tell if you're putting me on or not."

"OK, maybe I didn't get saved. I don't know. But I was flipping TV channels, and ended up watching about a half hour of Billy Graham's thing."

"And?"

"And what?"

"Well, what happened? What did you think?"

"What can I say? The guy made sense, what he was saying and all. And then afterward — " Dan says, suddenly glancing up when he hears his name being called. "Hey, Jessica," he shouts with a wave.

"Who's that?" Shirley asks, eyeing the blousy blonde.

"Jessica Bell," he says, watching her till she disappears into the distant hall. "She just made cheerleader for next year."

"You were saying?"

"Yeah, well afterward I actually dusted off an old family Bible, and stayed up half the night reading it and thinking."

"About what?"

"About my life, our relationship . . ."

"Forget our relationship. What about your life?" she asks. "The commitment you've apparently made is the most important decision you'll ever have to face."

"I know, but let's talk about our relationship," he insists.

"Dan, you drive me crazy!"

"Crazy crazy, or crazy with passion?"

Shirley shifts on the bench, and then suddenly stands. "OK, let's get this out in the open, once and for all," she sighs. "This going together business is driving me crazy. *Crazy* crazy, if you want the truth."

"No, go ahead and lie a little," he says, rising to stand beside her. He watches her chocolate eyes. Her eyelashes are longer than he'd remembered.

"I'm just not up for any kind of relationship. Period. Maybe I'm gun shy because of past losers I've been involved with, I don't know. But I don't even *want* a steady boyfriend at this point."

"Your eyes scream desire."

"Please, Dan. All I can tell you is how I feel. And I feel that the most important relationship in my life is my relationship with the Lord. I don't expect you to understand, but Jesus is more important to me now than anything or anybody else. And He should be to you, too. He *is* my life, Dan — my reason for being. And I don't want anything to stand in the way of my relationship with him. Not even you."

"Talk about heavy duty competition," he says, turning away momentarily.

"Huh?"

"In past relationships, my competition has always just been other guys. I've never been up against God before. What chance do I, a mere mortal, possibly have?"

"You act as if being friends is some kind of tragedy."

"On par with being shot through the head."

"Come on, I'm not shutting the door in your face. I wouldn't have stopped by the store yesterday if that was my intention. I want to build an honest friendship with you, but that's about it for now." Shirley pauses, searching for words. "I don't know what will come of it. Who knows, maybe it will develop into something stronger. I'm not saying it will; I'm not saying it won't. But without first building a solid foundation, you can have no true, lasting relationship — not with me or with anybody else. So, to answer your question — "

"I didn't ask a question."

"You keep asking if I'll go with you!"

"Right. Drum roll, please."

"I'm very content just being friends."

She looks at Dan. Dan looks at her. "I figured you'd probably say that," he shrugs. "I didn't think you'd make me late to class to say it, but I'm not surprised. Of course, you *can* change your mind," he smiles. "In the meantime, *Pal*," he says, draping his arm around her, "how about lending me a little moral support?"

"For what?" she asks.

"Front row center for opening night Friday," he says, pressing a ticket into her hand.

"Sure. I'd love to."

"I love you, too," he says with a wink. And then he checks his watch and shudders. "Gotta make like a banana."

"And split."

"We'll talk more later. But my life is on the line now, because Mr. Payne is going to be hot." Dan backs slowly away and waves. Shirley waves back. He wheels around, sprints back across the courtyard, rounds the corner and dashes up the steps of the Little Theater where final play rehearsals are underway.

As Dan quietly slinks onto the stage, his drama instructor looks up with cold eyes. He fingers his beard, and glances at his wristwatch. "Hold it, hold it!" he bellows, slamming the script on his desk top. "What's going on here? Don't you know it's just four more days till opening night!"

"I'm sorry," Dan says. He looks around at the other students and shrugs his apologies.

"Sorry? You going to tell the audience that?"

"I'm barely ten minutes late."

"Ten minutes today. And how about tomorrow? I can't tolerate this, Krainert. Nor can I tolerate the fact that as of our last rehearsal, you still didn't have your lines down. Last week, you flubbed your cues and — "

"I already explained that my boss has kept me working late every night for the past several weeks. So my study time has been tight."

"Incompetence has plenty of excuses."

"I'll get the lines down — I always have," Dan says. "You don't need to worry."

"I'm not worried," his teacher huffs. "But *you* should be! It's your name that's broadcast all over campus every morning on the Daily Bulletin."

"Otherwise known as the Daily Bull," smirks Charlie Hughes, trying for laughs.

"Don't wise-guy me, Hughes," the teacher snaps, turning around.

"Come on, Mr. Payne, calm down," Charlie says, raising his hands and stepping back. "You're always on everybody's back, riding us like we're a bunch of irresponsible idiots. You get so worked up before an opening, but we've never let you down. We always pull things off."

"Quote, '*Never* let me down,' unquote," the teacher says sarcastically. His cold steel eyes glare. "And you, quote, '*always* pull things off,' unquote. Well let me tell you something. The only reason you pull anything off, Hughes, is that your two-bit performances are always done for an unsophisticated audience of teenage jockstraps and their lollygagging parents who don't know the difference between a good play and a poached egg."

"I don't believe what I'm hearing!" Charlie storms.

"You don't *want* to believe it!"

"This is getting out of control," Dan says, stepping between the two.

"Credit male menopause!" Charlie blasts. "The old man's gone over the edge! Senility strikes again!"

"Charlie!" gasps his girl friend Nicole.

"Well you heard what he said!"

The teacher paces the stage. "What I'm trying to say — and it's apparently not sinking in — is that opening is just four nights away. *Four nights away,* and nobody knows their lines. And the star, the illustrious Dan Krainert who is supposed to carry the show, is missing every cue that comes his way. Let me count it off for you," he snarls. "Tuesday! Wednesday! Thursday! Friday! Four nights and you go public with this nonsense."

"I'll be fine by Friday," Dan says, pushing an unruly shock of hair off his forehead. "Like I said, I've been under the gun. There's been a lot of pressure."

"Well the pressure is on now, young man. The clock is ticking and you've got four days to prove you're right!"

Charlie drapes his arm around Dan's shoulder and draws him aside. "Take a deep breath," he says. "The old man rants like this the week before every play. But you'll do fine. Take another breath. That's right, you're a star. Even *he* got that right. You're a star, Krainert! But you've got to stay humble. Humility's the word. Can't let it go to your head. But you won't have a problem with that, Star. You'll never have a

problem with humility. And you know why?" He squeezes
Dan's shoulder. "You know why, Star?"

Dan shakes his head.

Charlie looks him square in the eyes and smiles. "Because
your fly's down, Star."

Dan pushes him away, as everybody laughs. He tugs up
his zipper, smiling sheepishly.

Mr. Payne glances from face to face and then heaves a
sigh. "Look, everybody take five. Get intelligent, wake up,
grab a Coke — whatever it takes you to concentrate. And then
get back here. I'll be calmer, you'll be smarter. We'll back up
and start again with act two, scene two."

Dan quickly pulls a pencil and scrap of paper from his
shirt pocket, tallies food orders, and sprints out the door toward
the cafeteria. He looks for Shirley but she is gone. On his
way back, carrying a tray laden with malts and chips, he
suddenly blanches. He takes slow, deliberate steps. He looks
up at the door to the Little Theater but sees only snowflakes.
Stopping, he takes a deep breath. Exhale. Inhale. He takes a
few more steps, feeling pressure rising in his chest. He walks
quickly now, following the path he knows by heart. Left turn.
Straight ahead. Up the steps. Through the door. He is panting,
and there is a wild look in his eyes.

"Food everybody!" he shouts. And then he stumbles.

"Dan!" Charlie shouts, grabbing him by the arm and
steadying the tray. He removes the tray from Dan's hands and
passes it to another student. "What in heaven is wrong?"

"The pain," Dan says, massaging his chest. "It's all across
my chest." He grunts the words out, fighting for breath.

"Nicole!" Charlie shouts. "Mr. Payne!"

"I'll be fine," Dan pants.

"Walk around," Charlie commands, slipping his arm beneath Dan's. He guides him back and forth across the stage.

"I can't see!" Dan cries. His arms flail the air.

"What is it, Dan?" Mr. Payne says, rushing over.

"I can't see!"

"We'll get help," his teacher says. "Dan, everything will
be fine. You'll be OK. We'll get help." He grabs another

student, says something in his ear and shoves him toward the
door. "Everything will be fine," he repeats nervously.

"It's the same thing I felt before." Dan's eyes fill with tears.

"Talk to me, Dan," Charlie says, leading him back and
forth. "Talk to me, Star."

"Maybe he should sit down," Mr. Payne suggests. "Do
you want to sit, Dan?"

"Now it's going down my arms!" Dan sputters.

"Hold on to me, Dan!"

"My arms are stiff!"

"OK, I've got you," Charlie says. "I'll hold on."

"My neck is burning!"

"Do you want to sit?" Mr. Payne says, trying to keep his
voice calm. "Somebody get a chair! You can see he's having
trouble! Get a chair!"

"No, it's better if I walk," Dan mumbles.

"How do you feel now?" Charlie asks. "Take a deep,
slow breath. Blow it out. Again. That's right."

"That helps," Dan grunts, stroking the biceps of his right
arm. "That helps a lot."

"Good. Keep breathing."

"If I quit breathing, I'd give you a real scare," Dan says,
forcing a laugh.

"A scare," Charlie huffs. "What do you think you're giving
us now, a comedy routine?"

"Don't," Dan says. "It hurts more when I laugh."

"Look at everybody," Charlie says in his ear.

Dan looks up. Other students are gathered around the
stage staring at him.

"They're scared spitless. So keep breathing or they'll all
pass out."

"We've called your mother, Dan," Mr. Payne says, walking
beside him. "She'll be here in a few minutes."

"No need to get her worked up," Dan says. "You know
how mothers are."

"How's your eyes?" Charlie asks.

Dan stops pacing and rubs his eyeballs. He looks up and
swings his head around in a circle. He rubs his eyes again,

and then squeezes them shut. He takes a deep breath and blows it out. "Better," he says. "Everything's coming back to normal."

"Is the pain gone?"

Dan fills his lungs again. His fingers massage his shirtfront. "Getting there," he says. "Can I have some milk?"

"Milk!" Charlie shouts. "The star wants milk!" He looks around, and then turns back to Dan. "You didn't buy any milk, Idiot. How about a milkshake?" he says, grabbing a cup from another student. "A chocolate milkshake. Thick as sludge and tastes about as good. Made with the finest petroleum products, and the best artificial additives. Contains nothing you'd recognize in real life, but it will make you feel great!"

"Give me a swig," Dan says, elbowing Charlie aside.

"How does it taste?"

"Not bad."

"Hey, all right! Applause everybody. The star is feeling tough. Tough enough to drink carcinogens and not blink an eye!" Charlie looks around and holds up his hands. "Are you guys deaf or something? Applause for the star! Applause!"

Everybody claps. Mr. Payne steps over, guiding Dan to a chair. Dan shakes his head. The backstage door bursts open. Dan's mother rushes in. She dashes over to his side, and says something in his ear. Dan nods. She puts her arm around him. He smiles and nods again. And then the two walk off the stage, arm in arm.

On his way out the door, Dan glances back at Mr. Payne. "Count me in for Friday," he says. "I'll be ready."

Mr. Payne nods without saying a word, and watches him slowly descend the stairs. He stands motionless, staring at the empty stairway long after Dan is gone.

In the waiting room of the doctor's clinic, Dan thumbs through *People* magazine while his mother fills out the necessary forms. She hands the clipboard back to the receptionist and takes a seat beside her son. He looks up at her and smiles. Her eyes are glued to his, searching deep for meaning to the pain that has plagued him.

"How do you feel?" she asks, stroking his arm.

"Not too bad."

"Say it again."

"I'm fine. Really."

She looks at her watch. Dan stands and retrieves another magazine.

"You've been having problems for some time, haven't you?" she says.

He puts down the magazine. "Nothing that I was worried about."

"And now?"

Dan shrugs. "I'm only seventeen. What can be wrong? I've just been worn down. Between work, the play, trying to figure things out with Shirley — maybe it's gotten to me. Maybe I worry too much. And I haven't been getting as much sleep as I should, I suppose."

"We'll get some answers soon," his mom says, checking her watch again, "if they ever get around to seeing us."

"No hurry, I actually feel fine now."

His mother nods absently, rises and walks over to the receptionist's window. She and the woman behind the glass exchange a few words, and Mrs. Krainert takes her seat again. Moments later, a nurse opens a side door and calls Dan's name.

He and his mother are ushered into a small examination room where Dan is asked to remove his shirt.

"The doctor will be with you in a minute," the nurse says, closing the door behind her. But it opens again instantly and a doctor strides in. He is tall and angular, his dark curly hair coiled tight as a Brillo pad. He scans Dan's chart momentarily and smiles.

"You a Giants fan?" he asks, placing his stethoscope against Dan's chest.

"When they're winning," Dan says.

"Nothing to root for last night." The doctor moves the cold circular instrument around. "Take a deep breath and hold it. That's right. Very good."

Dan sits atop the end of the examination table. Goosebumps rise on his arms. His face turns purple. "Can I breathe now?" he gasps.

"Take another breath and hold it. They ought to unload Knepper if you ask me."

"Knepper?" Dan says. "He's the only decent pitcher they've got."

"If that's the case, the owner ought to sell the team," the doctor says, booming a hearty laugh. "Now, what seems to be the problem? Nothing's wrong with the old ticker."

"I've been having headaches. Seeing white spots. And these pains, they sort of come and go."

The doctor nods. "What exactly are these pains? What do they feel like?"

"Like I've been hit by a bus. And then everything gets cold and stiff. My fingers. My toes. They go numb."

The doctor prods and squeezes Dan's stomach. "There. Does that hurt?"

Dan nods.

The doctor stands up, flashing a fatherly smile. "Just like I thought," he says. "Probably just a nervous stomach or a spot of heartburn." He drapes his arm over Dan's shoulder and smiles again. "Ninety-nine percent of the people I've seen today would trade places with you in an instant. You're a strong, healthy kid, and have nothing to worry about. Nothing that couldn't be relieved by taking a couple of Rolaids . . . or simply kicking a few trash cans."

"Kicking *what*?" Mrs. Krainert asks.

"Trash cans. Something to let the steam off. Your son needs to release his nervous, pent-up emotions."

"And that's all it is? As a child, you know, Danny had serious heart problems."

"Best as I can tell, those early problems were a misdiagnosis. Your son's heart is as strong as yours or mine — and undoubtedly a great deal stronger. So please," he says, "please trust me."

"But what about his pains? The white spots in his vision? The headaches? The numb extremities? Things seem to be getting worse."

"Probably a cold. Give it time. It'll run its course. Coupled with the pressures he's facing at school, well . . ." his voice trails off as he shrugs. "You have to watch it, but it's nothing serious. Like I said, Mrs. Krainert, your son is fit to beat the band. The numbness could just be a signal to him to get more exercise."

"He's had this cough," Dan's mother argues. "And it seems to be getting worse."

"A cough could be anything," he says. "Do you smoke?" he asks, turning to Dan.

"No."

"Then perhaps an allergy of sorts, especially at this time of year. If it doesn't clear up, make another appointment and we'll run some allergy tests. As for his heart — it's beating strong as a bass drum. And on that matter you've simply got to trust me," he admonishes, flashing another paternal smile.

"Thanks," Dan says, smiling. He looks sideways at his mother, but she looks worried. "I'll lay into some trash cans tonight."

"That a boy." The doctor's deep laugh rises from somewhere near his toes. "But it's not you that needs help. It's those Giants. If you're rooting for them, you've got to root a little harder. They could use whatever help they can get."

Later that night, long after Dan has excused himself from the dinner table, his parents remain seated before half-eaten meals. "I don't know," his mother says, twirling her fork through a plate of cold spaghetti. She looks up at her husband. "George, there's something *else* wrong with Danny. He's nearly collapsed twice now, and not even a doctor can tell me that's due to a nervous stomach."

"He's a strong kid, Libby."

"Strength has nothing to do with it. You've seen how he is in the evening. Tired. Limp. He just drags. And his eyes, I only need to look at them to know something's wrong."

"You're right. He looks awfully haggard."

"And I can't help but think it has something to do with his problems as a child. Perhaps his heart disease, rather than being a misdiagnosis, has merely been in remission."

"After all these years?"

"That's my suspicion," she says.

"Did the doctor talk about that?" Mr. Krainert asks.

"Not really. He just said that whatever Danny has or doesn't have, it's not due to his heart. Said his heart's 'fit to beat the band.' But I didn't want to carry on in front of Danny. He has enough pressure as it is, without taking on my fears, too."

"He was definite about the heart?"

"He only listened to it for a few seconds."

"Doctors can be wrong," Mr. Krainert says.

"Danny's talked about the heavy lifting he's done at work lately. Maybe that has strained his heart."

"Well, don't worry yourself unnecessarily, Libby. The only thing to do is take him in for a second opinion."

"I don't trust the doctors at the clinic."

"Can we afford anything else?"

"No, but you get what you pay for."

Dan, who is standing on the scale in the hall bathroom, hears their discussion through the closed door. From his wallet he extracts the weight chart he's been keeping and inks a small red dot on the graph paper. Down another half pound — a drop of 16 pounds the past month. He stares at himself in the mirror — his dull hollow eyes are filled with fear.

When he steps out of the bathroom, his parents look up and smile.

"Feeling better, son?" his father asks.

Dan ignores the question and steps to the refrigerator.

"We'd like you to visit another doctor," his mother says.

"Fine with me, but after the play."

"Tomorrow."

"Can't. If I don't learn my lines, I'll bomb Friday," Dan says, slamming the refrigerator door and stalking down the hallway.

"Whatever the star wants!" his mother shouts after him, trying to smile. She cocks her head, listening for a response. But all she hears is the crash of his bedroom door and, much further in the distance, the slow, sad, tolling of church bells.

DRESS BLUES

Each breath Lloyd Chambers takes is hard and deep. His lungs heave, as if with each running step he is surfacing in a pool after being under water too long. Water. That's what he tries not to think about. Water. That's all he can think about. Each step increases his agony. Blisters crown his toes. His feet are stuffed inside heavy, steamy, black leather boots, one of the two pair issued weeks ago on that first nightmare night in the Marine Corps. As he runs, he thinks back about Stinko. About the mattress-kicking. About the puddle in Stinko's pants after being pushed off the tower. About saving Stinko's life. "Water off a duck's back." Water. Lloyd can't shake the thought. Water.

After three miles the DI's voice slices through the cloud of dust.

"OK, girls, gunna do us some CHANTS. Gotta play cheerleader here, cuz I can TELL you boys still GREEN. And the CORPS can't use you green. They need you LEAN. They need you MEAN. The CORPS need lean, mean, fighting MACHINES. So you gotta keep running through the pain. No pain, no GAIN. And to keep running, you gotta CHANT. And CHANT so they can hear you from TJ up to Hollyweird. Got it? OK, let's GO. After me!"

Low and loud, his voice booms over their heads as their
boots pound the dirt trails:
Chesty Puller was a good Marine,
And a good Marine was he.
He called for his pipe
And he called for his bowl
And he called for his privates three.
"Who will swab the deck?" said the general.
"We will swab the deck," said the privates,
"Happy men are we!
The Army's fair,
But it don't compare
To the Marine Corps Infantry!"
"Very good, girls. But I like to see SMILES when you
run. You all having FUN? OK now, gunna teach you another.
Follow along, and lots of SMILES!"
His chanting voice again cuts the air:
C-130 rolling down the strip,
Recon Rangers gunna take a little trip.
Stand up, buckle up, shuffle to the door;
Jump right out and count to four.
If my main don't open wide,
I got another one by my side.
If that chute don't open round,
I'll be the first to hit the ground.
For the next several miles, everybody is silent. Nobody
smiles. Nobody chants. The halfway marker comes and goes.
But the barracks are still five miles away. Lloyd's boots feel
like cinder blocks. Other platoon members chug painfully beside
him. Sixteen rows of young men, each merely trying to survive
this ten mile run, their eyes are glued to the shoulder blades
of the recruits in front of them. Each stride is measured.
Regulation left right left, 15-inch running steps, 180 steps per
minute. Dust clogs their lungs.
Suddenly, two rows in front of Lloyd, a recruit stumbles
and falls. He goes down stiff. His knees hit the ground first,

and then his face plows into the dirt. It's Lomangino, the kid from Nevada who's always bragging that his dad's killed three people. The ranks part. Lloyd reaches down to lift him up. But the DI shoves Lloyd away.

"It's just a FAINT!" the DI snaps. "Hands OFF and KEEP moving!"

"Sir, his face!" Lloyd protests. "The kid's bleeding!"

"MOVE IT, CHAMBERS!" the DI bellows at Lloyd.

Reluctantly, Lloyd rejoins the other runners. Running up a short rise, he looks back as the DI dumps a canteen of water in Lomangino's face, drags him to his feet and kicks him hard in the pants. The young private shakes his head and stumbles ahead, trying to get his feet to work. The DI gives him another boot in the rear. Lomangino picks up his pace. Two miles further down the trail, the DI and the bloody private catch up with the pack.

"Let's pick up the PACE!" the DI yells. "Just a couple more MILES, and then home sweet home. Get HUMPING! Let's GO, pick it UP!" And then his voice rises again, in the familiar chanting cadence:

Mister Monkey jumped up from the coconut grove,
He's a good lookin' dude, you can tell by his clothes.
He wears a four button jacket, and his pants are tight,
He's got a fun-lovin', girl-chasin' appetite.
He chased a lady monkey up a coconut tree,
And said, "Ooh ooh, Baby, I like what I see."
He lined a hundred others up against the wall,
And bet his last banana he could tree them all.
He treed ninety-eight till his tail turned blue,
Then he jumped down, turned around and treed the other two.
They stayed up the tree till the day he died,
Then they crawled down slowly, and moaned and sighed.
On his grave the lady monkeys wrote in green:
"Here lies a tail-waggin' U.S. Marine."

Back in the barracks, the privates fall onto their beds.
The DI disappears, but only for ten minutes. Suddenly he
reappears, banging the steel bedframes with a stick. He's wearing
a clean uniform, and looks like he has showered and pampered
for a party. On the contrary.

"Come on, girls! Everybody UP and smiling! You've got
twelve minutes to clean up, change clothes, grab your rifles
and assemble outside for pre-lunch inspection. And SIX minutes
have already passed! On your FEET! MOVE IT!"

Pandemonium ensues. Lloyd whips off his boots. His toes
are red and raw. Lomangino races for the john and sticks his
face under the faucet. Wincing, he wipes away the blood with
his hands and then darts back to his footlocker. Lloyd scrambles
into his reserve uniform. He buttons his shirt with one hand,
and pulls on clean boots with his other.

At the thirty-second warning, the privates snatch their
rifles from the locked racks and, polishing their buttons and
buckles on the way downstairs, dash into formation.

As the inspection commences, the DI moves slowly from
man to man, examining their uniforms and rifles. To each
recruit he barks rapid-fire questions.

"Caliber SHELL used in the M-16? Private Young!"

"Sir! U.S. .30 caliber, Sir!"

"SHOOTing distance of M-16? Private Bolinder!"

"Sir! Thirty-five hundred plus yards, Sir!"

"EFFECTive range of M-16? Private Fickett!"

"Sir! To 600 yards, Sir!"

"Spot! Number MEN in a fire team?"

"Sir! Four, Sir!"

The DI spins and goes nose to nose with the private.
"Number FIRE teams in a squad?"

"Sir! Four, Sir!"

"Number SQUADS in a platoon?"

"Sir! Four, Sir!"

"Number MEN in a platoon?"

"Sir! Sixty-four, Sir!"

"Aw, Spot," the DI winces, hanging his head. "Nothing but fun and games together this morning, and now I'm hurt!"

"Sir! This private does not understand, Sir!"

"Does not understand? Spot, you LEFT me out of the count as if I'd disappeared off the FACE of the earth. Forgot to ADD me in with the sixty-four! And I can only think you did it intentionally, with premeditated malice. Is that what you did, Spot?"

"Sir, no malice intended, Sir."

"You got a problem with me, boy?"

"Sir, no, Sir."

"Can't tell you mean it, boy. And something else. You're standing here at inspection without your rifle!"

Spot glances around for support. When his eyes again catch the DI's, he looks penitent. His eyes bleed remorse.

"Don't eyeball me, Spot!" the DI barks, thrusting his finger at the large mole on the private's cheek. "GIT your ugly dalmatian face BACK into the barracks, and give me fifty trips up the steps with your footlocker. NOW! And then get back down here with your RIFLE! ON THE DOUBLE! GO! SCRAM!"

The private scampers off, and the DI turns to Lloyd.

"Code of Conduct, Article *ONE*! Private Chambers!"

"Sir!" Lloyd snaps to attention, " 'I am an American fighting man. I serve in the forces which guard my country and our way of life. I am prepared to give my life in their defense,' Sir!"

"Private Lomangino! You call THAT a shoe shine? Give me thirty pushups! NOW! And count them out!"

"Sir! One . . . two . . . three . . ."

"Let me hear your chest BOUNCE!"

"Sir! Yes, Sir! Four . . . five . . . six . . ."

"LemonJello! The diRECtion the platoon now faces?"

The private darts a glance at the sun. "Sir! To the north, Sir! Seven . . . eight . . . nine . . ."

"The direction the sun SETS?"

"Ten . . . eleven . . . Sir! In the west, Sir! Twelve . . . thirteen . . . fourteen . . ."

"Where you FROM, LemonJello?"

"Fifteen . . . sixteen . . . Sir! Private Lomangino is from Reno, Nevada, Sir! Seventeen . . . eighteen . . . nineteen . . ."

"The diRECtion your home in Reno faces?"

"Sir! To the . . . uh, to the east, Sir! Twenty . . . twenty-one . . . twenty-two . . ."

"LemonJello!" the DI bellows, squatting with his nose inches from the private, "If the platoon's facing NORTH, and the sun sets here in the WEST, and your home faces EAST, then in what direction does the sun SET over your home?"

"Twenty-three . . . Sir! That would be . . . twenty-four . . . let's see . . . twenty-five . . ."

"Spit it OUT!"

"Twenty-six . . . twenty-seven . . . Sir! To the . . . twenty-eight . . . to the south . . . twenty-nine . . . thirty . . . Sir!"

"WRONG, LemonJello, WRONG! Give me thirty more. NOW!"

Spot returns from his footlocker duty, clutching his M-16 tightly. His face is red and bloated; his uniform soaked with sweat. He slips into line, trying to be as inconspicuous as possible. But the DI spots him and fires him another question.

Spot! The WEIGHT and LOAD of an M-16?"

Sir! The gun weighs 9.7 pounds and fires eight rounds, Sir!"

"VOLUME!"

"SIR! THE GUN WEIGHS — "

"The WHAT?"

"SIR! THE GUN — "

Spot is summoned front and center, facing the entire platoon. "What you've got over your shoulder, Spot, is your *RIFLE*. Got that?"

"Sir. Yes, Sir!"

"Don't get confused AGAIN, understand?"

"Sir. Yes, Sir."

OK, loud and clear, repeat after me . . ."

Swallowing hard, Spot repeats what the DI commands: *"This* is my rifle — "

"EVERYBODY!" the DI says. "Spot in the lead, let's MARCH. Across the parade deck to the MESS hall. RIFLES on your shoulders. Let's GO!"

And so they march toward lunch: regulation stride behind Spot. The DI struts beside them, his eyes straight ahead and his anvil head held high.

Given just ten minutes to eat, the recruits snort down their food and scramble back into formation. On the way out, Spot grabs extra Oreo cookies and stuffs them beneath his cap for later consumption.

Outside, a stiff wind is blowing. As the privates march back across the parade deck, a practicing color guard cuts ahead of them. Snapping to attention, Spot loses his hat in the gale. He snatches it back, but not in time to save the Oreos. One rolls toward the flag bearers like a runaway yo-yo; the other hits the DI's shoes, stopping dead at his feet. Spot cringes. Another private behind him kicks him in the pants. The DI stares at the cookie for a long, painful moment, and then turns slowly, very slowly around. He nods his head up and down, and there is a knowing look in his eyes.

"Would the private who belongs to this . . . this cookie kindly reclaim it," he says calmly. He waits for somebody to come forward. Nobody moves. He repeats the command. All eyes stare straight ahead, unblinking. "Who OWNS the COOKIE?" he asks, his voice rising. Spot's ears flush, and the corner of his mouth begins to twitch. But he stands stiff as the butt of his rifle. The DI nods again, and then steps from man to man, asking each in turn if the cookie is his. Each says no. Spot lies.

"Very well," the DI says, and then orders all men to hoist their rifles above their heads and, with full stomachs, to double-time it to the confidence course for more "fun and games."

Ten minutes later, he draws the platoon to a stop beside the obstacle known as the "Bridge Over Troubled Waters."

"Fess up and we'll be DONE with it," he says as his foot taps impatiently on the edge of the narrow footbridge which spans the deep lagoon. He rolls his tongue around inside his mouth, and then clears his throat. Nobody moves. "So be it, girls," he says. "Before this is over, you're going to wish you'd died in your sleep," he says solemnly. "If nobody's man enough to fess up, we'll just have to FIND our man another way. Isn't that right, Spot?"

Spot blanches. "Uh, Sir. Yes, I suppose, Sir," he says, averting his eyes.

The DI quickly divides the platoon into two teams, issues football helmets and pugel sticks.

"Needless to SAY, this no GAME!" he bawls against the wind. "In the event of war, particularly if you encounter the enemy hand-to-hand, you've got a CHOICE. That is, you can die for YOUR country or make the OTHER gook die for HIS! So heads up. It's on this bridge you learn hand-to-hand. And I expect you to FIGHT here like your LIFE depends on it! OK, first two men, LET'S GO!"

Lloyd steps confidently onto the plank, walks straight toward his opponent, and with three swift jabs sends him sprawling into the water. Lloyd bests his next opponent, though not without taking an unseen blow to the head and suffering a bloody nose. By the third round, only eight men in the platoon remain dry. Lloyd dabs the blood from his nose and again heads up the plank, this time to face Private Lomangino. Lloyd steps closer and looks in his face. The blood has dried from his earlier fall, but the wound still looks bad. Lloyd moves in with his pugel stick held high.

"Hope you know how to swim," Lloyd says.

"Don't need to know," Lomangino snarls, eyeing him coldly.

Lloyd steps within range and his opponent bats him away. Lloyd comes at him again, fakes left and smacks him hard in the neck. Lomangino coughs and backs off. Lloyd lunges, driving his weapon into his gut. Lomangino grunts, then returns the blow. The strike is tentative. Lloyd laughs, sticking his head out and points to his chin. Suddenly Lomangino is on him, screaming like a Banshee. Bam. Bam. Bam. He swings hard and furiously. Each strike hits the target. Lloyd takes five straight blows. His nose is really bleeding now, but he maintains his balance, ducks a sideswing and shoves Lomangino back with his foot. Lloyd wipes the blood with the back of his hand, takes a deep breath and then charges with fierce and renewed determination. He launches a left, a right, followed by another quick left-right combo, a belly jab, then a stunning haymaker to Lomangino's head.

Lomangino's pugel stick clatters on the bridge and splashes into the water below. Then he wobbles a moment. His eyes roll up. Lloyd watches him fall. He goes down hard and stiff, his head banging against the bridge with a sickening crunch. Lloyd reaches for his arm, like earlier in the day, to prevent him from tumbling unconscious into the water. But Lomangino hits flat. His weight is evenly distributed on the bridge. His mouth hangs open, with his tongue sticking out like a dog that's been hit by a car.

"Let's GO, LemonJello!" the DI yells. "On your FEET!"

Lloyd turns around, shaking his head. "Sir, he's out cold."

"Not again!"

Lloyd nods.

"Give him a couple swats in the face and wake him up," the DI says.

Lloyd reaches down and slaps him lightly across the face. He waits, but nothing happens. He slaps him again. Still no response.

"Roll him overboard," the DI says. "That should do it."

"But Sir, he's out of it."

"Don't CROSS me, Chambers!"

"But Sir — "

"Don't 'But Sir' me, BOY! I said ROLL HIM OVER-BOARD! NOW! And GET that STUPID look off your MUG!"

Lloyd stares down at Lomangino's putty face. His tongue rests against the wooden planks, and his arm is twisted at a funny angle. Lloyd reaches down and pulls the private's arm up. He rolls his head over and blows in his face. He slaps him again.

"NOW!" the DI barks.

Lloyd looks back over his shoulder and nods. Hunching low, he tips Lomangino's body up, trying to roll him over. His head hangs back like a kewpie doll. His arms are rubbery. Lloyd balances the body on the edge, unwilling to let go.

"NOW!" The DI moves toward the bridge.

Lloyd purses his lips. He lets go of the body. But not before draping the limp arm around his own shoulder. Together, they take the four foot drop, plunging into the frigid lagoon. The cold water slaps Lomangino awake. But he is disoriented and grapples with Lloyd. His arms flail the water as he gasps for air. His wet fatigues and boots pull him down. Lloyd shoves him back toward the surface.

"Calm down, man!" he sputters, swallowing water himself. He yanks Lomangino's hands from around his neck. "Calm down, Idiot, I've just saved your life!"

Lomangino backs off, kicking on his own now. He looks at Lloyd. Then he turns and looks at the bank where the others are standing. The DI is board-stiff, with his hands on his hips. Lomangino takes a few painful strokes toward the edge of the bank and crawls on his belly out of the water. Lloyd waits behind him, and then pulls himself out. He kneels beside Lomangino and slaps him hard on the back. Lomangino coughs hard, spitting up water. His lungs fight for air. He rolls over, grimacing as he rubs a knot at the base of his head. He looks up at Lloyd.

"Thanks," he says, coughing again.

Lloyd nods.

The DI steps to his side and stares down at him. Lloyd keeps his eyes on the ground.

"What's the MATTER, Chambers?" he smirks. "You think you're at some KIDDIE pool? Trying to play MISTER Lifeguard? Huh? You think you're MACHO? Well I'll TELL you something, Private. You ain't TOUGH. And you ain't MACHO. If this was

Gookland, you'd be *DEAD*, Bozo! Your head just been skewered! Understand? You show MERCY and you lose your LIFE. And you don't WANT to lose your life. You don't want to DIE for your country, got it? You want to make the other gook die for HIS! Understand?"

"Sir. Yes, Sir," Lloyd huffs, dragging himself upright. He coughs up some water, swabs a trickle of blood from his nose, then stretches his hand down to Lomangino. Lomangino grasps his palm tightly and Lloyd pulls him to his feet.

Days blur into weeks, and the final month passes with Lloyd never having enough personal time to do anything but wash his reserve uniform, keep his spare boots polished and ready for inspection and to write his parents to say he'd soon be graduating. Of his original sixty-four platoon members, sixteen recruits have dropped out by the day commencement rolls around. Yet the forty-eight that remain have been toughened together into a disciplined team — a group of boys turned into a brotherhood of men. Grungy boots, they call themselves.

During the last days of training, final testing is done to determine who the ranking recruits will be for graduation. Lloyd Chambers, the cocky, once-aimless kid from Sillwater, Oklahoma, finishes at the top, and is awarded a set of dress blues to wear at commencement, a day which dawns bright and clear.

Inside the vast MCRD auditorium, packed with friends and relatives of the eight departing platoons, Lloyd's name booms over the loudspeakers as one of the five recruits in his platoon who have received a meritorious promotion to the rank of Private First Class. Moments later he hears his name again, echoing inside the hall, as the commanding officer announces that he has been named Honorman of his platoon. Lloyd rises to his feet. As he mounts the stage to accept the commendation, members of his platoon burst into a chant.

"GRUN-GY! GRUN-GY! GRUN-GY!" they shout in unison.

He glances back over his shoulder, smiling like he's never smiled before and wishing that Marilyn, and perhaps even his old boss at Moon-Lite Bowl, could be there to see him now. His eyes sweep across the sea of bodies, each in their go-to-church best. And then suddenly he spots familiar faces. High up above in the first row of the balcony, his mother is on her feet, clapping and screaming his name and blowing him kisses. He waves, and his father flashes a silly salute. Lloyd snaps to attention, chin up, chest out. His heels click. His palm snaps to his eyebrow. And standing there, eye to eye with his parents, he feels a surge come over him — a flush of emotion so intense that for the first time in eleven weeks, he feels tears well up in his eyes. But he dare not cry in front of United States Marines.

Following the final dismissal of recruits, Lloyd's parents rush to his side. His mother's face is smeared with mascara. She takes his face in both hands and plants a kiss on his mouth.

"I can't tell you how proud we are!" she says, beginning to cry. She pats his cheek, burying his face against her shoulder.

"Just a second, Mom," he says, stiffening. He takes a step back. "Go easy on the huggy-kissy stuff. I've got a reputation around here to maintain."

She pulls him back and gives him another kiss. "Well, son," his mother finally asks, "how does it feel to be a United States Marine? And the Honorman at that!"

"Like I can whip the world!" he says, smiling for his father's Instamatic. "Though I walk through the Valley of the Shadow of Death, I shall fear no evil," he expounds with a wink, "because I am the toughest grungy boot in the Valley!"

"And now we'll treat Mister Grungy Boot Okie Marine to lunch at the nicest restaurant in town," his father proudly announces.

"Yes, Sir!," says Lloyd. "I've got five days freedom before I have to report to Camp Pendleton. And I don't want to miss a minute . . . or a meal."

"Hear that?" his father crows, turning to his wife, "My own kid's calling me *Sir*! Do me a favor and say it once again."

"Yes,*Sir!*"

"There's hope for you after all! Once more — louder."

"Yes, SIR!"

"That — that right there is what you call music. Either music . . . or a miracle! Now, let's go eat. We passed a McDonald's on the way in."

Chapter Seven — DAN

"I THINK I'M DYING"

The corridors of Vintage High are beginning to fill with students changing classes. Dan, wearing a pair of faded denims, white Adidas and a Velour long-sleeved pullover, pushes through into the quad. Surrounding the courtyard are grey concrete buildings, concrete benches and concrete planters filled with institutional shrubbery that remains greenish-brown year-round.

On one of the planters, a boy and girl sit close together beside a tower of school texts. He wears black running shoes, black socks, black jeans and a Porsche-red flannel shirt with the sleeves rolled up to the elbows. He is tall and thin with an afro of rust red hair flaring out around his pale face. He looks like a zinnia. Pulling a limp pack of Marlboros from his pocket, he lights up and then passes a ragged cigarette to his girl-friend. She wears brown suede hiking boots with waffle soles and red laces lined with white hearts. Her blond hair is perfectly straight and hangs halfway down her lavender blouse. She takes a deep drag, smiles, gives him a peck on the cheek, then blows smoke out her nostrils.

As Dan passes, the boy looks up and waves. "Great play Friday!" he yells. Dan waves back and keeps moving.

Two girls, wearing their boyfriends' football jackets, exchange looks as he approaches. They both stop. "The play was dynamite, Dan," says the one wearing oversized glasses with rose-tinted lenses. Her friend pushes a lock of brunette hair behind her ear and smiles.

"Thanks," Dan says, hurriedly. "I don't want to seem rude or anything, but I've got to run. My mom's waiting for me out front." He glances at his watch, excuses himself and picks up his pace.

Suddenly he feels a tap on his shoulder. He spins around.

"Whoa, Hollywood!"

"Sorry, Jessica," Dan says. "My mind's in outer space and I didn't see you."

Jessica Bell is a pretty junior with immaculate blond hair that curls to her shoulders. Two braids are joined behind her head with a frilly blue ribbon. She wears a tight white sweater and navy slacks that are pleated in front.

"Congratulations!" she beams.

"On what?"

"On *what?*" she says, bursting into a ready, contagious laugh. "Your wonderful performance! The standing ovation!"

"Walk with me," Dan says. "I'm running late."

"Where you headed, off to talk with Broadway producers?" she bubbles, running to match his strides.

"To shoot some pool."

"Serious, what's the big hurry?"

"Doctor."

Her smile disappears. "Because of what happened last week?"

"You heard?"

Jessica nods.

"It's no big deal."

"I talked to Charlie."

"So he's spreading vicious rumors around campus?" Dan asks.

"Filthy lies."

"What'd he say?"

"Just that he was pretty scared about what happened in drama rehearsals."

"Only thing scares Charlie is waking up and looking in the mirror."

"Said you had these horrible chest pains. Like a heart attack or something. Twice."

"Exaggeration. Doctor says it's just a nervous stomach because of the fire I've been under recently. Me, I don't know what's wrong. Maybe it's a hangnail that's cramping a pressure point and interrupting the flow of blood to my brain. But I'm heading out now to get a second opinion, for what it's worth."

"We'll all be rooting for you," she smiles.

"Been hearing some vicious rumors myself lately. Something about you making cheerleader for next year."

"All last week waiting for the results, was I a basket case or what?" she says, laughing easily.

"You didn't have any competition."

"Tell me about it. The other girls were fantastic."

"Accept a compliment. You're hot stuff."

"I'll try to remember that next time I'm sitting home alone on a Friday night feeling like warmed over oatmeal."

Approaching the front of the school, Dan's eyes sweep the curb. He spots his mother's car and waves. "Well, looks like the ambulance is here," he says. He turns to Jessica and gives her shoulder a light squeeze.

"Take care at the doctor's. And hope you're feeling better."

"No big deal. Just a little — " His words erupt into a choking cough. " — a little stomach problem."

"You're a terrific guy, Dan," she says, helping him into the car. She closes the door and sticks her head through the open window. "And we're all proud of you — especially after Friday night. Wasn't he fantastic, Mrs. Krainert?"

"So-so," she smiles. "Actually, in my objective opinion, he was the best."

Dan screams suddenly and grabs his head.

Jessica jumps. "What's wrong?"

He looks up, laughing. "All this flattery, I thought my head was going to explode."

"A vacuum *implodes*," his mother says, waving to Jessica and pulling away from the curb.

Inside the clinic, Dan's mother again fills out the paperwork. Dan flips absently through the familiar stack of magazines
until his name is called. His mother follows him into the
examination room, where they are joined by a short Chinese
doctor wearing round gold-framed glasses. He has a matching
round face, with a new mustache sprouting from his cherub-like
mouth. His wrists are thin, and his fingers very long.

"So how you doing?" he asks, moving his stethoscope
around Dan's chest.

"Good question," Dan shrugs. "You tell me."

"This must be boy's mother," he says, without lifting his
eyes from his instrument.

Dan shakes his head. "Boy's girl friend."

"Ah hah! Velly funny boy," the doctor laughs. When he
laughs, his eyes squint shut and his shoulders shake. He makes
no sound.

"How's the heart sound, Doc?" Dan asks.

"Heart still beating. Ah hah!"

Dan looks across at his mother. She closes her eyes and
shakes her head.

"Have you lift velly heavy things recently?" the doctor asks.

"At work. Everything from fifty-pound bags of dog food
and rock salt to even heavier cases of canned goods. The dolly's
been busted."

"Dolly?"

"My other girl friend."

The doctor takes a step back, eyeing him skeptically.

"Uh, dolly. Actually it's a thing with wheels that you
carry heavy boxes on. Refrigerators. That kind of thing. But
it's been broken and I've had to carry and lift everything."

"Right. I see. I see," the doctor says, nodding hard. "Well
you be careful of body. Body cannot do what dolly should.
Your heart now clear. Velly strong. But physical strain make
hernia. I think that your problem. Hiatal hernia. You go home
and talk to boss. Tell him strain cause problem. Tell him no
more heavy lifting or you quit job."

"Music to my ears," Dan says. "I'd love to quit, and
there's no better reason than doctor's orders."

"Just a minute, Doctor," his mother says. "Your diagnosis, you say, is a hiatal hernia?"

"Doctor not always right. But I tink so. We give it couple weeks to see if trouble clear. If not, we operate boy to repair damage."

Mrs. Krainert nods. "And here that other doctor suggested Dan's problem could be cured by Rolaids or . . . trash can kicking. Imagine!"

"Ah hah! Kick trash cans? Ah hah!" he laughs, his shoulders shaking like an old car. His laugh is contagious, and Dan and his mother begin laughing with him. Suddenly the doctor stops and grows very serious.

"What's the matter?" Mrs. Krainert asks.

"I tink about what other doctor say. He means problem may be *psychosomatic*. Sometime body hurt if boy keep worry and problems inside. But cannot do, just like cannot keep ball under water. Ball must come to surface. Worry the same way. Sometime worry cause physical problem that not easy for doctors to diagnose. Other doctor tink if boy kick trash can, maybe no more worry. And, well . . . " his voice trails off as he shrugs his shoulders.

"Yes?" Mrs. Krainert asks.

"Well, maybe other doctor right. Maybe not. It big mistake to rule any doctor out," he says, smiling benignly. "Me, I tink problem be hernia."

"But you're definite it's not Danny's heart?"

"Mrs . . ."

"Krainert."

"Mrs. Krainert, I practice general medicine since time you little girl. I have long career in United States and China. How many babies you tink I deliver during life?"

"Doctor, I don't care about — "

"Five hunner seventy-tree babies I deliver. How many tonsillectomies you tink?"

"Your missing my — "

"Two hunner eighty-nine tonsillectomies. I lose number for appendectomies, but I tink a hunner or so. Tree tracheotomies, and oh so many vasectomies. But if too many vasectomies, no more babies. Ah hah! No more number for boils and cysts, but I amputate eleven legs, tirteen arms and hands, one hunner fifty-six fingers — mostly of soldier boys during bad war. So believe me, Mrs. — "

She looks at him, rubbing her temples.

"Krainert," Dan volunteers.

"Tank you. Now Mrs. Krainert, believe me. I know human body inside out, top to bottom. And I know bad heart. So don't worry mind with such thought," he says, rising and guiding them to the door. "Otherwise *you* need kick trash cans. Ah hah!"

"Thank you for your time, Doctor," she says dryly.

"Please, trust me. My business is human body. Some things doctor don't know. But I do know if engine bad when I listen. And I listen to them long time — forty-tree years next September. So trust me. Boy's engine run smooth like Datsun!"

"Do me a favor," Dan says. "Make it a Ferrari."

"Ah hah! Velly, velly funny boy!"

Several nights later, sitting around the dinner table at home, Dan stares at the chicken casserole on his plate and tries to feel hungry. He shifts his fork around in the light, playing with his reflection on the four tines. The image is distorted and upside down. He counts forty-nine green peas, and then spaces them out like pearls of a necklace around the perimeter of his plate.

"What did your boss say when you gave him the news?" his father asks.

"Let's just say we didn't part as friends. He was his same old charming self."

"Try to be a little more specific," his dad says. "It's a concern of mine since the grocery is on my bread route."

"Well, let's see," Dan begins. He waits for his father to look away, and then slips a chunk of casserole beneath the table to his dog.

"Yes?"

"I told him, you know, about what the doctor said, and he got a little peeved. No, *very* peeved. Thought I was an ungrateful son-of-a-you-know-what to just up and leave, regardless of what the doctor said."

"So you told him about the hernia?"

"No, I told him I had the bubonic plague."

"Don't be a wise guy. What else?"

"I don't know. He kept chomping the wet, green end of his cigar like it was gum or something, and blowing smoke in my face. And saying stuff like if I walked out now, I'd never be hired by a grocery store again. Not if he had anything to do with it. You know, he was just real nice about the whole thing."

"I'll probably lose the account."

"Tell him you disowned me."

His father ignores the comment. "That's it? Anything else?"

"Yeah. He said not to ever ask him for a recommendation. And then, you know, we hugged and I jumped on my horse, said 'Hi ho, Silver,' and galloped off into the sunset. End of story, end of dinner," Dan says, pushing his plate away and standing up.

"You've hardly touched your food," his father says.

"I took a couple bites."

"Oh, really?" his mother says, giving him the eye. "The dog seems to be putting on weight recently."

"Wish I could say the same," Dan responds.

"Maybe you would if you ate more of your own meals and shared less with the dog."

Dan shrugs, gathering his plate and silverware together. He places them in the sink, hikes up his sagging pants and heads outside into the backyard.

Mrs. Krainert waits until she hears the door close, then turns to her husband. "I don't know, George. But I've got a feeling we're dealing with more than a hernia or anything else the doctors have said."

"I'm not a doctor, Libby."

"Well, you see how he looks. And it's not getting any better."

"I know that."

"What are we going to do?"

"That's what I don't know. Have you tried calling Dr. What's-his-name?"

"Who?"

"The pediatrician in Vallejo who diagnosed his heart disease when he was a baby."

"Keith Vincent. Not yet. I first wanted to — " She breaks off suddenly and cocks her head. "What's that awful racket?"

"Sounds like people beating each other with shovels. Let's go. It's out back."

Springing from the table, they race for the door. They follow the sound around beyond the swimming pool. The dog barks wildly. Neighbors peer out their windows. Rounding the back corner of the house, they both stop suddenly. They look at each other and burst out laughing. Poised over the aluminum trash can, Dan boots it up against the fence. It clatters to the ground and he lands a fierce sidewinding drop kick. Startled by the laughter, Dan glances up. His eyes move from his parents to the trash can, back and forth.

"Well, I've got to admit," he says, shifting on his feet, "this does feel a little stupid."

"The question is, do you feel any better?" his mother asks.

"Yeah, like I'm ready to take on a tree next. Or maybe the side of the house."

His father walks over and stands the crumpled trash can upright. He tries to bend out the huge dents, but quickly gives up and wipes his hands on his trousers.

"Doctor's orders," Dan says.

His father looks at the trash can, saying nothing.

"Look on the bright side," Dan says almost smiling. "The IRS will probably let you write it off as a medical prescription."

Walking back inside the house, Dan flops down on his bed, picks up the phone and calls Shirley.

"Hey stranger," he says, and then fills her in on the doctor's latest diagnosis, his possible hernia operation and quitting work.

"Sounds like things have been more exciting for you at home than they have been at school. How long are you going to be out?"

"I'm feeling better. So if things go OK tonight, I'll probably be in tomorrow."

"Last week of school, you know."

"I know."

"Everybody's asking about you," she says gently.

"They ask *you* about me?"

"For some reason people link the two of us together. But I'm sure you wouldn't have any idea why that is."

"I'm stumped."

"Right."

"On the other hand, I've told a few people — but only a couple dozen — that you're the girl of my dreams."

"Probably the same couple dozen that have asked me about you."

"And what do you tell them?" Dan asks.

"That you've become a born-again Christian and have quit school for a pilgrimage to the Holy Land."

"Tell me something about this born-again business, Shirley. You know, I honestly don't feel any different . . . or for that matter, very Christian. Same old Dan when I look in the mirror. Not even a halo. And after watching Graham on TV, I didn't feel fireworks in my toes. No Fourth of July tingles. No voice from heaven. Not even any flashing lights on the Goodyear blimp. So I guess . . . well, maybe I don't understand what being a Christian is. And as for the born-again analogy that everybody talks about, it honestly sounds a little silly. I'm not even sure what it means."

"For starters, Dan, everybody has different ideas about what being a Christian means. Some describe Christians as people who *believe* certain things. For example, that Jesus was born in a Middle-East cow stable. That He turned water into wine. That church is a good place to hang-out on Sundays.

"Others would describe born-again Christians as those who *do* or *don't do* certain things. They talk to God. They don't tell dirty jokes. They read the Bible. They don't do drugs in the school restrooms." She pauses. "Dan, are you still there?"

"I'm listening."

"Still others would describe Christians as basically *good* people," Shirley tells him. "They send birthday cards to their grandma. They actually sing the Star-Spangled Banner at ball games. They turn in class papers on time. They smile a lot."

"So if everybody has a different idea," Dan says, "who's right?"

"Poll a hundred people, and you get a hundred different opinions. But the key is not what people think, but what the Bible says. And in the Bible, Jesus describes Christians as those who have been born again. That's *His* analogy, Dan, not something Billy Graham came up with. It comes straight out of the Gospel of John where Jesus says, 'I tell you the truth, unless a man is born again, he cannot see the kingdom of God.' "

"Fine. But that still doesn't explain what it means."

"Well, when Jesus first used the term, He was speaking with Nicodemus, a Jew who was big in religious politics. Nicodemus didn't understand what the term meant either. It triggered a ridiculous image in his mind of a grown person curling into a fetal ball and re-entering his mother's womb to be reborn. But Jesus was not trying to be funny when he used the analogy. Rather, he wanted to convey some key spiritual concepts."

"Such as?"

"For one thing, that your spiritual birth, like your physical birth, marks a new beginning. You were given a new Father, a new home, a new family. That is, a whole new identity. You're a new creation. The problem is — and you're right — you still look the same in a mirror. No halo. And the zits are still there."

"So you noticed. I was hoping perfect skin was part of the deal."

"Dan, your outer characteristics don't change. But your inner characteristics do. As you get to know God better, some of His personality and traits rub off on you. It's not a conscious thing. One day you begin to notice that some things you once enjoyed now seem empty and pointless, things like attending wild parties. Or reading *Penthouse*. Or getting stoned. Or making crude jokes about others. Things like these no longer have the same attraction they once had."

"Or wearing togas to school?"

"You said it, not me," Shirley says.

Dan coughs. "I'm not bothered by those things. What about me?"

"One day you'll notice your attitude changing toward others — your parents, for example. Or you'll find a new sense of hope and peace about the future. You'll realize you can trust God with . . . well, with what you're going through right now — these crazy health problems you're having."

"Can you guarantee that?" Dan asks.

"In the Bible, the book of Joshua, it says, 'Be strong and courageous. Do not be terrified; do not be discouraged, for the Lord your God will be with you wherever you go.' " Shirley pauses. "And the Bible says Jesus will never leave you, Dan, or forsake you. He's *always* there."

Dan shifts the phone to his other hand. "Go on, Shirley."

"Dan, at the heart of the born-again analogy is the idea that there's nothing you could ever have done to *earn* or *deserve* God. Being a Christian is not something you do or think. Being a Christian is not living idealistically and doing good deeds. It's a relationship. And like physical birth, spiritual birth stems from an act of love. It's through Jesus, and Jesus alone, that you've become a son of God."

"You're amazing, Shirley. Maybe you should be a preacher. Or rather, a preacher*ette*. But if it wasn't for you, I wouldn't feel the way I do now."

"Which is . . . "

"I've never really given much thought to any of this stuff before. But for the first time in my life, religion — or whatever you call it — makes sense. *Jesus* makes sense. You and Graham ought to team up."

"So you can honestly say, Dan, that you believe in Jesus? That He died — for you? That He rose again?"

"It sounds sci-fi, but I think I do. Yes, I do. I really believe. But when I come up short, you've got to help me."

"I'll be there, Dan."

"I wish you were here now."

"I think I know what's coming. And I think I'm glad you're there and I'm here."

"Shirley?"

"Yeah?"

"Someday I'd like to kiss you."

"Goodnight, Dan."

"I really would."

"Goodnight, Dan."

"Don't hang up."

"It's late."

"Who cares?"

"Goodnight, Dan."

Reluctantly, Dan replaces the phone in its base. He rolls out of bed, wanders into the living room and flips on the television. Laying on the couch with the remote control, he clicks through the channels for an hour.

Dan's father sticks his head through the door. "Don't keep switching channels. You'll wear the remote control out."

"You can't wear it out," Dan says, flipping channels again. "It's a radio signal."

"If nothing's on, go to bed."

"I'm not tired."

"How do you feel?"

"I wish you'd quit asking me that."

"Fine. Your mother and I are going to bed. Suggest you do the same."

"I'll be along."

"Goodnight."

"I actually feel OK."

"Maybe you can go back to school."

"But my foot's a little sore."

"Foot?"

"Accidently kicked the rim of the trashcan."

Laughing, his father disappears down the hallway. Dan runs through the channels one last time, and then turns the set off. Rising from the couch and walking into his bedroom, he feels a twinge in his chest. Undressing slowly in front of the mirror on the back of his door, he tries to ignore the pain.

Soon it is gone. He compares his reflection in the mirror with snapshots on his dresser taken the previous year: a picture of him snagging a line drive during a softball game, a stage shot, another of him doing a back flip into his family's backyard pool. In all of the shots his face and body are full; even his clothes fit. But now he must wear bulky sweaters to disguise his loss of weight. Now his pants hang on his bony hips. His ribs protrude. His eyes are deep and dark. Setting the picture cube down, he turns off the light and climbs slowly into bed.

Unable to sleep, Dan stares at his clock radio, watching minutes drag into hours. His stomach growls. He reaches for the half-empty jar of Rolaids on his nightstand. But suddenly his arm jerks rigid. His fingers claw the air, toppling the bottle of tablets. It's the same pain, but worse. He grabs for his chest, gasping for breath. Sweat pours.

"Dear God, please!" he gasps, trying to massage the fire from his chest. But the pain blazes across his torso. His head threatens to explode. Fighting off the covers, he stumbles to the door. Snowflakes cloud his vision. He grabs for the dresser, knocking a lamp to the floor. His parents burst in, their faces ashen.

"Same thing," Dan grits.

"Where does it hurt?" his mother asks, putting her arm around him.

Dan motions to his chest. "It's not indigestion. And it's no hernia. The pain is in my heart!"

His parents help him to the couch and ease him back into the cushions.

"No!" Dan yells. "I've got to sit up. It's worse laying down."

His father grabs a pillow from the chair and stuffs it behind Dan. He lays an afghan over him.

"I . . . I think I'm dying!" Dan grimaces.

"Libby, call the doctor!"

"And I'm only seventeen," Dan's voice quakes.

"Hush. Don't talk like that," says his mother, her eyes brimming with tears. She takes his temperature, wipes his brow, fluffs his pillow, adjusts his afghan.

"I'll call the doctor," his father says. "We can drive Danny in tonight."

"A *real* doctor this time. Dr. Vincent."

"Vincent!" Dan grunts. "He's a kid's doctor."

"But he knows his medicine. And he knows your heart."

"Do we still have the number, Libby?"

"Try information. Vallejo."

Mr. Krainert darts for the phone in the kitchen.

"What time is it?" Dan asks.

"Almost four-thirty," his mother says. "But doctors have answering services. They'll wake him up."

"It's too hot," says Dan, kicking his cover off.

"Do you want something to drink?"

Dan shakes his head. Squeezing his eyes shut, he massages his arm. His breaths are forced and heavy.

"How is it now?" his mother asks.

Dan shakes his head.

Mr. Krainert returns from the phone with word that Dr. Vincent is out of town.

"No!" his wife cries.

"Vacation. But he's expected back tomorrow. Actually today," he says, glancing at his watch. "His answering service said to call the office in a couple of hours to set up an appointment."

"We don't wait, George. Go get dressed. We'll run Danny into emergency now."

"I'm not going to any hospital meat ward," Dan says.

"You're going. And you're going now," his father says.

Dan shakes his head. "The pain's letting up."

"Danny, don't be silly," his mother says. "If you could just see yourself!"

"I have. And I know what's wrong."

"We're your parents, son."

"But it's my body, and I'm not going to some M.A.S.H. ward."

"You've been watching too much TV," his mother says, dabbing his forehead with a cold washcloth. "How do you feel now?"

"Like a trashcan."

His mother wipes his face again.

"But getting better," he says. "It always hits hard. But after fifteen minutes or so, the pain starts backing off."

"It's been twenty," his father says. "What do you say, Libby?"

His mother looks at Dan.

"I can make it through till morning," he says.

"OK," she says, throwing up her hands. "Why don't you go back to bed, George. I'll stay with him. And if anything else happens, we'll go in. Otherwise, we'll wait for Dr. Vincent."

"Are you sure?"

"I'm not sure about anything."

"I'll be fine," Dan says. "Trust me."

"Trust me," his mother mimics. "I heard the same thing earlier this week from the doctor. And look where it got us. Just a few minutes ago, you said you were *dying*."

"Maybe you're right," Dan says. "Maybe I do watch too much TV."

CAMP PENDLETON

Fastening his duffel bag onto the back of a gleaming black Yamaha 400, purchased by his parents as a boot camp graduation gift, Lloyd guns the engine to a low whine. His parents move in with their Instamatics clicking, and then hug him goodbye.

"Write us," his mother says.

"I'll try to do better."

"Stay true to your roots, son," says his father. "You can take a man out of the country, but you can't take the country out of a man. Even if he lives in California."

"Once an Okie, always an Okie," his mother says, wiping a tear from her cheek.

"Hey, this ain't a funeral!" Lloyd says, reaching out and squeezing his mother's arm.

"I'm not very good at goodbyes," she sniffles, rummaging through her purse for a handkerchief.

"Goodbyes are one thing," he says. "But now you're crying like you're paying final respects. Smiles, everybody."

"I'll be OK. But here, take this," she says, handing him an envelope. "It was in my purse, and I almost forgot to give it to you."

"What is it?"

"Letter from Marilyn. She heard we were coming out, and dropped it off the night before we left."

He opens it, skims the first couple of paragraphs, and then tears the stationery in half. "A 'Dear John,' " he says, shoving the remnants into his back pocket. "When I left she was talking marriage. And now this."

"Has she written before?"

"During the first weeks, quite a bit. But then I didn't hear from her for a month. After that her letters were pretty strange. I suspected something like this was coming. Have you seen her with anybody?"

"There was somebody waiting in the car when she stopped by," his mother says. "But I didn't want to say anything."

"Just as well," Lloyd says. "California girls are better, anyway."

"California isn't the only place in the world," says his father. "Remember, you've always got a job back home with me if — "

"Sorry, Dad, but I'm in this for keeps. Got me the heart of a Marine."

"A lifer?"

Lloyd nods.

"Then be the best, son."

"And if anybody ever shoots at you, be sure to duck," his mother adds, struggling to smile.

Lloyd nods again. "Like I said, 'though I walk through the valley of the shadow of death, I shall fear no evil.' For I am the best and the toughest grungy boot in the Valley."

"Put on your helmet," his mother says, giving him a final hug.

He runs his hand over his closely cropped red hair. "Gotta let my buzz job breathe," he laughs. "Been wearing a helmet for the past eleven weeks." And then he revs his bike, pops into gear and squeals across the parking lot with a wave.

"Your helmet!" his mother yells, but her voice is lost in the roar of the engine. Shaking her head, she turns to her husband. "Maybe we should have bought him a car instead."

"He would have just traded it in for a used go-to-hell

bike like he's got back home, and then pocketed the difference.
Better we got him a new one now."
    "Maybe he'll settle down someday."
    "Nice thought."
    "When he gets older?"
    "Possible."
    "Perhaps when he reaches Captain."
    "Our son? Impossible!" he chuckles.

    It is a lazy summer day — bright sun, clear sky, big
surf — as Lloyd roars up the Pacific coast on Interstate 5
toward the Marine Corps base at Camp Pendleton. With a
couple of hours to spare before checking in, he circles down
Harbor Drive to Oceanside's sailboat-jammed marina. He parks
in the lot fronting Cape Cod Village near Helgrens Sport Fishing
and scans the boats, sunbathers and gulls through a dime-for-
three-minutes telescope. Across the harbor he spots a sun-
bleached blonde fishing off the Villa Marina jetty. She wears
cut-off denims, a blue-checkered blouse tied high on her waist,
and no ring as best as he can tell. Sniffing at a fish pail beside
her sits a golden cocker spaniel.
    When the telescope suddenly goes black, Lloyd reaches
for another dime, but then changes his mind. He hops back
on his bike and whips around by the jetty. Perched on a nearby
stoop sits a woozy old drunk with three-day whiskers, sipping
lunch from a bag-covered bottle. At the man's feet staggers a
matted, flea-bitten mongrel that laps at puddles of sweet wine
which the man periodically replenishes. Lloyd swings to the
curb to survey the plastered pair, and then steps off his bike
and ambles over. The man is singing a Don Ho song.
    "Hey-o," Lloyd says.
    The man stops singing and turns around. He squints hard
at Lloyd, nodding as he steps closer. "Affernoon," he slurs,
swiping at his drippy nose with the back of his hand. "Yerr
juss (burp) in time ferr Hawayee concerr. Pull up a shair (burp)
an I'll sinn some more sonns. You lie . . . like (burp) Don Ho?"
    Lloyd sticks a ten dollar bill in the man's veiny hand. "I
need to borrow your dog for a half hour. Go buy yourself
some decent wine."

"Mush oblige, Misser. Than-you. Than-you verr (burp) mush." He downs a final swallow of his bagged brew, pours the last drops for his dog and hands the frazzled rope leash to Lloyd.

As the old man staggers off toward a bar, Lloyd hustles the mutt into the nearby men's restroom. Scrounging tiny slivers of discarded soap from the shower floors, he gives the animal a quick bath, fluffs its fur beneath the wall-mounted air dryer, and then, with the intoxicated dog in tow, strides purposefully down the jetty toward the girl. She watches him cautiously as he approaches.

"Any luck?" he asks, motioning toward her fish pail.

The girl glances warily at Lloyd and his dog, which suddenly stumbles onto its face.

"What's wrong with your dog?" she says, trying not to laugh. She is soft and lean, with a beach complexion and a light sprinkling of freckles across her nose. She wears no makeup. Her lips are full, and her cheeks are accented by a matching pair of dimples.

"Wrong? Uh, nothing," Lloyd says.

The girl raises her eyebrows and points at the animal.

"Well, this is no ordinary dog," he begins as the dog again trips, landing on its ear. "It, uh — those are impersonations she's doing. She's working on Gerald Ford right now," he says, reaching down to lift the mutt back to its feet. The dog promptly rolls onto its back with a crooked grin and burps. "And that's Dudley Moore she's doing."

"She? Your dog's a *he*."

Lloyd darts a look down at the sodden-minded animal. "Plain as day. Can't argue anatomy."

"And he looks drunk," the girl says, breaking into a light giggle. Her dimples seem to glow.

"This conversation isn't going like I intended," he says. "OK, I fess up. Actually it's not my dog. I borrowed her . . . *him* from an old drunk down the street. You see, I'd spotted you in the marina telescope, and thought . . . you know, you had a dog and it seemed like a good way to meet you. So here I am. How's that for honesty?"

"You're a Marine." She says it as a statement, not a question.

"My buzz job, I know."

"It'll grow back."

"Not while I'm in the Corps. They're into scalp."

The girl reels in her line and recasts.

"What's your dog's name?" Lloyd asks.

"Blossom."

"Here, Blossom," he says, holding out his hand. "Here, girl."

Blossom ignores his hand, takes a hesitant sniff at the other dog, and then draws quickly away.

"Nice dog, but uncomfortable around a party animal," Lloyd says, turning his attention back to the girl. "Caught anything?"

"If you call that something," she says, pointing at a scrawny bass in the bottom of her bucket.

"Did you catch that, or is that your bait?"

"Fish in the marina are all small."

"It's their junk food diet — kids tossing them Cheetos and marshmallows and bits of Velveeta. Place to fish is beyond the breakers. Out there they've got honest meat on their bones."

"You sound like the voice of experience."

"Used to get seasick on paddleboats," Lloyd confesses with a shrug. "Guess that's why I'm a Marine instead of a Swab. But maybe I'm over it. In fact, I'll take you out deep sea fishing . . . if you'll go."

"Now?"

"Next weekend. Or whenever I can get off. Don't know my schedule yet."

"Grungy boot?"

"Yeah. Just graduated."

"So you haven't met my father yet?"

Lloyd raises his eyebrows. "Father? Haven't even met *you* yet. My name's Lloyd Chambers."

"Lisa," the girl says.

"And just who's your father?"

"Base commander. Everybody knows him . . . or of him. And most people hate him."

"Great," Lloyd swallows. "And I've got a date with his daughter?"

"I never said yes."

"Well?"

"I don't know."

"I'll pay."

"Talk to my father."

"Be serious," Lloyd says.

"Standing rule. He says any Marine I go out with must first deal with him."

"What can happen on a fishing boat?"

Lisa smiles.

"Uh, right," Lloyd says. "Where do I find him?"

"Anybody on base can tell you. Just ask around."

Lloyd glances at his watch. "Gotta head that way now," he says. "And I'll track him down this week. Save the weekend."

"*All* weekend?" Lisa asks, eyeing him coyly.

Lloyd looks her over and smiles. "I think we're going to get along."

"Think so?"

"I do."

"You seem rather cocky."

"Oh?"

"Sweet dreams, soldier," she says with a wink.

Lloyd waves, moaning to himself as he turns to leave, dragging the dog behind him. On his way back to his bike, he spots the old drunk and hands him the leash. "I'm grateful," he says. "You've got a real champion."

The man squints at the animal with its newly washed and fluffed fur and shakes his head. He gives the frazzled rope back to Lloyd. "Thanss, Misser. But thass not mine. I'm sor . . . (burp) sorry, but thirss been some triffic miss-up. My dog dunn look that . . . (burp) good."

"Take it," Lloyd insists.

"Iss not my — "

"It *is* your dog," Lloyd insists, forcing the leash back into the drunk's hand. "Just smell it's breath."

Wheeling to a stop at the main gate fronting Camp Pendleton, Lloyd hands his papers to the guard on duty. The man
points him down the road to the Joint Reception Center and
snaps a salute. Lloyd returns the salute, and then peels past
him in a fifty-foot wheelie. He blasts down a straightaway and
takes a sweeping turn 20 m.p.h. too fast. Rounding the bend,
he glances to his right. Looming off the edge of the roadway
is a six-foot metal stake, topped with a headstone-shaped sign.
The sign is lettered *KIA*, dated, and marked with a cross. He
passes three more before arriving at the Center for check-in,
and asks the woman at the desk about them. She's a stout
civilian employee with football shoulders, short brown hair,
heavy jowls and a deep mannish voice. Lloyd wonders if her
arms are tattooed.

"Oh, those," she says, processing his orders and registering
his motorcycle. "They're 'Killed in Accident' signs. They mark
where Marines have died. Mostly drunk driving."

"Bodies planted right there?"

"No bodies. Just markers," she says, handing back his
papers and a gaping information folder. "You're to report to
Bravo Company, Camp Horno, home of the First Marines. It's
a seventeen-minute drive from here." She gives him a map,
and Lloyd turns to leave. "You have a motorcycle helmet,
private?" she calls after him.

"On the back of my bike."

"I handle check-ins and check-*outs*," she says. "And I'd
prefer not to deal with you again. So wear the helmet."

"Check-outs?" he asks.

"Paperwork for the KIA bodies. Final roster, understand?
Most of the KIAs are motorcycle related, so — "

"Funny," Lloyd interrupts, approaching the desk again.
"You don't look a thing like my mother. But you sure do sound
like her."

"Just a word of advice, private."

"If you don't mind, the only advice I need right now is
how to get to the nearest liquor store, bar or commissary,"
Lloyd says. "In the space of a few hours I saw my parents
for the last time, got dumped by my girl, was serenaded by a

wino, gave a drunk dog a shower, hustled the daughter of the
brass, and have now met you. I could use a drink."

"I do not support the alcohol industry, nor personally
commend those who do," the woman says. "So I cannot in
good conscience provide the information you request. However,
the government does, and you'll find it contained in the folder
just handed to you."

"A little advice of my own," Lloyd says in a confidential
tone. He leans across the desk until he can count the blackheads
on her nose. "Do yourself a favor someday and get absolutely
pickled. You'd be a better person for it, guaranteed."

"Good day, private," she says calmly. "Speed limit on
base is 35 m.p.h., and the roads are patrolled."

"You probably don't personally condone speeding."

"No."

"I didn't think so." Lloyd blows her a kiss, walks back
outside and mounts his bike.

Heading for Camp Horno at nearly twice the speed limit,
Lloyd detours to Lake O'Neill, the base recreation area. Winding
up his engine, he wails up a dirt trail and skids to a stop on
a bluff overlooking the water. Nearby, couples neck beneath
giant eucalyptus trees, oblivious to the motorcycles and three-
wheelers roaring up and down dirt trails which snake through
the surrounding hills. The lake, peppered with ducks and row-
boats, reflects wisps of cotton candy clouds. The far shore is
lined with fishermen, and beyond them towers the Regional
Naval Medical Center.

Lloyd scans the area for several long minutes, filling his
lungs with long, deep breaths. Suddenly his mind is disrupted.
Gazing out over the water, his head clouds with a faraway
thought. He feels a dreamlike déjà vu sensation as if he's been
here before. He shakes his head. No, it's something else. A
thought, a feeling he can't quite place. He closes his eyes,
trying to focus his mind. His stomach tightens, and he starts
to sweat. Rubbing the side of his head, he wonders if perhaps
he is dreaming. But when he opens his eyes, the lake is still

there. Disquieted, he glances over his shoulder and notices his helmet. He thinks about what the woman told him, and then brushes her advice aside. Yet the helmet seems to mock him. He quickly unstraps it and tugs it over his head. He sits there a moment longer, trying again to capture the plaguing thought, but it is gone. Lloyd watches a crow cut against the wind in the distance. It flies closer, but with an imperceptible lift of one wing, disappears behind a bank of oak trees. Lloyd reaches for his key and pops the clutch. His mind clears with motion. Nevertheless, he moves cautiously down the trail back to the main road, feeling like a student driver approaching an intersection. But upon hitting pavement, he laughs at himself and guns the engine.

As Lloyd steps off his bike in the lot fronting the Bravo Company barracks, a huge khaki chopper circles overhead. Dangling from its belly on a long rope are seven Marines, and from where Lloyd stands he can hear their screams and shouts. He watches the helicopter until it passes behind a far ridge, and then steps inside the barracks where other newly-arrived privates are milling about, polishing shoes and buckles, writing home and playing poker.

"Chambers!" somebody yells.

Lloyd recognizes the voice and spins around.

"Chambers, what the bleep are you doing here?"

"Hey-o, Bart Thompson! No kidding, you're Bravo, too?"

"This is like some kind of bleeping reunion," Bart says. "Throw your stuff on the top rack next to me. Can you bleeping believe it? Just like old times, but without Stinko, Spot, Lemon-Jello and those other pansies. Not to mention that bleep of a DI." Small, but heavily muscled, Bart is barefoot and wears a pair of old Levis and a white football jersey cut off at the waist. His abdomen ripples, and his biceps strain the sleeves. He bears the chiseled good looks of Tom Selleck, but without the wrinkles.

Lloyd walks to the bunk, introduces himself to others in the vicinity and begins to undress when the company sergeant strides through the door.

"Attention!" he barks.

Lloyd, clad only in boxers, snaps a salute with the rest.

"At ease," the sergeant orders. "And welcome to Bravo Company, home of the First Marines. You'll be proud to know that the First Marines is the oldest, most decorated division-sized unit in the Corps," he says. "We've fought proudly in some of the bloodiest battles on this planet, beginning with action in Haiti in 1915. The story of the Marine Corps is the story of the First Marines, a story written with courage. The courage of young men like yourselves," he continues.

Lloyd elbows Bart. "Courage?" he whispers. "All I feel is hungry."

Suddenly the sergeant whips around.

"Identify yourself, soldier!"

"Sir! Private First Class Lloyd Chambers, Sir!"

"A PFC, but you forgot your manners already?" he thunders. "Give me fifty! Now!"

Lloyd pounds out the required pushups as the commanding officer drones on with his history spiel. He then dismisses the men, giving them liberty until the next morning at 0530 hours.

"As for you, Chambermaid," the sergeant says, drawing a toothbrush from inside his boot, "take this and clean the johns. And shine them bright as my boots. I'll be back to inspect them."

Five hours later as Lloyd is buffing the last toilet, two privates stumble drunk into the barracks. They head straight for the bank of clean stalls.

"NO! No, not there!" Lloyd yells, trying to herd them to the urinals instead. But it's too late. The stomach of one private explodes, splattering one seat. The other relieves himself, but can barely stand on his feet, let alone hit his target. Lloyd buries his face, afraid to look, as the two stagger back toward bed singing in drunken unison: "I wish I were an Oscar Meyer wiener . . . ."

Moments later the sergeant whips around the corner and kicks open the first stall. His lip curls. "I thought I gave you a job to do!" he steams. He kicks open the second stall. "Get over here and get to work!"

"Sir, I can explain — "

"No excuses! I want these spotless by morning!"

"Sir. Yes, Sir," Lloyd answers wearily. And with a toothbrush that now contains but a half-dozen bristles, he digs in for the night.

Chapter Nine — DAN

THE $100,000 SOLUTION

Dr. Keith Vincent clips the fresh set of X-rays to a light panel on the wall of his Vallejo office and carefully examines each of the six exposures. He is medium-built, with thinning gray hair, a salt-and-pepper beard, and droopy eyes that give him the perpetual look of one who has just crawled out of bed. His long face is lined with concern as he turns back to Dan and his mother, who sit stiffly on the other side of his desk.

"I'll give it to you straight," he says. "Dan, you're a sick young man. As you've suspected, your problem has nothing to do with indigestion or a hernia."

"No," Mrs. Krainert says, "I didn't think so."

"My heart," Dan states matter-of-factly.

"Seventeen years ago, I detected a leaking mitral valve in your heart, Dan. Because the valve doesn't shut completely, the blood sloshes around the heart chamber a little more than we'd like, causing what's described as a 'third' heartbeat. In technical jargon, it's called a long apical systolic ejection murmur — something we've always known you had. And in itself, it's not an overtly serious problem." He pauses. "But what I hear now is something different — an irregular rhythm . . . a weakening beat . . . fluid in the lungs. The X-rays show that your heart is hyper-enlarged."

"Bigger than it should be?" Dan asks.

"Much bigger. These findings, coupled with other symptoms such as your severe chest pains, near collapses, migraines, cough and blurry vision, indicate — "

"Doctor, I don't think I want to know," Dan says, looking away.

"Your originally-diagnosed heart muscle disease, which has been in apparent remission all these years, has flared up."

"Exactly what does he have?" Mrs. Krainert asks.

"Cardiomyopathy or, more specifically, endocardial fibroelastosis. Dan's heart muscle is deteriorating."

"After all these years, why now?" Mrs. Krainert asks, her voice quavering. She takes Dan's hand, tightly clasping it atop the physician's desk.

"Only God can answer that," he responds gently, placing his hand atop theirs. "When you were a child, Dan, I told your parents that I didn't expect you to live through your first birthday. And now you're seventeen. I don't know why the cardiomyopathy went into remission then, and I don't know why it's come back now. It's these 'why' questions that are the hardest, and I wish I had answers for you."

"Are you saying — " Dan bites his lip, unable to continue.

"That you may die?"

Dan nods.

"We'd like to avoid that possibility, Dan. Your heart is in serious trouble, and we've got to move quickly. I want you in the hospital today for tests."

"Today?" Dan says. "There's just a couple days left of school. Give me at least until Monday."

"For you, Dan, school's already over."

"Please, Doc. I've got a lot of friends that I — "

"I have already phoned Dr. Saul Robinson at the University of California Medical Center in San Francisco. He's the same cardiologist who saw you as a child and, as a specialist, he will know better how to treat you. A room has been arranged for you at Moffit Hospital — Dr. Robinson will be waiting for you there. I want you admitted by three o'clock this afternoon. Three o'clock. No later."

"That's barely three hours from now," Mrs. Krainert says. "And it's a good two hour drive to San Francisco."

"You have time to drive home and pack a bag," Dr. Vincent says.

"Is there any chance of a mistake in your diagnosis?" Dan asks quietly.

"I wish there were. But I'm afraid not," he says, rising from his chair.

"What about the other doctors — the indigestion and hernia they thought I had?"

"I wish it were that simple, Dan. But . . . well, I suggest you leave immediately. As I said, Dr. Robinson is expecting you by three."

Dan and his mother make the drive from Napa Valley's wine country, across the Golden Gate Bridge and into San Francisco in silence. They arrive at Moffit Hospital ten minutes early, pulling to the curb fronting the emergency ward. Just inside the automatic glass doors, a short, silver-haired man with the polished looks of a corporation president paces the floor in his lab coat. Dan checks his name tag as he passes.

"I suppose you're waiting for me." Dan says.

"Dan Krainert?"

"Yeah. But right now I wish I was somebody else."

"Dr. Saul Robinson," he says, shaking first Dan's, then his mother's hand. He motions at a nurse, who promptly rolls a wheelchair to Dan's side. Another nurse ushers Mrs. Krainert to the desk to begin paperwork.

"Take a seat, young man," the doctor says. We're going upstairs."

"I'm not an invalid yet. I can walk."

"Sit down," Dr. Robinson repeats firmly.

One look at the doctor's face and Dan knows he is accustomed to getting his way. Without another word, Dan eases into the wheelchair, and is quickly rolled by the nurse to the sixth floor pediatric ward. The walls are painted with butterflies and flowers, and large appliqués of Winnie the Pooh smile down from the doors. Young children play in the game room, while others, bedridden, cry through open doors down the hall.

"Shouldn't I be in another area or something?" Dan asks.

"Later, perhaps," the doctor says, walking beside the wheelchair. "But I want you here for now."

"How long am I in for?"

"Minimum two days for tests. Depending on what we find, your stay could be extended."

"There goes school," Dan says, shaking his head. "Couldn't this have waited a few days?"

"There are more important considerations at this point," the doctor replies, but does not elaborate.

"What's on the menu?" Dan asks.

"You'll be on a liquid diet for the duration of the tests," Dr. Robinson replies.

For the next two days, Dan undergoes a battery of tests: including EKGs and his first cardiac catheterization. During the catheterization, a wire connected to tiny clippers is inserted through an artery in Dan's groin and snaked to his heart, where it snips tissue samples for later lab analysis. Between tests, Dan passes the time by entertaining his six-year-old roommate with Mr. Rogers impersonations, and by making Play-Doh dinosaurs which he hardens on the radiator for the child.

"Are you my babysitter?" the boy asks.

"No, the laugh doctor," Dan says, suddenly jumping out of bed and rushing over to tickle the young boy.

Released from Moffit Hospital with his cardiomyopathy confirmed, Dan returns home on a strict medical diet of twenty pills a day. He lines the array of bottles along the kitchen counter, and begins reading the labels. He has memorized the purpose for each pill. Digoxin, heart stimulant. Quinidine, antiarrhythmic. Isordil, chest pain reliever. Lasix, diuretic. Coumadin, blood thinner. Hydralazine, blood pressure stabilizer. Klorvess, mineral supplement. Nitroglycerin, chest pain reliever. Lidocaine, antiarrhythmic. And then he opens a library copy of a medical encyclopedia and begins comparing his prescriptions to the side effects outlined in the text.

"What are you doing?" asks his mother as she passes by.

"Getting loaded," he says, flipping pages. "Here, listen to what they say about my blood pressure medicine: 'Coronary artery disease, arrhythmatic heart disease or known allergy to this drug prohibits its use.' I'm no Quincy or Trapper John, but I think it says that if I've got the disease I've got, don't take this stuff." With a shrug, he tosses one of the Hydralazine pills up in the air and catches it in his mouth.

"Don't play with the medicine, Dan. It's expensive."

"It's also deadly. Want to know the side effects of Quinidine? Straight out of the book: 'Possibly fatal reaction may occur.' " He looks at her, smiles and throws another Quinidine into the air. It bounces off his chin and rolls beneath the kitchen table. The dog races for the round tablet, but Dan snatches it away.

"Daniel Krainert, what did I say?" snaps his mother.

"If my heart doesn't get me, my medication will," Dan says. He wipes the pill off on his shirt and then swallows it.

"I want you to stop talking this way," she says, her hands on her hips. "Death and dying — that's all we've heard from you since you've been home from the hospital."

"Well?"

"Well what?"

"Do you know something I don't?"

"The doctors have not said you're dying."

"Read between the lines."

"Danny, please."

"You're not the one who has to eat this stuff or be poked full of holes by the doctor."

"It's hard on me, too," she says, wiping her eyes which have suddenly filled with tears. "The times I've prayed that I could take your place, you can't imagine. And you'll never know what it's like for a parent to — "

"That's right," he says, wheeling around suddenly. "I'll never know, because I'll never get the chance to *be* a parent." He tosses another pill in the air.

"I'm not going to tell you again about those pills!"

"OK, OK," he says, turning back to his book. "But it just seems that if I'm going to OD on this stuff, I ought to be able to have a little fun doing it."

His mother walks over and picks up one of the vials and examines the label. "Danny, I know this is hard for you. It's hard for all of us. And I don't want to fight. I just want you to know that I love you."

"I know, Mom."

"Why don't you stop thinking about all of this. Call a friend and go out. Get away from the house for a little while. Do something to relax. Maybe Shirley's free tonight."

"Can I borrow the car?"

"If you gas it up. It's riding past empty."

"Can I borrow some money?"

"Maybe I misunderstood you," she says, smiling. "Just a minute ago I thought you said you were *loaded*."

"You're a real wit, Mom. Where's your purse?"

Pulling into a corner Chevron station, Dan pumps seventy-five-cents worth of gas in the tank. He pays with a ten dollar bill, pockets the change, then drives to pick up Shirley.

"What do you want to do?" he asks, after they've been on the road a few minutes.

"What do you want to do?"

"I asked you first."

"I don't care. You tell me."

"We could go up in the hills and neck."

Shirley bursts out laughing. "Crazy as you are, Krainert, I've missed you."

"Really?"

"Really. How was the hospital?"

"Not bad if you don't mind being a pin cushion. But let's not talk about it. I've just been through it with my mom."

"What do you want to talk about?"

He winks at her, hooks a left turn and heads up a narrow winding road overlooking Napa. On the horizon, the sun retires for the night behind a bank of flaming, popsicle-colored clouds.

"Where are you going?" Shirley asks, eyeing him suspiciously.

"Calm down. I just want to get some altitude; drive up where I can clear my head and get a little perspective. Or if you want, I can turn around and we can go sit on my roof. I imagine we could see the sunset from there, too."

"It's gorgeous," Shirley says, watching the final light of day blink out.

"In the hospital, I realized I had absolutely never watched the sun go down over Napa. I mean, I'd seen it hundreds of times. But I'd never stopped to really *watch* it. I tried to picture it there in my bed — to picture *this*," he says, motioning out the side window as he enters a sweeping S-turn. "How the hills and trees glow purple right before sunset, and all the little white lights of the city. But I couldn't even remember what it looked like."

"Sometimes you forget to notice."

The car suddenly sputters and dies.

"What's wrong?" she asks.

"I think I'm out of gas," he says, pulling to the shoulder atop the hill.

"What now?"

Dan stretches his arm behind Shirley to lock her door. "Just a precaution. You never know where the Chain Saw Killer will strike next." He then drops his hand to her shoulder and lightly fingers her blouse.

"Dan, I don't think — "

"Shhh," he whispers. "Don't talk now." His finger moves to the base of her neck. "Shirley, I — " But he loses the words in his throat. He turns toward her, his eyes roaming over the smooth curve of her cheeks, her warm eyes, her soft brown hair that curls lightly upon her shoulders. He eases closer and drapes his arm around her.

"You wouldn't deny a dying man his last request, would you?"

She looks at him sternly, but can't smother a smile. She glances away, but immediately turns back. Her lips begin to move, but no words come out.

Dan slips his hand gently behind her head and draws her to himself. He looks deep into her eyes. "I'm going to kiss you now," he says.

Shirley nods, taking him in her arms. But after a long moment, she eases away, brushing strands of hair from her eyes.

"I've wanted to do that for a long time," Dan says. "All I could think about in the hospital was you." He turns her face to him again, but Shirley places her hand against his lips.

"What's wrong?"

"I'm sorry, Dan," she says quietly. "But I can't do this."

"You just did. And you came up for air smiling."

She looks at him and nods. "I know."

"So?"

"I'm scared for you, Dan."

"Please, Shirley — "

"No, let me talk for a minute. You just got out of the hospital. And I know this isn't what you want to hear, but I haven't really changed my mind. I still simply want to be your friend — the absolute *best* friend you've ever had."

He turns away and stares out the window.

"Dan, listen to me! I love you more than you realize, but I want to protect that love. You know yourself that relationships come and go. And when they go, there's a lot of hurt. You don't need any more pain at this point in your life."

"What I need is you."

"But not the way you think you do. You don't need a girl friend now. You *want* one, but you don't need one. What you need is somebody who will listen, somebody you can talk to and share anything with, somebody who can help you draw closer to God. And I want to be that person, Dan. I want to be there for you, helping you along in the months to come. And to guarantee that, I need to protect our relationship. To guard my heart. To help you guard yours. Look, you've just been diagnosed with an *incurable* heart disease! And I know that deep inside you're bleeding your guts out. I know, Dan, because I can see it. It shows in your eyes. You're afraid for your life. You think you're dying."

Dan squeezes his eyes shut, but the more he tries to fight back the tears, the faster they flow. "I don't think I'm dying," he blurts. "I *know.*" His voice cracks, and he suddenly begins to sob. "Here," he says, pulling his secret weight chart from his wallet, "Look at this. Even with the pills I'm taking, I still lose a couple of pounds each week. I'm skin and bones, and people talk to me as if I had a cold that will go away next week. You're right, what I've got is incurable. And these pills I'm taking, they'll just . . . all they'll do is just make me die slower." He breaks down again, and Shirley takes him in her arms. "You've got to help me," he cries. "I feel like I'm all alone. And I'm scared. Very scared."

"I'll help you, Dan. You know I will," she says, holding him tightly.

"You've got to."

"I will. You're not alone. I'll be there every step of the way — no matter what happens."

In a moment he is quiet, and Shirley releases him.

"It was awful in the hospital," he whispers. "I needed you there to talk with."

"You know I don't have a car. If I did, I would have been there every day. And when school starts this fall, I'll have classes to attend. There will be times when we'll be apart. But God won't leave your side. He'll be there with you every moment, and He understands more than anybody your deepest hurts and fears. Your relationship with Him is now the most important thing — the very most important thing, whether you live — "

"Or die?"

"Yes. Or die. Either way. Nothing can separate you if you just trust Him will all of your heart — "

"Or what's left of it, anyway."

Shirley reaches out and takes him in her arms again. "Let me just hold you for a minute, and then we can go," she says, wiping a tear from his eye. He kisses her lightly on the forehead, inhaling the sweet smell of her hair. And then Shirley eases away.

"I feel much better," Dan says.

"I do, too."

"I'm glad. But now what?"

"Now what?"

"We're still out of gas," she says.

"I need your help to push us off the shoulder. I'm not feeling up to it. If you can get us off, we can coast down. There's a station at the bottom of the hill."

"At the bottom of the hill! You knew that all along, Krainert!" she says, taking a playful swipe at his face. She climbs out, walks behind the car and leans against the bumper. The car doesn't budge. "Put it in neutral!" she yells.

"It is. Push harder!"

The car inches forward and begins to roll. Shirley races around to the door, but Dan has locked it.

"Open the stupid door!" she yells, trotting alongside and banging on the window.

Dan honks the horn and laughs as the car picks up speed. She begins running faster.

"I'm warning you!" But his hands don't move from the wheel. "Krainert!"

"Jump on board!"

"Are you kidding?" Now she is really running.

"Be a sport!"

Taking a pair of long, quick strides, she leaps with a scream onto the hood of his car. Dan honks again. Clutching tightly to the frame, she makes faces at Dan through the windshield as together they glide quietly through the warm and peaceful summer night.

Despite more tests, more pills, new pills, Dan's weight continues to plummet over the next two and a half months as his heart weakens. His skin is flabby, pouchy in spots — his hazel eyes lifeless. The times when he used to swim in his family's backyard pool, lift weights or play softball seem like long-ago memories, even dreams. In late August, Dr. Robinson turns his care over to Dr. Brian Strunk, one of the nation's leading cardiologists, and Dan is admitted to Moffit Hospital again. A tall, intense, bearded man with premature gray hair, Dr. Strunk enters Dan's room, nods a greeting to his parents, then sits on the bed beside Dan.

"I have reviewed every test result, every X-ray, every bit of data collected on you by anybody from infancy to the present," Dr. Strunk begins, draping his hand across Dan's leg.

"I'd be dishonest if I told you things look hopeful. They don't. You need a valve job, but that's a relatively straight-forward procedure. My real concern," he says, "is the matter of the cardiomyopathy. The disease, Dan, has progressed rapidly — "

"Just tell me how long I've got," Dan says, trying to blink away his tears.

"Perhaps a year if no further action is taken."

"Further action?" Mr. Krainert blurts. "We've done everything. *Everything!*" His jaw is twitching.

"Let me rephrase that. If no more *advanced* action is taken."

"What are you suggesting, doctor? What else can we do for our son?"

"I'd like you to consider a heart transplant."

"And without it?" Dan asks.

"Without it, it's just a matter of months," Dr. Strunk says, looking Dan straight in the eyes. "I'm afraid we've reached the point where nothing else can be done."

Dan nods.

"The operation would be performed at the Stanford University Medical Center, where nearly 200 patients have received new hearts since January, 1968. So it's still a fairly new procedure. But in a relatively short time, the transplant has become an established therapeutic measure in certain patients with end-stage heart disease." He pauses, then says, "Of course, that doesn't mean it is a cure, or that everything would be roses after a transplant. There are definite risks. But survival rates of five years and up are now considered the norm in nearly half the cases."

"Meaning the other half don't survive that long," Mr. Krainert states.

"Yes. But those rates could jump considerably with new drugs. Doctors are particularly optimistic about one in particular. Cyclosporin-A. And from what I've heard, the FDA is within months of giving final approval for its human testing. We hope it's the breakthrough drug we've been looking for."

"What drugs are used now?" Mrs. Krainert asks.

"Steroids. But unlike steroids, Cyclosporin-A suppresses the immune system just enough to prevent rejection of a new heart, but not enough to interfere with normal healing. Yet Cyclosporin or no Cyclosporin, a heart transplant is not a cure-all. It is, simply, the final alternative. And it's your decision, Dan. Yours alone. I can't make it for you. Nor can your parents."

"And if I say yes?"

"First of all, I don't want you to say yes now. I want you to think long and hard about it. School starts for you in a few weeks, and I want you to go back. Take a full load, a half load — whatever you feel comfortable with. But when it gets to the point where you can no longer attend classes, give me a call. Tell me your answer then.

"To qualify for a new heart at Stanford is not a simple matter," Dr. Strunk continues. "Not simple at all. You've got to be sick enough to need a transplant, but well enough to survive it. And that's a very fine line. There is also a required psychiatric evaluation to determine the degree of your 'will to live.' You'd face medical battles for the rest of your life. Tough ones. And the transplant team needs to know . . . well, that you could endure such rigor. I'll be blunt. Not all transplant patients have been able to cope with what comes afterward. Several suicides have been recorded. And Stanford doesn't want any more.

"There are other considerations. I should also explain that if you say yes, that does *not* guarantee a new heart. It's a numbers game of sorts. Only one-tenth of those who apply for a transplant at Stanford are accepted. And a third of those who actually make the waiting list die before a suitable donor heart is received. The odds aren't encouraging. But I know many of the transplant surgeons at the University. And I will do my utmost to get you on the list if you decide you want to go through with it. I can guarantee that."

"Doctor, you've got to be frank with us," Mr. Krainert says. "What kind of money are we talking about for such a transplant?"

"It doesn't come cheap — somewhere in the ball park of $100,000. Also, Dan would be in the hospital several months and would need family support. That means at least one of you would need to take a leave of absence from work and rent a nearby apartment in Palo Alto. And a small two bedroom now runs about $700 per month. Is that frank enough?"

Mr. Krainert opens his mouth to speak, but the words die in his throat. He glances at his wife, and then turns back to the doctor with his eyes lowered. "I don't . . . I don't know how that would be possible," he says, swallowing hard. "We're not the Rockefellers, and . . . the kind of money you're talking about is out of our league."

"Then I'd suggest that you check into your company's insurance policy. Policies differ widely, but you might find you're in luck."

"And if we're not covered?"

"These things have a way of working themselves out," the doctor says. "All you need is the faith of a mustard seed, or so the Good Book says."

"And a benefactor with a million bucks," Dan's father adds, rising to pace the floor.

Chapter Ten — LLOYD

SEA BREEZE

Wrenching a gas mask over his head, Lloyd takes a couple of preliminary breaths and looks around at the other hooded members of Bravo Company. He smiles to himself, feeling like a character in some B-rated Japanese thriller. The air inside the mask smells like a trunk of old clothes. He fills his lungs again and coughs. The company sergeant says something which Lloyd doesn't hear, but the line starts to move and he follows the group single file inside a large steel chamber. The door swings shut and locks with an audible click. Suddenly the room feels more crowded than it is.

From behind a glass-paneled room, the sergeant speaks into a mike. His voice booms from a single speaker hung high on the wall. "Welcome to the gas chamber," he says, smiling broadly. "You've undoubtedly heard about this aspect of training, and I'd like to assure you that those stories, they're all true." He pauses a moment, waiting for the guffaws to stop. "In the event of chemical warfare, you would be exposed to gasses or agents significantly stronger than those which you will experience here in a few moments."

Greeted by a chorus of groans, he flips a lever. Fans inside the chamber switch on, belching a thick fog over the heads of the masked Marines.

"I was a bleeping idiot to ever sign up," laments Bart behind Lloyd. "The few, the proud . . . the *stupid*. Am I bleeping retarded or what?" Lloyd ignores the voice, and doesn't turn around.

"Exhibit A," the sergeant drones on. "You are now surrounded by the aforementioned gas, similar to that used by riot cops and S.W.A.T. teams. But with the masks on, you notice that you can breathe without discomfort. If the enemy were to use nuclear, biological or chemical agents in time of war, you would be required to fight in such masks, plus full body suits that would protect your skin and clothing from contamination.

"However," he continues, "with your gas masks *off* inside this chamber, you would experience violent sneezing, coughing and burning eyes. You would feel extremely nauseous and dizzy. Your mucous membranes would react as if you'd eaten a couple jars of jalapeño peppers. Your head would feel as if you'd been clobbered by an alley thug with a blunt instrument. Of course, not everybody responds alike to the gas. But thanks to the goodness of the American taxpayers and your commanding officer," he smiles, "you will now have the opportunity to experience individually how *your* body reacts. Should the need arise, there is a retch basin — also known as a common urinal — attached to the wall outside."

He flips another switch and green exit lights flash through the dense fog. "You see where the exit is. Now, children, remove your masks and . . ."

Lloyd slips the mask off hesitantly, holding his breath as long as possible. Suddenly he is being shoved. He takes an elbow in the side. Somebody is standing on his feet, coughing as if he's dying of emphysema. Lloyd pushes back and, at the same time, expels the last of his oxygen. His first gasp is shallow, but the burning in his lungs is immediate. His eyes are aflame, and there is a taste in his mouth that he can't spit out. A hot flash sears his chest and radiates to his extremities. All around him, fellow Marines choke and gag.

". . . and starting with the front row, recite your names, ranks and serial numbers. That's it. Exit quickly. Keep moving. And when you've done your thing in the basin, you strike payoff. Liberty, children, until 0500 hours tomorrow."

"Let me the bleep out of here!" screams the voice that Lloyd knows all too well. "Bleep! Bleep! Bleep!"

Lloyd cannot talk. He cannot see. But he can follow the voice toward the exit. And moments later, following the trail of expletives, he bursts through the door and races for the basin. His eyes stream acid tears, and his legs feel spongy. He tries to control his stomach, but suddenly it explodes. And then his knees buckle and he goes down hard, like a department store manikin dislodged from its perch.

When he wakes up, he is back in the barracks. He glances out the window. There is still at least two hours of light. So he strips down, showers and changes into clean utilities. After making a quick phone call, he borrows a squirt of Visine for each eye, grabs a quick lasagna meal in the mess hall, and then bikes across base to a square stuccoed building. Taking the elevator to the third floor, he is met by a secretary who is a good head taller than him. She wears no makeup, and her sandy hair is pulled back in a tight bun. She is as lean as a yardstick and about as pretty.

"I'm here to see the base commander," Lloyd says.

"Do you have an appointment?" she asks. Her lips are thin, and barely move when she speaks.

"I just called. Private First Class Lloyd Chambers."

"Yes, of course. He is expecting you."

She steps around her metal desk and guides Lloyd down a short hall. She stops in front of a hulking oak door, marked with the major general's name, knocks once and then turns quickly away, leaving Lloyd by himself on the threshold. Wiping his belt buckle with the sleeve of his uniform, Lloyd heaves a deep breath, pushes hesitantly against the heavy door and steps inside. The office looks like the lobby of a successful Victor- ian restaurant. It is paneled in large rectangles of dark walnut, with textured maroon drapes at the long window. The carpet is a thick maroon pile, and the furniture is black leather.

The man Lloyd assumes to be the major general is stripped to his waist and glistening with sweat as he stoops over a barbell. His short hair is gun metal gray, and his eyebrows are like two small wire brushes. Though the man easily looks twice Lloyd's age, he has the build of a tank, with arms like cannons.

"Sir, Private First Class Lloyd Chambers, Sir," Lloyd says, introducing himself again as he moves two strides closer. He waits for the man to respond, but when he doesn't, Lloyd counts the iron rings on the barbell. There are two 50-pounders on each side. Coupled with the weight of the bar itself, he figures the man is dealing with at least 220 pounds of iron.

Ignoring both Lloyd and his salute, the major general squares his polished shoes in front of the weights, adjusts his hands carefully and, with a throaty rumble, cleans and jerks the barbell over his head. He holds the pose for a long moment, his muscles taut and steady, and glares at Lloyd.

"My daughter is my jewel," he suddenly grunts, his voice grinding like the busted gearbox of a jeep.

Lloyd looks up with a start and says, "Sir, I understand, Sir."

Slowly, with precise control of his bulging arms, the major general lowers the weights in one smooth motion and settles them to the floor with hardly a clink. Wiping his face and hands on a towel, he then steps to face Lloyd. "Look me in the eye, soldier," he says.

"Sir, yes, Sir."

"That's better. Back to my daughter. As I said, she's a precious gem. And I expect you to treat her as such. Understand?"

"Sir, yes, sir."

"And never forget who her father is."

"Sir, I could never forget, Sir."

"If you mess with her, you mess with me. And I suspect you know better than to do that."

"Sir, my intentions are honorable, Sir."

The major general stares hard at Lloyd and then points down at the barbell. "Come over here, soldier," he growls, motioning him closer. "Show me what you can do with these weights."

"Sir?"

"I want to see you pump some iron. Go ahead, give it a try."
Lloyd rolls up his sleeves, tightens his belt and steps to
the bar. With a grunt he lifts the weights to his abdomen. He
pauses a moment, adjusting his hands to the load. He clears
his throat and looks at the man. And then he takes a sudden
step back and beneath the bar, raising it to his chest. "Hey-o,"
he breathes, trying to smile. But his face is tight. And then
his arms suddenly come to life, quivering and shaking. He can
press the bar no higher.

"Here, set it down," the commander says, stepping to
Lloyd's side and assisting with the weights. "I thought you'd
be able to get it up."

Lloyd nods, mopping his forehead with his sleeve. "Almost,
Sir."

"All or nothing, soldier. Almost never counts, except with
grenades."

"Yes, Sir."

"Very well," he says, glancing at a small digital clock on
his desk. The desk, which is as large as the officer's door, is
cleared of everything but the clock, two red folders and a
miniature United States flag. He looks back at Lloyd and clears
his throat. "I believe we've taken care of our business with
each other."

"Sir. Thank-you, sir," Lloyd says, snapping a salute.

"One more thing, soldier."

"Sir?"

"Just remember that I can make your life miserable."

"Yes, sir."

"Cross me once on account of my daughter, and you'll
wish you'd never been born."

"Sir, yes, Sir," he says warily, saluting again.

The following weekend, Lloyd hugs the rail of the *Alaskan*
and retches over the side as it bobs and tosses its way to sea.
Having been through the gas chamber, he thought he knew
what *bad* felt like. But that was before the boat left the dock
of the Helgrens Sport Fishing dock. He wipes his mouth and
glances up at the stern where Lisa stands, watching the coast

of Oceanside disappear into the distance. Her hair is blowing behind her head like a loose scarf. She is in jeans, with a pink Windbreaker covering a yellow T-shirt. Two fishing poles rest in the notched rail at her side.

"This was a great idea," she bubbles, walking over to where Lloyd is hanging his head.

"Lousy idea," Lloyd groans. "This is why I didn't join the Navy."

"Have you taken anything?"

"No Dramamine aboard this wreck."

Lisa fumbles in her purse and pulls out a small bottle. "Try this."

"Prescription?"

"Midol," she smiles. "It's the best I can do."

"Isn't that for — "

"Menstrual cramps," she says, trying not to laugh. But suddenly she is laughing very hard.

Lloyd shrugs. "Desperate men seek desperate solutions. Give me three." He tries to laugh along, but his stomach hurts too much. So he pops the pills and just stands there, trying to remember what dry, steady ground feels like.

Two miles out, the boat slows and the bait tank is opened. Lisa nets a four-inch anchovy, but is squeamish about baiting the hook.

"Here," Lloyd says, taking her hook and the bait fish in hand. "You've got to hook it right through the brain, like this — just behind the eyeballs. Give the hook a little tug, like so, and pull the tip right out its snout. You can also hook through the lips, but this lobotomizes them so they feel no pain when Fat Albert bites."

"It's easier in the harbor," Lisa says. "You don't have to worry about lobotomizing marshmallows."

"In the harbor, the only worry is what you'll catch if you *eat* what you catch," he says, smiling at his play on words. "Now, watch it when you cast," he cautions, stepping aside. "I don't want to be smacked in the head."

Lisa flings her pole backward, pauses, and then jerks the line above her head and over the rail. The anchovy snaps free and strikes a deckhand in the back.

"Bombs away!" she yells, fighting a laugh.

"One thing's for sure," Lloyd grins, pulling another bait fish from the tank. "They don't make anchovies like they used to."

For most of the afternoon, Lloyd sprawls in a deck chair with his head on the rail — too ill for little more than standing up and retching overboard.

"For what I had to go through to get this date, I don't think it's worth it," Lloyd groans.

"My father's not that bad."

"You didn't tell me he was King Kong. The guy acted like he'd bust my knees if I look at you twice."

"No."

"You should've heard him."

"He'd never break your knees," she says, shaking her head again.

"No?"

"He'd shoot you."

"No doubt."

"He's actually pretty nice. Really."

"And I'm Jacques Cousteau."

"He's had a bad year," she says, a far-off look clouding her eyes. "My mother was killed ten months ago — in a car accident with another man. The guy was a junior officer, and he basically walked away with bruises. That is, until my dad found out about the affair. Anyway, now it's just the two of us at home — dad and me. And I'm no shrink, but I suppose he gets hyperpossessive because he doesn't want to lose two women. Losing one was bad enough."

"What happened to the other guy?"

"Dad had him reassigned. To Okinawa," she giggles, reaching to adjust the zipper on her Windbreaker. "I think he was killed over there — got bit by a banana spider or something stupid like that."

"What's that?"

"Banana spider?"

"No, your T-shirt. The little figure."

"Oh that," she says, unzipping her jacket to reveal the logo of a dancing girl above her left breast. "It's my company shirt. I'm an aerobic dance instructor."

"Mmmm," he croons, eyeing her shirt. "Don't know whether it's you or the Midol, but something's working."

Lisa rolls her eyes and smiles as she rezips the jacket. Suddenly, her line goes taut.

"I've got one!" she screams.

Lloyd jumps to his feet, but thinks twice about it and sits back down.

"What do I do?"

"Keep your tip up," he shouts, "and just reel the mother in."

"If I land it, you clean it."

"If I clean it, you eat it."

"*I* eat it?"

"You eat it."

"Don't you like fish?" she asks, cranking hard on the reel.

"Not after today."

"I've got a James Beard recipe for fillets," Lisa says, darting a glance over her shoulder. Lloyd is holding his stomach. "You'll feel better once we're off the water. And if you're up to it, you're welcome for dinner tonight."

"The *three* of us?"

"Dad's never home for dinner."

"Suppose he shows up and I'm there?"

"Hello, Okinawa."

The late summer sun has settled into the ocean by the time they arrive back at Lisa's condo, which is nestled on a hillside overlooking the Oceanside marina. Gazing westward out the living room window, the thought crosses Lloyd's mind that a major general makes a few dollars more per month than a private first class. A sea gull glides on the wind, banks, slows, and then drops to a perch on the fencepost outside. Lloyd watches it until he realizes that sea gulls don't do much worth watching. So instead he looks around the condo. More leather, but thankfully no maroon. There are two black leather couches with low soft backs, and a free-form endtable made out of glass and some sort of treestump that had been sanded and heavily lacquered. Lloyd walks over and takes a deep sniff of the couch. The smell reminds him of a shoe store. The floors are all hardwood parquet tiles, with ivory-and rose-colored area rugs arranged neatly around the room. Two stuffed pheasant stare glassily from the mantel above the brick fireplace; on the hearth her spaniel, Christie, is curled up like a cinnamon roll. Lloyd is rubbing his fingers across the grain of a three-foot tall Fisher speaker cabinet, one of four in the room, when Lisa appears in the doorway. She has cleaned up and changed into a pair of shorts, topped by another aerobic dance shirt. She wears a pair of white Reebok shoes, with short athletic socks rimmed in red.

"How about a dance demo?" Lloyd asks.

"There's nothing much to really see," she says. "Just a lot of hopping and jumping."

"I'll force myself to watch."

"Dinner's almost ready."

"No pre-dinner entertainment? What kind of a cheap joint is this anyway?"

"Light the candles," she says with a wink, throwing him a book of matches. A fleeting part of his mind thinks, "What if the major general shows up?" But the enduring majority of his mind says, "Yes, Yes, Yes," as he watches her disappear into the kitchen.

Baked sea bass with a twist of lemon. Rice pilaf. Whole grain bread with honey and fresh raspberry preserves. That's part of the menu. But the part Lloyd concentrates on is the beverage: a bottle of Cabernet which Lisa has pirated from her father's special reserve. Finding them sharing a candlelight dinner would be one thing. Finding them sharing a bottle of his special reserve quite another. So Lloyd tries to make the best of a bad situation, and drinks the evidence so the bottle can be quickly thrown away. What surprises him is when Lisa opens the second bottle.

After dinner, Lisa plugs in the coffee. Lloyd retires to the living room sofa, stretching out on the leather cushions as if in his own home. Outside it is very dark. The lights of the harbor flicker rainbow colors across the water and a half moon hangs in the sky. The dog rises slowly from her spot beside the fireplace, stretches, and then walks slowly over to the dining room table and sniffs the floor for scraps. Lisa comes out, shoos the dog away from the table, and finds a quiet station on the stereo.

"Entertainment time," Lloyd says. His voice is deep and husky.

"You like the music?"

"Music's fine. But you promised a dance demonstration."

"I didn't promise anything."

"You sort of promised."

"Not on a full stomach," she says. "It's not good for you."

"I still feel queasy," Lloyd says. "And watching you would be good for me."

"OK, something short," she says, fumbling through a stack of records in a mahogany cabinet by the fireplace. She slips the theme song from the motion picture "Fame" onto the Gerrard turntable, clicks the sound up a notch, and throws in more treble as the music starts.

Lisa kicks right, takes two steps, kicks left. Her hands move like feathers through the air. Her legs are lean and very tan, and when she rolls with her hips Lloyd feels his head tingle. She dances through the first stanza, and then stops abruptly and steps to Lloyd's side as the music plays on.

"You look a little pale," she says, kneeling at his side to adjust his pillow. Her face is two inches from his own, and he can feel her warm breath.

"Yes," he says. He looks her deep in the eyes. The corner of his mouth starts to twitch.

"Do you feel sick?"

"Sick? I don't know."

"I'm the nurse. Tell me where it hurts."

Lloyd points to his stomach. Leaning over, she brushes her lips against his shirt.

"And here," he says, pointing to his head. She pecks his forehead. "And here," he says. She kisses him softly on the eye. "And here," he says. She looks at his finger beside his lips and smiles. She leans closer. Lloyd rises to meet her, planting small kisses on her lips.

"Are you sure we're OK?" he whispers in her ear.

"Uh huh."

He eases her up on the couch, kissing her warmly. His hand strokes her waist, feeling her softness, and then moves slowly up her side.

Suddenly there is a crash in the dining room by the door. Lisa screams. She whips around, falling off the couch. Lloyd's heart lunges. He blindly scrambles to his feet and salutes. And then Lisa is laughing. Laughing hard. On the floor lies a shattered wine goblet. Atop the kitchen table stands Christie, wolfing down a cube of butter and wagging her tail wildly.

Chapter Eleven — DAN

THE BOTTOM DOLLAR

During the first days of his senior year at Vintage High, Dan is quizzed about his health from friends he hasn't seen all summer. In the locker hall during the second week of classes, he is stopped by Diana Panigazzi, a slim-waisted 17-year-old with petite features, cat green eyes and tousled blonde hair which she constantly brushes behind her ear with her fingers. She wears a burgundy polo shirt, and Calvin Kleins which look as if they have been painted on.

"Like I don't know what it is, Dan, but there's something different about you," she blusters. "Didn't see you much last year, and now . . . like, you look great! Like you've lost a lot of weight or something, you know?"

Dan looks at her blankly, pausing a moment to check his heart rate with a stethoscope given him by Dr. Strunk.

"Are you into jogging now? Or like, you know, doing aerobics?" Diana asks, combing her fingers through her hair.

Dan shakes his head. "I'm dying."

"Come on, what's with the stethoscope? Are you like rehearsing for another play or something?"

"I'm dying," he repeats.

"Like be serious," she giggles, brushing away a fly that circles her head.

"I am serious," he says dryly. "But look, Diana, I've got to run. Have a wonderful life, huh. I'll be sure to write you into the will."

Diana stops and stares after him, with a puzzled look on her face as if deciding whether or not Dan is joking and whether or not to laugh. And then she shouts down the locker hall at his back, "Like if it's not a joke, Dan, it's not funny." Turning to a classmate standing nearby, she shakes her head. "You know," she says, "I don't think Dan's putting me on. He says he's *dying*. And like I think he's serious."

"Welcome to Planet Earth," the girl says.

"He's *dying*? Not Dan."

"Earth to Panigazzi, come in please. Earth to Pani — "

"You're serious, aren't you?" Diana says, looking her classmate deep in the eyes. "I can tell you're serious by your face, because like you didn't even blink. I don't believe it! Dan Krainert is *dying*. Dying at 17, and now I know. That's awful! And here me and him were like that," she says, crossing her fingers. "Tight as that, and I didn't even know. This is unbelievable! I'm so dumb I could, you know, like kill myself!"

"If you need an accomplice," the girl says, "look me up."

Walking to his car at the end of class that same day, Dan hears somebody shout his name. He turns around as Jessica Bell, the cheerleader, bounces up.

"Haven't seen you for awhile," he says. "You look great."

"Cheer practice has taken up most of my time. Are you coming to the game Friday?"

He doesn't answer immediately. And when she turns to look at him, he is biting his lip.

"I don't — " he begins, but he loses the words. Dan suddenly stops by the flagpole. His face pales, and he grabs her shoulder for support.

"What's wrong, Dan?" she pleads, stumbling beneath his weight.

"Jessica," he grits, fighting for breath, "I don't think I can . . . make it to my car." Instantly his legs go limp, and he collapses in a heap in front of the school office.

"Oh God, no!" Jessica screams, dropping her books.

"Somebody run for help!" she yells to nearby students. "It's Dan! Somebody quick — call an ambulance!"

Shirley, who has already boarded the school bus, is oblivious to the commotion until the ambulance screams to a stop at the curb. Craning her neck out the window, she watches the attendants dart through the crowd. Moments later the throng parts again as the gurney rolls back to the ambulance. A knot of apprehension grows tight in her stomach as she strains to see. She catches a sudden glimpse of Dan's pallid face.

"Dan!" she screams, tears flashing in her eyes. Those surrounding the ambulance turn and look. But Dan remains still, his chin cocked straight to the sky. Grabbing her books, Shirley scrambles madly up the aisle. But it's too late. The bus pulls away with her trapped inside. "Dear Lord, please help him," she cries, her tears streaming down the glass panes of the door. "Dear Jesus, be with him."

Rushed to Napa's community hospital, Dan spends a fitful night wired to beeping, buzzing monitors. The words of Dr. Strunk continually course through his mind: *"When it gets to the point where you can no longer attend classes, give me your answer then."*

The following day, accompanied by his parents, Dan ·is transferred to the intensive care ward at the University of California Medical Center in San Francisco. There, flat on his back with IVs in both arms and a tube down his nose, he informs his parents and Dr. Strunk of his decision.

"A new heart is my only chance," he says. "I want to go for it. I want to live."

"Then we'll go for it . . . and get it!" Dr. Strunk says, gritting his teeth. "You're a prime candidate. Now we just have to convince Stanford of that."

"What's the game plan?" Dan asks.

"I want you transferred tomorrow to the Stanford University Medical Center. That will be your hospital home from now on. If we're going to get you on that list, I want them to see you every day. I don't want them to forget for a moment that Dan Krainert needs a new heart. And that'll be hard to do if you're under their noses day and night."

"Stanford University," Dan says weakly. "I might not be smart enough to get admitted. But I guess I'm sick enough."

"It's better this way," his mother says. "What do you want, a diploma or a new heart?"

Dan's father is staring at his feet. He looks up at the doctor and shakes his head. "I told you before that we've done everything possible for Danny. Everything. But now I'm frankly scared about the bills. Stanford is — well, it's *Stanford*. And my job just doesn't — "

"You checked the insurance?" Dr. Strunk asks.

"I called the main office. They said the policy would pay to a limit of only $40,000, because a transplant is still considered experimental."

"Leaving us $60,000 or more short," Mrs. Krainert adds.

"*Experimental*. But I did some checking and found that other policies would pay every cent to help some screwball pervert get a sex-change operation. They'll support you 100 percent if you want your gonads rewired, but not if you need a new heart. I don't get it. It's nonsense!"

"Did you try the Red Cross?" Dr. Strunk asks.

"Called Red Cross, and they suggested I try United Way. So I called United Way, and they suggested I try Red Cross. That's what I'm running into. Back and forth. The response is always the same: an apologetic no with best wishes. I even tried the big newspapers and area TV stations, asking if they'd do a story or something about Danny."

"And?"

"Same thing. 'I'm sorry, Sir. But this isn't the kind of story we do. After all, your son has not yet been accepted by Stanford.' But Danny can't get on Stanford's list until we have $100,000! It's cash on the barrel. The media people don't understand. By the time the story is *newsworthy*, all they'll have to report is Danny's obit." He wipes back angry tears. "Doctor, our son could be *dead* within a couple of months!" he says.

"You've gone to the big newspapers," Dr. Strunk says. "But what about the smaller ones?"

"They're throwaways."

"Try the local paper."

"People don't read it. They all read the *San Francisco Chronicle*."

"Believe me," Dr. Strunk says. "Start with the local paper."

"I'll do anything. It's our last hope. But all the doors are slamming in our face."

"Journalism is not my field," the doctor says, "but there's one thing you can be sure of."

"Yes?"

"Every paper, no matter how small, is at least read by the editors of the larger papers. They don't want to be scooped on a good story. And if you can get some initial interest stirred up, you may find reporters standing in line. Believe me. I've seen it happen before. These doors that are slamming, sometimes they have signs saying, 'Push.' So just lean a little harder, and you may find them swinging open."

The following week in the lunch yard of Vintage High, Jessica Bell is surrounded by a small group of friends. On her lap is a copy of the *Napa Register* with Dan's picture and a story about him, written by Kevin Courtney, on the front page.

"We can't just sit back and let Dan die," she says. "We've got to do *something*. You guys read the paper. Dan needs us. He needs all the help he can get — especially financial. And we're his friends."

"So? What can we do?"

"I don't know. Car washes, walk-a-thons, paper drives, can drives . . . "

"Come on, Jessica. Be realistic. That's just nickel-and-dime stuff," her friends say. "None of those things would even raise a couple hundred bucks at most. The *Register* said he needs a hundred *thousand* bucks."

"Somebody's got to start somewhere. The librarian had an idea. He suggested a blood drive. What about that? He'll probably need lots of blood," she says.

"As you say, we've gotta start somewhere."

"We can do posters and flyers," Jessica says. "And have the bloodmobile out here October 10th, the day of the Big

Game. Maybe get Dan to say something at the pep rally. I think the TV station would go for it. The students definitely would. After all, we wouldn't be asking for money. Most kids don't have any, anyway. But they've got blood. And that costs nothing to give," she says. "We owe at least that much to Dan. After all, he's a Vintage Crusher. He's one of us."

Inside the Vintage High gymnasium on October 10, the bleachers fill to capacity as the band explodes into a round of foot-stomping spirit songs. Football players, proud and uniformed, file into a bank of chairs facing the podium. The cheerleaders, sparking adolescent fires with their hip-shaking, high-kicking routines, form a backdrop for the on-camera lead-in by KRON TV's Greg Lyon. Then the TV lights blaze upon the podium as Jessica parts ranks with the cheerleaders and steps to the mike.

"Tonight, a lot of courage will be required of our Crushers when they go head-to-head against the Vacaville Bull Dogs," she says. "Everyone knows that football players are brave. They have to be. But I'd like to introduce you to somebody who's even braver. You all know him. He's one of us. DAN KRAINERT!"

Screams and applause thunder within the gymnasium as Dan, fresh out of Stanford University Medical Center, crosses the hardwood floor to the mike. He is gaunt and pale. His clothes hang loose as curtains on his thin frame. The klieg lights of the minicam seem to shine right through his skin.

He clears his throat, shades his eyes against the lights and smiles. He clears his throat again, and then begins to speak.

"When I was a kid, I was told I had heart disease. But it was never a big deal, because it went into remission. That is, until recently. I was fine until the end of last year. And now I'm not so fine any more. My doctor tells me I need a new heart if I am to live to see graduation in June. A new heart and a hundred thousand bucks," he says, his words punctuated by an irritating cough.

"My doctor also says that Stanford accepts only ten percent of those who apply for a transplant, that thirty-three percent of those accepted die before a donor heart can be found, and that more than fifty percent of those who actually receive a new heart die within five years of the operation. Now, I'm no whiz at numbers — in fact, I got a C-minus in my last math class — but I punched those figures into my calculator." His voice trails, "And I found that Texas Instruments gives me only about a one percent chance of surviving long enough to receive my college diploma."

He pauses, looks down. His chalk-white hands grip the podium. Then he focuses again on his classmates. He wipes his dry mouth with the back of his hand. "But the other night I was thinking about these odds. About my future. Or, perhaps, my lack of it. And I opened my Bible. And some things I read struck me very deeply," he says, pausing to wrench a pocket New Testament from his back pocket. He quickly flips it open and begins to read. "What is impossible with men is possible with God.'

"*Impossible.* I know what that word means. It means fighting off death at 17. And that seems impossible — especially when I'm lying on my back over at Stanford and poked full of needles and tubes. But it's not impossible to God. And so you see, my challenge is really an opportunity. An opportunity to let God turn my impossibility into a possibility.

"Of course, that doesn't mean I'll make it. I want to. I want to be around until I'm 18 and 20 and 25 and 105. I want to live! And if I do, I will live for God. If I don't, I will die for God. Either way," says Dan, "I will fulfill God's plan — His unique purpose for my life . . . however long it lasts.

"But before I sit down and they turn these TV lights off, I want you all to know one thing. I couldn't go through this transplant without your support. I don't know all of you. But I know all of you are behind me. That gives me courage. And knowing God stands beside me gives me strength.

"So . . . well, I don't know what else to say right now except thank-you. Thanks for being here when I need you most. I love you. I couldn't do it without you." And then he takes a step back from the podium. He smiles awkwardly and waves, unsure of how to respond as the student body erupts with a thunderous standing ovation. It's a sound unlike he'd ever experienced, even after a good play, and it reverberates and grows louder within the packed gymnasium. He glances over at Jessica for help, but she is clapping and crying louder than anybody else.

Suddenly football coach Burl Autry steps to the mike to rescue Dan. A small man with a rugged but friendly face, he holds his hands up to still the din. "Do me a favor," he says. "Make me as happy as you've just made Dan. Bring some of this enthusiasm out to the stadium tonight. I expect to see you all there. This game's the Big One. And it'll be one of our toughest. But we're going to go out there and CRUSH the Bull Dogs! We're going to win! And we're going to win it for DAN KRAINERT! Dan, this one's for YOU!" he yells as the gymnasium again erupts. He bolds his hands up again. "Just a second," he yells over the noise. "Hold it down, please. I'm not through. I want to tell all of you something. I want to tell you to quit crying now. Tears make gym floors warp. Besides, Dan doesn't need your tears. He needs your *blood*. And the bloodmobile is waiting just outside the gymnasium doors!"

That evening, following the television report of the pep rally and blood drive, several other TV stations and newspapers from surrounding areas phone to set up interviews.

"I can't get over this telephone — it's ringing right off the hook!" booms Dan's father. "And to think they said you weren't newsworthy. Before this is over, those guys are going to be eating their words!"

"Calm down, Dad," Dan says. "If I'm to get my heart, we need the media's help — whenever it comes."

"I know that. I'm just saying it's interesting they're playing 'Follow the Leader' now that you're becoming a celebrity. That's all."

"I'm nothing of the sort. I'm just a dying kid who needs a heart. Period. To pay for the heart, I need the money. To get the money, people need to find out about me and my problem. It's as simple as that. God is beginning to open the door. Don't lose sight of that."

"Maybe we could have the TV crews come to the house. They'd probably want to interview your mother and me as well. And it wouldn't hurt business a bit. As business improves, we'll be that much more able to pay for the transplant. Understand what I'm saying?"

"No, but I *see through* what you're saying," Dan says.

"From what I saw on TV, you probably could line up some speaking engagements, and really start spreading the word. Especially at churches. And maybe you could even arrange for me to sing where you speak. People would go for that kind of thing. What do you say?"

"I'm going to bed."

"OK, be that way. But mark my words. Before this is all over, you're going to be famous around here!"

As October merges into November, Dan's story breaks wide open. All of the area papers and TV stations report regularly on his condition, and prowl the halls of Vintage High gathering testimonials from his friends and student leaders. And a special Dan Krainert Trust Fund is established at the local Bank of America to collect the rising tide of contributions.

Under the ongoing leadership of Jessica Bell at Vintage High and Julie Moore at nearby Napa High, students bolster the fund by staging benefit dances, car washes, and conducting widespread can, paper and bottle drives. They pass "HAVE A HEART" buckets during half-time at football games and canvass local businessmen for contributions. Other area high schools and even the junior highs and elementary schools join hands to slate fundraisers of their own. A Dan Krainert Walk-a-thon/Bike-a-thon attracts hundreds of participants and boosts the trust fun by several thousand dollars, while more than $20,000 is given by residents of nearby Vallejo in a campaign spearheaded by Bev Stringer, wife of Dan's former Little League coach.

Before long, the area fire and police departments, Chamber of Commerce, civic organizations and neighborhood groups all pitch in their support to raise money, and community spirit climbs to a frenzy. Invited to Napa by the mayor, the then-world champion Oakland Raiders send their off-season basketball team to town to play a benefit game in Dan's behalf. A few weeks later, the entire Stanford University basketball team drives to Napa for a special barbecue, clinic and scrimmage, with all proceeds pumped into the Krainert Fund. The highlight of the fundfests is a massive 600-person testimonial dinner in Napa, attended by community dignitaries, townspeople, and served by a host of Vintage High students. Dan's father, a closet opera singer, provides the entertainment for the evening, and Dan, growing weaker by the day, gives the keynote address. His message: Though his body is weak, his spirit is strong. And his hope, come life or death, is based solely and completely on God.

However, officials at Stanford University Medical Center don't take kindly to the media hype, especially when it spills over the hills from Napa and the story is picked up by the San Francisco TV stations. Ired by the publicity, Stanford officials order Dr. Strunk to have the Krainerts break all contact with the media.

"We've got reporters calling Stanford every day," he is told, "and the boy is not yet even on our transplant list."

"I understand, but the family — "

"You will simply have to tell them no more TV. No more articles. Either they play by our rules or they don't play at all. We don't have time for all of this. We're a medical center, not a city hall."

"I'll see what I can do," Dr. Strunk says quietly. But when he relays word to the Krainerts by phone, they can barely choke back their tears.

"But Danny is dying before our very eyes," Mr. Krainert blurts. "He can't even walk the length of the hallway without gasping for breath. He's on the verge of death, and we're still short the money for the operation. Should we just sit back and watch him die? Trying to stop the media now, even if we could, would probably do Danny in," he explains, his voice quavering.

"I know that. And don't think for a moment that I'm not on your side," the doctor assures. "But there's also the matter of transplant politics. If Stanford is crossed, they might . . ."

"Might what?"

"Well, let's just pray for the best. Danny has enough faith for all of us, and somehow the money will be there. For now, though, we'd better sit tight and let this blow over. In the meantime, I'll do what I can to speed things along and try to hasten Stanford's decision."

"Why the delay?" Mrs. Krainert asks. "Danny's going downhill fast and we're both terrified."

"The delay, sadly enough, has a lot to do with the availability of donor hearts. There are not enough to meet the growing demand at Stanford, or anywhere else for that matter."

"What about the Anatomy Gift Law, or whatever it's called? You know, the sticker on the back of driver's licenses? Doesn't that help?"

"The Uniform Anatomical Gift Act," the doctor says. "When it was enacted it was somewhat helpful. Yet relatively few people have taken advantage of the opportunity to give. After all, most people do not plan on dying, nor do they plan on the disposition of their body parts. And given a choice about donating them, most simply choose not to choose."

Reluctantly, the Krainerts honor the request for their silence. But when a major San Francisco TV station picks up on the forced gag, they send a camera crew to trail Mr. Krainert on his bread route during the first week in November. Intercepting him on the job for an interview, they ask about the sudden hush.

"I'm sorry, but I can't talk about it," he says.

"Surely they gave you reasons," the reporter says, sticking a microphone at him as he loads his truck.

"No, I don't know why."

"No explanation?"

"They've simply requested our silence."

"They expect your *silence*? The silence of a father when his son is critically ill?" The cameraman zooms in for a closeup.

"I can't . . . " he struggles to answer, but loses his voice. Suddenly he breaks down. "The politics of this whole thing are . . . are *killing* my son. All I know is that he's dying . . . and desperately needs a new heart. My boy is dying!" he weeps.

The story airs that evening throughout the San Francisco Bay Area. And in apparent response to the broadcast, Stanford officials notify the Krainerts through Dr. Strunk that Dan should come immediately to the Medical Center for a psychiatric evaluation and further tests to determine his suitability for a heart transplant. Dan sails through the interview, receiving a thumb's up from the psychiatrist. But trouble is encountered during the cardiac catheterization.

Transported from his room to the cath lab, he is moved onto a flat table under a large X-ray machine. A doctor he doesn't know applies small electrodes to his legs and arms, while another cleanses and shaves his groin.

"You're going to feel a sharp sting," the doctor says through his mask.

Dan winces. "What was that?"

"The local. Now we are going to thread this catheter through the vein in your groin," the doctor says, holding a long, hollow, flexible tube into the light. "You'll feel some pressure as it is inserted."

"Ouch!" Dan cries.

"How are you doing?"

"That's *pain*, not pressure!"

"Everything's fine. We'll dim the lights, and in a minute you'll be able to see your heart and coronary arteries on the TV monitor to your left."

"I'd rather watch 'Happy Days' if I've got a choice."

"Take a deep breath and hold it. That's good. We're injecting the dye into your heart now." The automatic X-ray film changer begins clacking loudly. A camera in the unit whines.

"I can feel it."

"What do you feel?"

"A warm flush."

"Smile, you're on camera. Watch the monitor."

"Your head's in the way."

"I'll move in a minute. Just a little more dye."

"Now it's getting hotter. Ooh, Doc!"

"What's the matter?"

"A hot flash all over, spreading from my heart. Like I just guzzled taco sauce."

"The flush accompanies the spread of the dye. Within a

minute it should recede. Please take another breath and hold it. Stay perfectly still."

"What are you doing?" Dan grits through his teeth.

"No talking, please."

Suddenly Dan's eyes bulge. He grabs his chest.

"Please hold still! Some discomfort is expected," the doctor says, moving Dan's arm away from his chest.

"Something's wrong in here!" Dan gasps, clutching his chest again. "Help me!"

He hears the doctor curse.

"Doctor!" Dan breathes. His voice is airy, as if he has just run up a long flight of stairs. "Doctor! The pain! It's . . . my chest . . . everywhere, Doctor . . . the pain!"

Somebody slips a tablet under Dan's tongue, and he feels a prick in his arm. The electrocardiogram monitor begins to buzz.

"We've got atrial fibrillation," he hears the doctor say. And then, "I think it's the J-wire straightener. The tip has embolized in the left pulmonary artery."

"Doctor!" Dan says through his teeth, "What is — "

"Complications, Dan. The tip of the catheter has dislodged in your chest."

"Am I . . . Doctor, please . . . dying?" Dan pants, struggling to speak. Sweat pours from his body, yet he feels strangely cold. And then he throws up on the table and feels the light of consciousness fade.

He is whisked into the operating room, and for the next nine hours, various doctors take turns trying to fish the delicate wire back out. But it can't be hooked, and with Dan's vital signs wavering on the operating table, the doctors decide to abandon the catheter tip where it lies.

Three days later, Dan's condition has stabilized and he is discharged to return home. Two weeks pass as his family prepares for Thanksgiving. But the day before the holiday, suffering with extreme chest pain and cardiac arrhythmia, Dan is rushed by ambulance from Napa to the U.C. San Francisco Medical Center. Pain is his constant companion, and every breath is a battle. And the battle is one which he seems to be

losing. That night, despite a host of drugs, Dan suffers a
massive cardiac arrest. Code Blue alarms blast throughout the
ICU ward. Doctors scramble to his bedside.

"No pulse!"

"Stand back!" Dr. Strunk orders, slapping electric defibrillator paddles on Dan's chest. The charge is applied. Dan's body
lurches.

"Again!" The paddles hit his chest. Again he bucks. His
pulse and breathing are restored, yet Dr. Strunk stands over
him sadly. His condition is failing, and there is little else that
can be done. On the last day of November, he again suffers
a full cardiac arrest. Though the paddles revive his heartbeat,
Dan's vital signs hover on the dark verge between life and
death. His skin is cold and clammy; his eyes, glazed.

"He's still here, but just barely," Dr. Strunk says. The
doctor has seen death before, and it looks like Dan. "Somebody
get on the phone, call his parents. And get a priest up here quick."

Racing down the rain-slick streets of San Francisco toward
the Medical Center, the windshield wipers of the Krainert car
beat a dull rat-ta-tat against the night.

"Why? Oh God, why?" Libby Krainert cries, her eyes
flooded with tears. "Why does it have to end like this!"

Her husband George steers silently, crying openly, as they
speed downtown. Ahead, rising through the shroud of fog and
rain, towers a church steeple.

"Let's stop for a minute and pray," George says, pulling
to a stop at the curb.

"No," Libby answers. "Danny needs us. You heard what
the nurse said."

"Please," he says gently, placing his hand atop hers. "Just
for a minute."

Inside the quiet chapel, they kneel together. With tears
streaming down his face, George prays aloud.

"You, of all people, know the pains and fears we face.
And You know the sufferings of our son, because you experienced the sufferings of Your own son, the Christ. Please . . .
please hear us now. We have no other hope but You. Our Danny

is near death. Please help him. Please give him time. And strength. Please . . . ." Beyond words, George pauses. Not willing yet to leave, they wait, and a deep, silent comfort gently enters into them. They feel their prayer has been heard. Wiping away their tears, they walk quickly out of the church to their car.

Arriving at the Medical Center, they catch an elevator and sprint down the hall to Dan's room. The doctor, nurse and priest huddle together around his bed.

"How is he, Doctor?"

Dr. Strunk nods. "Danny refuses to give up. He's got a fighting spirit, and seems to be stabilizing. His heart is very weak now, but his pressure is rising. We almost lost him, though. He was dangling by a thread."

Suddenly Dan's eyelids flutter. He looks around the room, his eyes wild. He coughs hard, gagging on the tube the doctors inserted down his throat, and throws up on the bed. His mother grabs a towel and wipes off his mouth. With a wet washcloth she strokes his forehead.

"That's a good sign," Dr. Strunk says. "A very good sign. At least he is well enough to get sick."

MOUNT HORNO

Deep in the cavernous Mount Horno range of Camp Pendleton, thunderheads pour sheets of rain, and ferocious winds snarl through the manzanita and scrub oak. The earth smells musty and dank. From horizon to horizon, the clouds are locked in place, and the mountains are shut up. On this dark December evening, the first night of a three-day practice "search and destroy" mission, Lloyd and other Bravo Company members are entrenched in foxholes swamped with three feet of water.

"It's just like my recruiter said," Lloyd mutters, trying to stomach a small can of chili from his evening C-rations. "You eat out of a can and sleep under the stars. But you wouldn't feed these rations to your dog if you cared about your dog. And the stars have blown to Kansas by now."

"No bleep," says Bart Thompson, who shares Lloyd's foxhole. "Those bleeping recruiters sell their souls, but sleep sound as angels. Me and my bleeping patriotism. This is where it gets me — in a bleeping snake pit up to my yin yang in slime. And to think I bleeping volunteered!"

"You're a *bleeping* idiot," Lloyd mimics, drawing hoots from Bart. He takes another bite of chili, but spits it out. "This'd gag a hungry dog."

"And choke a bleeping garbage disposal."

"My high school cafeteria had better food."

"No bleep."

"Remember high school cafeteria ladies?"

"I'm still trying to forget."

"Remember their hair nets?"

"Yeah."

"There was this one cafeteria lady when I was in school," Lloyd says. "Should have worn her hair net on her arms. She had more hair there than on her head."

"That's Oklahoma for you. A land where the men are men, and so are the women."

"Hey-o, no flies on Oklahoma," Lloyd says.

"Flies couldn't find it. It's bleeping lost out there in the middle of nowhere."

"Talk about lost," Lloyd says, eyeing the wet blackness that envelops the heights. "We're lost. When do you think this storm's gonna blow?"

"When the sarg says so."

"And until then . . ."

"Until then we bleeping tread water."

Lloyd listens to the wind howl. It kicks at the leaves on the ground and whips in his face. He pulls the collar of his jacket up.

"Why did you sign up, anyway?" Lloyd asks.

"Why?"

"Yeah."

"Beats working for a living."

"Be serious."

"Why not?"

"That's a good reason."

"I don't know, sometimes I surprise myself and do something really stupid."

"Think we'll ever fight?"

"Bleep no. We'll just hump around Pendleton for a couple years, playing combat like we're doing now. But never any real ammo. It's all pretend soldier, you know. Make believe. But makes my old man proud. He runs around telling his

bleeping friends that I'm out fighting Commies, when all I'm
really doing is fighting a bleeping cold."

"I suppose."

"What about you?"

"I don't know. Does seem like make believe. Like we're
just playing soldier. You know, like *bang! bang! you're dead.*
But sometimes I think about what it would be like to really
fight. Shooting somebody, you know."

"Or being shot. Them bleeping gooks got guns, too."

"You live. And then you die," Lloyd says.

"That's a bleeping downer. But speaking about dying, did
you see the *Scout* a couple days ago? The story about the tank?"

"Didn't think you could read."

"Bleep, man. I read all the time."

"Comics, maybe."

"Serious, front page of the base paper. Two Marines
checked out over at Pulgas Lake when their tank went down
a 45-foot ravine. They were pinned underneath."

"Oh yeah, heard about it."

"One of the guys who died, a lance corporal with Company
D, First Marines, his girl friend had some bleeping heart
problem. Anyway, a couple weeks before the accident he had
this feeling, you know, that he was going to check out. And
he told everybody he wanted her to have the heart if something
happened to him."

"That was weird. Like ESP or something."

"No bleep, man. He had a premonition. After they pulled
him out from under the tank, they got him to the hospital and
transplanted his heart into his girl friend."

"Some of the guys were talking about it, but I thought
they were pulling my leg. His *heart?*"

"They got it now where you can recycle practically your
whole bleeping body after you die."

"No joke?"

"Heart, eyes, kidneys. Just about everything."

"They just cut you open and take them?" Lloyd asks.

"I mean, big deal. You're already dead. You gotta sign a
card or something first, though. The DMV gives stickers out
that you put on the back of your driver's license."

"You got one?"

"Not yet."

"Maybe we could go down together."

"Tell you what, Chambers. You get one of them cards, just promise not to give away your bleeping brain. Your heart's OK, but don't make some poor sucker stupid."

"Funny," Lloyd says. "Let's talk about something else."

"Like what?"

Lloyd shrugs. He peers out at the iron-gray sky for a while. The rain slams harder. *Bang, bangedy, bang, bang.* It hits the earth like rifle fire. The boding clouds hang very near the earth.

"Hey-o, Thompson, you want to buy my bike?" he suddenly asks.

"That bleeping wreck of yours?"

"Brand new. Just a couple thousand miles on it."

"Thought you just got it."

"I did."

"And now you want to unload it?"

"Maybe. Been thinking about buying something bigger. Like a Honda XR 500. Either that or another Yamaha. Maybe even a Kawasaki. Or else just bank the money and get married."

"Sounds like you got your bleeping mind all made up," Thompson laughs. "Got it narrowed down to a choice between three bikes and a broad. A real decisive guy, Chambers — the kind that probably drives the bleeping waiters nuts in restaurants. Is that the bleeping truth, or is that the bleeping truth? I've got you nailed, don't I? A bleeping basket case inside."

"Give me a break."

"Who you going to pay to marry you?"

"Didn't I tell you about King Kong's daughter?"

"What about your 'Hog of the Week' the DI used to razz you about? She give you the bleeping ax or what?"

"Just stopped writing — was too eager to get married and pregnant."

"Or pregnant and married."

"No, with her the order was important. She wanted about a dozen kids, and I . . . well, forget it. Let's just say we axed each other. She's past tense. It's Lisa now. Have you seen her? She's got a body that could put this storm to rest in minutes."

"No. But a little advice: forget marriage. You're just . . . what, 18?"

"Nineteen. Had me a birthday."

"Well, I've seen some of them bleeping young Marine brides with stomachs out to here and a couple other snotty-nosed kids tagging along and screaming their bleeping lungs out. These broads don't got nothing to do at night but sit home alone watching Richard Dawson on . . . .what's that bleeping show of his, anyway?"

"I don't know. Magnum?"

"No, no. Bleep, man, where you been? Dawson's that old crotch who's always kissing the broads on that bleeping game show of his."

"Wheel of Fortune?"

"Bleep you're dumb, Chambers. Sonofa . . . what is that . . . 'Family Feud'! That's it, 'Family Feud.' And that's all these Marine widows have to do at night, but watch that bleeping show of his and change diapers and wipe noses and try to stare down the bleeping ceiling at 3 A.M., wondering if their old man's still alive or if he's blown up or rolled over in a tank . . . or drowning like us in some foxhole up in the mountains somewhere. Chambers, you're too bleeping young to get married. Wait till you're a sergeant or something. And if you sell your bike, buy a Harley. Not some toy built by the bleeping Chinese."

"Japanese."

"Same bleeping difference. Honda, Yamaha, Kawasaki — sounds like some kind of bleeping Japanese law firm," he laughs. "How much do you want for your bike, anyway?"

"I don't know. Maybe sixteen."

"Hundred?"

"Yeah, or sixteen-fifty. But for you, a fellow Marine, an even seventeen."

"Bleep."

"It's a great bike — an XT Enduro. You can ride it around town or take it up in the hills. Been kept in the garage and only my grandma's driven it."

"Maybe I'd consider it for eleven-fifty. Twelve, max. It's probably not worth a bleep."

"Really, it's a great bike, and I've kept it up. I'll let you test it next weekend if we don't drown up here tonight. Maybe we could take it up in the hills behind Lake O'Neill. You know how to ride?"

"A little. But I don't have no bleeping sixteen hundred bills."

"We'll work something out."

"That's the bleeping weekend before Christmas, you know."

"Next weekend? So?"

"I'm just saying it's the bleeping weekend before Christmas, that's all."

"So buy yourself an early Christmas present."

"Bleep."

"You like that word, don't you?"

"Bleep?"

"Yeah."

"It's got a certain ring to it."

Entrenched in their foxhole, battered by the raging wind and rain, Lloyd and Bart talk through the night, unable to sleep. At 4 A.M., with the sky dark as pitch, the sergeant blows his whistle. Visibility remains near zero. Lloyd and Bart pull themselves out of their hole, dripping wet and covered with foul gray mud. They gather in loose formation with the other company members. The early morning is cold, but the coldness has more to do with the wind and the rain than it does the temperature.

The sergeant quietly reviews strategy for the final assault on "Enemy Hill," which looms a mile in the distance, but which is now shrouded by darkness and clouds.

"Marines have fought in much worse weather than this," the sergeant barks against the wind. "Now let's move it! Spread out, but not beyond arm's length from the man next to you. This is one mother of a black night, and I don't want to lose anybody."

Together they trudge toward the hill, each man carrying his blank-loaded M-16 in a ready, fighting position. Water runs off Lloyd's nose. He wipes it with his sleeve. But that doesn't help. The chill rain pounds like an angry fist, and he lowers his head against the blows. The sky is iron above, and the wind slices to the bone. The everlasting downpour strips damp foliage from the trees, which stand naked as skeletons. Thick sticky mud sucks at Lloyd's boots. Suddenly, off to the right, he hears a sepulchral groan.

"Aaarrghhaadoo!"

It is a deep gargle that makes Lloyd shiver.

"That you, Thompson?" he says.

"I bleeping thought it was you," Bart says.

Lloyd hears the noise again — an eerie groan that rises through the wind.

"Aaarrghhaadoo!"

He stops, peering into the blackness.

"What the bleep was that?" Thompson breathes.

"Don't know," Lloyd whispers.

"Sounded like somebody just got their throat cut. There are drug runners who operate out of these hills, you know."

"It was probably just the trees."

The sergeant again signals for the line to move ahead. They walk in silence for several minutes. Ears are pricked, waiting. Suddenly Lloyd jumps. A wild bawl erupts through the darkness straight ahead.

"Haarrrooghhaadoo." Again and again. "Haarrrooghhaadoo! Haarrrooghhaadoo!" Something thrashes in the brush to the left. Nobody moves. Lloyd can hear his heart. Over and over the guttural noises rise above the howling wind. Nearer. Louder. Creeping forward by inches, the men steady their rifles.

"That's no bleeping tree," Thompson hisses.

"Shhh!" In the quiet that follows, Lloyd almost doesn't breathe.

Another groan splits the night, answered by yet another to the right. And then dead silence, except for the beating rain. The wind cries through the brush. A branch snaps. A low wheeze rattles near Lloyd's feet. Something warm and big seems to be very, very close. Too close. He freezes, his heart

beating tattoos in his throat. Whatever it is has a smell. It is
a zoo smell. Rot and fur and dung. It smells worse than a
kennel of wet, dirty dogs. Lloyd grips his rifle. His eyes strain.
But still, he can see nothing but blackness.

The sergeant signals with his whistle. Two short blasts,
pause, two more shorts. The signal has been prearranged, like
audibles called by a quarterback. Rifles are braced. Then the
sergeant pops the release of a rocket flare. A sudden *whoosh*
rips through the silence. Lloyd watches the tiny comet tail of
light. One-one thousand . . . two-one thousand . . . three-one
thousand. An orange fireball, bright as the sun, suddenly
explodes high in the clouds. The mountain flashes with brilliant
light. Five feet from Lloyd towers a buffalo. Its fur is black
as the night; its horns, long and sharp.

Lloyd's scream catches in his throat. The animal snorts.
Lloyd feels its hot nostril blast and drops his rifle. He turns
to run. The buffalo snorts again. Lloyd is running hard. He
hears hoofs pounding the soppy earth. The smell lingers in his
lungs. He tries to spit it out as he runs, but his mouth is dry.
Now he's really running. Clots of mud spin from his boots
with every wide, wild stride. The muscles in his legs snap and
tighten, snap and tighten. He sprints blindly through the blackness. The wind in his face blinds him. His feet can't move
any faster. A branch suddenly hits him across the cheek. He
stops, wheels and gropes for the trunk. His hands paw for a
branch. Finding one just above his head, he lunges. The limb
sinks underneath his weight. His feet scramble. He digs his
toes into the trunk's wet bark, pulling himself to safety. Hugging
the branch, he darts a glance below.

Light from the rocket flare lingers. In the pale glimmer
he spots the other Marines, laughing and pointing up at the
tree. And much further in the distance, illuminated in the fading
light, a small herd of buffalo rumbles toward the horizon.
Lloyd grabs the branch and swings down. He drops to the
ground and walks back. He is greeted with hoots.

"Almost got killed," he snaps, picking his M-16 out of
the mud. "What's so funny about that?" He looks around.
Everybody is still laughing.

"You scared the bleep out of the buffalo," Bart whoops. "How does it feel to have a face that starts a stampede?"

Mud and the bleak winter season lay all around, and the clouds hug the mountains. Rain beats against the puddles. Lloyd tries to laugh, but the laugh is stifled by the foul stench of the buffalo which lingers in his nostrils and the pounding hoofs which still echo in his ears. He looks back at the naked tree, which mocks him in the distance. There is no beauty in the mountains, and the only color is that of rot. The first leaden rays of dawn have slipped over the far range, and Lloyd shivers against the cold. He thinks of liquor and he thinks of Lisa, unsure of which he desires most.

Three days later while on liberty, Lloyd and Lisa stop by the showroom of an Oceanside motorcycle dealer. Inside, Lloyd caresses the smooth contours of a sleek new Honda XR 500.

"That's the one," he says.

"It's pretty," Lisa remarks, touching the black vinyl seat. The showroom smells metallic and clean. The shelves of the dealership are stocked with forks and chains and gloves and gaskets. Blue windbreaker jackets with Honda logos hang by the door.

"I'll buy it if I can unload my Yamaha to Thompson."

"Is he ready to buy?" she asks.

"He will be."

"You sound sure."

"Cash on the barrel by this weekend."

"Let's forget about this weekend and think about tonight," Lisa says, hooking him by the arm and leading him out the door. The storm has blown over, and the night is warm but moist. A lace mist hangs in the air, and tiny white lights glitter from the street lamp poles. "We need to get a tree," she says.

"Two blocks over," he says. "You can practically smell it from here."

"Our tree is normally up by Thanksgiving, but this year is different," Lisa says. "After Mom ran off, things weren't the same. Dad still hasn't sent out cards. And if we don't get the tree now, I think we'll go without."

Lisa hops on his bike, hugging Lloyd's waist as he pulls into traffic, turns the corner and slips to the curb fronting an empty lot now stocked with Christmas trees. The perfumed air smells like a forest, rich and warm. Lloyd takes a deep breath and helps Lisa off the back of his Yamaha. They walk hand in hand through the gate, and survey the lot. There are hundreds of trees, each leaning against a horizontal wooden brace.

"There," she says, pointing.

"Where?"

"There," she repeats, walking quickly toward a spruce that stands at the end of the nearest row. "That's it."

"No," Lloyd says, "that's not it." He holds the tree up and shakes it out. Thousands of brown needles fall to his feet. He turns the tree around.

"You're right. That's not it."

"There," he says, pointing down the aisle.

"Where?"

"There," he says. He sets the first tree down and heads down the aisle. "I thought I knew what a tree looked like. But that," he says, "now *that* is a tree."

She pulls the tree from the grasp of other neighboring branches and holds it up. He grabs the trunk and bumps it twice on the ground. Needles fall, but not enough to diminish his enthusiasm.

"What do you think?" he says. "Is this a tree, or is this a tree?"

"You may be right," she says. "I think it's a tree. Actually it's not bad."

"Not bad? This was the king of the forest until somebody laid into it with a chainsaw. What do you say?"

Her eyes move from him to the tree.

"How do we get it home?"

"Same way I intend to get you home," he says. "We just hold on tight."

Hauling the pine out to the sidewalk, they button their jackets against the cool December evening and hop onto Lloyd's Yamaha. Stars hang in the sky like glitter. Riding with the tree tucked beneath their arms, they return to Lisa's condo to decorate it.

Lloyd cuts an inch off the base of the tree and places it in a stand by the large picture window as Lisa makes hot buttered rums. When she returns with the steaming mugs, Lloyd is watching her. Her skin is soft and smooth. She steps to his side and hands him a mug. Her eyes glow like the lights on the harbor outside. He takes a sip.

"I'll get the Christmas boxes," she says quietly.

Lloyd shakes his head. He sets his mug on the long table by the leather couch. And then he removes the mug from her hand. Her eyes are intent.

"Where's your father?" he asks. His voice sounds hoarse.

"Out."

"How about the dog?"

"Caged."

He takes a step closer. She looks up and swallows. He reaches out and fingers her long blond hair. And then they embrace, easing down to the carpeted floor and lying together beside the tree as the lights of the harbor glimmer and mingle with the twinkling stars outside.

Chapter Thirteen — DAN

HEAD OF THE LIST

Inside the cardiac care unit at Stanford Medical Center, Dan rests in bed with an open Bible on his chest. Surrounding him is a jungle of high-tech, heart-monitoring equipment, which he has decorated with Christmas wreaths, bows and tiny elves.

"Shirley, they thought I was a goner," he says, cradling the phone receiver against his chin. "The hospital priest was even there . . . ready to usher me onward and upward. But I told him — I said, 'Stick around if you want, but I'm not going anywhere.' He was talking — the priest and somebody else, maybe the doctor — about the Giants game, and he practically jumped out of his robe when he heard me say that. Probably thought I was already over the edge.

"And now, they say, I'm at the *top* of the transplant list. Shirley, number one! No more politics. No more hospital shuffling. Now the wait is for real. I get the first heart that's a match. Today I even got my own transplant nurse, Seana Ferguson, who will be with me for the long haul."

"What's she like?" Shirley asks.

"Let me just read the Christmas card she gave me this morning. I don't know her very well yet, but the card probably describes her best. I'll read it if you've got time."

"I've got time, if you've got money," Shirley says. "It's your phone bill, Krainert."

"Here's what she wrote. Seana said:

Dear Danny,

You know that you are very special to many people. But you are that much more special to me. You are the first heart transplant patient that I've decided to be primary nurse for, and I'm really excited and looking forward to this.

I want you to understand that there will be good times. But there will also be bad times, and you must realize that the bad times will be just as rough on me as they are on you. But we will get through it all together!

Please feel free to ask me anything. I will be as open and honest with you as I can, and I hope that you will also be open with me. We'll be spending a lot of time together in the future, and I just want you to know that I am here not only as your nurse; I'm here also as your friend.

If there is anything you need or any questions or problems you have, please feel free to call me at any time. I will always be here to lend support when it is needed. At the same time, I, as your nurse, will offer you the very best of care, and work with you to make you the best heart transplant done so far. And that is the most important thing to me — that you get out of here and live a long, healthy and happy life.

Helping you attain this goal will be my Christmas present to you. Your present to me can be to work hard at getting well . . . and just being happy. So, Danny, here's to our first Christmas together and to many, many more to come. Have a very beautiful Christmas and a loving, peaceful and healthy New Year.

Your transplant nurse,

Seana

"Doesn't that rate some kind of award?" Dan asks. "Say, the Pulitzer Prize for Christmas cards?"

"It's beautiful," Shirley says, pausing to gather her thoughts. The phone goes silent for a moment. "So what about this 'top of the list' business, Dan? Are you scared now that you're next?"

"Scared? Not really. Relieved, yes."

"Not even a little scared?"

"About what?"

"Well, you know . . ."

"Go ahead and say it. About *dying* you mean? Sure, I suppose. But I believe God's got a purpose to all of this. My time's not up yet, and I think I'd know if it was. But I spend most of my time in bed. On my back, looking up. Looking up to God, so to speak. And it's my faith in God that keeps me going. I mean, I honestly believe that I'll make it. That all things will work together for good. But . . ."

"But what?"

"I don't know. There's always the statistics. And against the odds, my faith sometimes seems — "

"Illogical?"

"And impossible. Yet I'd be dead tomorrow without faith. *Dead!* I mean that. And it's because of you that I've got any faith at all. Shirley, you've been with me every step of the way."

"No, I'm not with you much. But I am with my prayers."

"I know."

"It's OK to be scared, though. You don't have to pretend with me."

"Sometimes I am scared. Every time I look in the mirror or step on the scale, I cringe. My body's a heap of bones. A skeleton."

"How's the pain?" she asks softly.

"Even with the drugs, worse each day. And now, I've got pain in places I never even knew I had places. Health is something I always took for granted when I had it. Playing ball, swimming, even just going for a walk. Not once did I ever stop to think that I was doing something other people couldn't do. But this hospital is filled with people who can't even get out of bed. As for me, I'm a physical basket case.

Just walking across the room is something that takes all the strength I've got left. Coping with the pain, that's the hardest thing."

"What do you mean?"

"The constant pain, it makes you think."

"About?"

"About my relationship with God. I want it to be real, Shirley, regardless of my circumstances. You hear about fox-hole or fire-escape conversions. You know, people who say they'll do this or that if God just saves them. I want to live, yes. But it's not important, really, whether I live or die." Dan clears his throat. "What's important for me now is to stand firm, regardless of what happens. It's like a test. And I think the true test of my faith is not how I face death, but like Job, how I face suffering. If I die, the test is over. I'll be in heaven with Jesus. But I want to know that very same closeness this side of heaven. I want . . . oh, forget it. Enough of my rambling. I get talking and — "

"No, please. I'm not bored. I want to know more about what you think and feel."

"Well, for starters . . . I think about you every day, and — "

"That's not what I meant."

"And I feel that I love you very much. I've never said that to anyone before, Shirley. You haven't changed your mind about us, have you? About our relationship?"

"Listen, Krainert. I would like to say I have, because I know that's what you want to hear. But I want to go through this operation with you as our relationship stands."

"Figured I couldn't lose anything by asking again."

"Krainert?"

"Yeah?"

"Ring the buzzer on the side of your bed."

"The buzzer?"

"Go ahead."

"Why?"

"Ring it. And when Seana comes, tell her you need a shower. A very cold shower."

Later that night as his mother sleeps quietly beside his bed, Dan switches on the TV and flips through the band of channels. The room glows in gray shadow until he clicks the set off and reaches for a magazine. But he quickly loses interest in that, too. Wadding up the McDonald's bag from dinner which his mother had brought, he heaves it across the room, missing the trash can. Flopping back onto his pillow, he stares at the ceiling tiles, each pocked with dozens of tiny holes. He begins to count . . . .

". . . seven hundred forty-five . . . seven hundred forty-six . . . seven hundred forty-seven . . ."

His transplant nurse, Seana Ferguson, suddenly walks through the door. She is a tall brunette, with long, shapely legs and a milk chocolate tan.

"Did she change her mind?" Seana asks, flashing a hopeful smile.

"Shirley?"

Seana nods.

"Not yet."

"That's the spirit. Just give her time," she says, bending over Dan to take his temperature. Her neckline drops open, and Dan glances up, his pulse racing. "Are you all right?" she asks, fitting a blood pressure collar around his arm.

"I think so."

"Your pulse is suddenly way up, and you look a little flushed. Better take a quick EKG."

"I'm fine. Really."

"Your color's not right."

"Nothing's wrong. I mean it."

"Just to be sure — it'll only take a minute," she says, opening his pajama top and attaching the jelly-backed suction sensors across his chest. She flips the machine on, watches the scanner for a moment as it moves across the graph paper, and then steps outside the room to run a quick errand. Moments after she leaves, Mrs. Krainert awakens and walks down the hall to get a drink of water, leaving Dan in the room alone.

Suddenly, a buzzer blasts in the nurse's station. Dan's room number flashes red. Seana's face goes white as she whips around to check the console EKG monitor. Flat line.

"No!" she screams, pushing the Code Blue alarm. Grabbing the emergency medical cart, she races down the corridor. Doors fly open as doctors sprint toward his room. Dan's mother follows in their wake, her face ashen as the eggshell paint of the hospital corridor.

Seana bursts into Dan's room. He lies in bed, still. The EKG needle pens a flat dark line. Grabbing his wrist, she checks his pulse. The doctor readies the defibrillator.

"Stand back!" he orders, poising the paddles above Dan's chest.

"Stop!" Seana yells. She elbows the doctor back. "He's got a pulse!"

Abruptly, Dan jerks upright in bed. Seana screams. Choking with laughter, Dan opens his hand and flashes the five tiny suction sensors.

Seana looks down, comprehending in that instant the trick Dan has played. Her eyes flood with tears. "That's not funny!" she cries. And then she slowly backs away from his bed, turns and walks quickly out of the room.

With Dan at the top of the transplant list, his parents have both taken extended leaves of absence from their jobs so they can be near the hospital when the donor heart arrives. They rent a small apartment on Sheridan Drive in Palo Alto — an area otherwise known as Life Row. Scattered throughout the same general vicinity in hastily rented apartments and hotel rooms, a dozen or so other transplant patients and their families maintain an anxious vigil, waiting for a special phone call, abiding their appointment with death or, more optimistically, their chance to cheat it.

Making the six-minute drive to the medical center on this bright December morning, Dan's parents arrive shortly before Dr. John Wallwork, one of the transplant surgeons, enters on his rounds. A plump Englishman with a cheeky boyish face, teardrop glasses and a near-bald head, the doctor strides quickly to Dan's bedside.

"Any news yet?" Dan's father asks him, rising from his chair.

Dr. Wallwork shakes his head. "Still waiting and hoping," he says. "The heart supply is a little lean right now. But that can change overnight. Maybe today's the day, you never know."

"Right," Dan says dryly.

"You've got to keep hoping."

"I am, Doc. But hoping this hard can make you crazier than despair."

"We just need the proper match, that's all. How do you feel?"

Dan ignores the question. "I've been at the top for two weeks now," he grumbles.

"I know. But one must, as Emerson said, 'Adopt the pace of nature: Her secret is patience.' "

"If my heart doesn't come soon, I want to go home for Christmas," Dan says. "I am bored stiff and want to get out of here, if only for a few days. There's absolutely nothing to do here."

"That's a harsh assessment."

"Nothing but count holes in ceiling tiles."

The cardiologist takes a seat on the corner of the mattress and places his hand on Dan's shoulder. He clears his throat. "I heard about last night."

"I figured you probably would. Seana nearly passed out."

"Not to mention your dear mother," Mrs. Krainert interjects.

"No more pranks like that, Dan," Dr. Wallwork says. "There are only so many hearts to go around. And we don't have a surplus for the staff and your parents, too. Now, enough said. However, I am glad your spirits are up."

"They're not. I'm going nuts, and want to go home for Christmas! And I'll get progressively nuttier until you say yes."

"This will all be over before you know it," Dr. Wallwork says, patting Dan on the shoulder.

"I'm going home for Christmas," Dan says.

Dr. Wallwork smiles and rises to leave. Dan abruptly grabs the doctor's necktie and jerks him down face to face.

"Don't you have a family?" he snarls, feigning anger. "Don't you have people you want to be with at Christmas?"

He tightens his grip. "Have compassion! I tell you, I'm climbing the walls. There are friends and relatives I want to see. I want to smell flowers, not Lysol. I'm tired of being cooped up in this prison, and I want out. I want to look at the clouds, play with my dog. Doctor, have mercy! I want to go home for Christmas!" He pauses before releasing his captive. "I know where your children go to school. I know where your wife shops. You don't want to jeopardize their safety, do you?" he snarls, slowly easing his grip.

Rising to his feet, Dr. Wallwork adjusts his necktie. His smile melts to seriousness. "Dan, you are critically ill. Don't forget that for a minute."

"If all I'm doing is waiting for a heart, I can do that at home."

The doctor nods. His eyes are understanding. "We'll watch you closely over the next few days. If your condition remains stable and your heart's still not in, we'll consider your request. And the key word here is *consider.* If you were to be released, I'd want you to remain in Palo Alto for several days before driving to Napa."

"Thank you, Doc."

"I can guarantee nothing. I mean that. However, I will at least consult with other physicians — the heart team — to see what they think."

Three days later on December 18th, Dan's heart has still not arrived, and Dr. Wallwork relays word that Dan can take a temporary leave from the Medical Center.

"Remember, I want you to remain in the Palo Alto apartment for several days. *In* the apartment, and that's a strict order."

"Yes, Herr Commandant," Dan says.

"We need to monitor you very carefully, so I'll insist that you call in twice a day, at 11 and 6. Also, get lots of bed rest. And only two visitors per day."

"Heil."

"Dan, keep in mind that your name could be scratched off the transplant list if you so much as contract a cold or come down with the flu."

"Doc, serious. I won't get sneezed on. I'll wear a mask and suck lemons if I have to."

"Three final comments," the doctor says. "One, stay healthy. Two, stay close to your phone. The heart could come any time, day or night."

"That's only two," Dan says.

"Three, have yourself a beautiful Christmas."

That night on Life Row, Dan lies in bed with the telephone perched beside him on the nightstand. He considers calling Shirley, but it is already past ten. Closing his eyes, his thoughts wander as he drifts toward sleep.

Suddenly the phone rings. Dan jerks awake. His parents race to his doorway, standing on the threshold of his room as they wait for him to answer it. Dan looks up. They are both in their bathrobes. It rings again. His mother motions at the phone. Dan reaches to pick it up, but his hand begins shaking as he touches the jangling receiver. It rings a third time. Then a fourth time.

"You answer it," Dan says. "I'm too nervous." The phone rings again.

"What's the matter with you two?" his father says, darting to Dan's bedside. "I'll get it!" He snatches the receiver. "Hello?"

"Yes, what time do you close?" the voice on the other end says.

"What time do we close?" Mr. Krainert snaps. "You're calling a private residence!"

"Sorry. Wrong number."

"I should say!" he snaps again. He hangs up the phone and glances around. Mrs. Krainert walks over and sits on the corner of Dan's bed.

"I was hoping . . ." he says.

"I know this is hard on you," his mother says. "It's hard on all of us."

"Yes," he says. His lips barely move. And then he closes his eyes again.

She looks down at him, his mouth slightly open as he drifts again toward sleep. She feels his pain, sees his wasted body, his pale gaunt face, his unruly hair. She watches his chest rise and fall, and silently urges him to take another breath, deeper and longer. She strokes his blanketed leg, thinking of how it was when she was pregnant with her son. The pregnancy then had seemed interminably long as she waited for her due date. Month after month, her body aching for delivery. Her ankles swelling with edema, her veins popping as they coursed with life blood for two, her internal organs cramping against her chest cavity as the baby grew. The final long days of the pregnancy were the most difficult, and each additional hour of waiting seemed like another day.

She continues stroking his leg, watching the covers rise and fall with each slight breath, praying that the breaths will continue until a heart arrives.

Rising to turn off the lights, her nerves suddenly go taut. Outside the apartment, screeching tires split the still night. There is a scream, followed by a collision. The windows shake, and Dan bolts upright.

"What was that?" he asks.

"An accident," his mother says, throwing open the curtains and peering out into the darkness.

"You never know," Dan says, scrambling out of bed and drawing the sheet around him, "that could be my heart." He ambles painfully to the door, trying not to strain himself. But even crossing the room has become a challenge. Each step is taken with increasing difficulty. When he reaches the door, his chest is pounding, his neck throbbing. He battles the lock and tugs the door open.

His parents peer over his shoulder, watching as two men jump out of the cars, waving fists at each other.

"Just a fender bender," Mrs. Krainert says. "Everybody back to bed."

Dan heads for his room, pauses in the doorway, and then turns to face his parents. "You know what I think about as I wait for this heart?" he asks. "I think, somebody out there is going to die. I don't know who it is, and I can't do anything about it, but somebody is going to die."

His father nods.

"I've thought the same thing," his mother says.

"I feel kind of selfish, hoping for it to happen. But somebody must die if I'm going to live."

His mother looks at him warmly.

"Our days are all numbered," he continues. "And wherever that person is, he or she still has some important things left to take care of. I believe that. He or she is still working through something and just isn't ready to go yet."

THE FINAL GIFT

Saturday dawns bright, with a sky so vast it seems to draw Lloyd and Lisa up into it as their rowboat edges across Camp Pendleton's Lake O'Neill. The sky and water meld into a single blue expanse that stretches out toward the distance. The glistening blue surface above is broken by a single puff of cloud; below by the splash of a paddle.

Propped in the bow with a stereo tape deck perched beside him, Lloyd pries the top off a small vial, pops two tablets and downs them with a can of Coors. He tosses the empty into the bottom of the boat, and reaches for a fresh can. Struggling at the oars, Lisa whips the water into a whirlpool, propelling the boat in circles in the middle of the lake.

"Don't drink too much," she warns. "I may need help getting us back to shore."

"Somebody's gotta drinn it," he slurs. "And if you won't drinn any, I can handle enough for two. Mustn't let anthinn go to waste, cuz too many hunry people inna world."

"My father would kill us both if he knew your condition."

"No, you have verr nice father."

"We should head back."

"Less not go yet. Less stay here — iss so pretty."

"You're drunk, Lloyd. And I don't like it when you drink like this."

"Drunn?" Lloyd laughs. "I'm juss trying get rid this blasted headache. That, and trying get uppa nerve ask you a serious question."

"What question?"

"Verr sneaky, verr sneaky! But I haffa get uppa nerve first."

"Isn't this a beautiful day?" Lisa says, changing the subject. "I got a letter this morning from my aunt back in Chicago. They're buried under a foot of snow, with a wind chill of minus twenty."

"Minus twenny? Thass worse than Oglahoma. Ann I thought Oglahoma was worse of anyplace."

"I've never seen anybody as drunk as you are now," Lisa says, splashing Lloyd with the oar.

"Bedder wash out, or you'll lectrocute us," he says, wiping a spot of water off the stereo. He looks at her and starts to laugh. "You're so drunk you can't see straight."

"I'm not drunn. Jussa happy soldier in the M'rine Coors. Get it? *Coors?*"

"Real funny. You're hilarious."

"Don't haffa be snooty. I'm juss having li'l fun . . . with a pun . . . inna sun . . . with my hon . . . the equal of none," he says, laughing harder.

"At least your headache's gone."

"Headache. No, don't remind me! Oh, my head, my aching head. I almose forgot about it. You, my hon the equal of none, can you get me nother aspirin?"

"That's not aspirin you're taking. It's Darvon," Lisa says, pointing to the bottle rolling about between his legs. "They're much stronger."

"Long's it isn't Midol," he laughs, downing another pill with a swig of beer. "My head's ready bust wide open."

"You really shouldn't be mixing the two — alcohol and pills — you know."

"Takes grenade hurt a M'rine. Not li'l pill and li'l can Coors. I'm tough as nails, you know." He downs the last of his beer, and then sings along with a stanza of "Fame" on the stereo.

Lisa hums along as she dips the oars. "Say, wasn't your friend supposed to meet you about now?"

"Frenn? Oh yeah, Thompson! What time is it?"

"Eleven."

"Already?" He spots Thompson sitting on shore, and stands up to wave. "Be rye there!" he shouts across the water, losing his balance and nearly toppling overboard.

Lisa grabs him by the shirt to steady him. The boat rocks wildly. "In your condition, you're not only not going to make it to heaven, but you may not even make it to shore," she says.

"Hah! I'll teach you how row," he says, turning cautiously around and switching with Lisa at the oars. "But once I get you on shore, you gotta wash out for my frenn."

"Watch out for Thompson?"

"He's crazy M'rine."

"I wonder what he says about you?"

"He bedder not say much, cuz I outrank him. But when he says anthinn, he has one-word vocablarry."

"What's the word?"

"Bleep."

"What?"

Lloyd laughs. "That's word. *Bleep.*"

He leans hard on the oars until the bottom of the boat noses up against the shoreline. Thompson walks over, grabs the bow and pulls the boat higher onto the bank.

"Where you bleeping been?" he asks, looking hard at Lloyd.

"Playing sailor," Lloyd says, squinting

"Man, you're bleeping pie-eyed! You didn't drink all that yourself, did you?" he says, eyeing the litter of aluminum cans in the bottom of the boat.

"I was kind thirssy."

"Apparently so."

"Come on," Lloyd says, draping his arm drunkenly around Thompson's shoulder. "My bike's over by the big euglyptus tree. Less go over there ann I'll let you tess-ride it. But firss," he grins, "firss, I gotta fine me a ressroom."

Five minutes later, Lloyd joins the others. He walks around the bike, flashing a big smile at Thompson. "Juss like I said. It's bess deal inna world! Bike's in mint shape. Everthinn works on this baby! Nothinn wrong, everthinn shiny!"

"Only thing that's got anything wrong is you, Chambers. You're more bleeped up, man, than I seen you before."

"I'm ready a deal," Lloyd drawls. "Bike starts inna flash, hot or cold, rain or shine. Good mileage. And fass. Fass? Lemme tell you about fass. Iss so fass — "

"Quit your bleeping hype, Chambers, and give me your best price."

"Eleven hunner . . . (burp) fiffy."

"You really messed yourself up, man. How many bleeping beers did you drink out there anyway?"

Lloyd flashes a crooked grin and begins counting his fingers.

"Nine beers, three Darvons," Lisa prompts. "And he took another two Darvons earlier."

"Bleep, Chambers! You're tossing beers down the hatch like a bleeping career Marine. If you're not careful, somebody's going to be glad you got that card of yours!"

"What card?" Lisa asks.

"Nothing," Lloyd says, waving her off. "He's juss talking like always."

"What card?" she asks again.

"M'rine secret," Lloyd says, winking at Thompson.

"You're gonna feel like you got hit by a tank tonight," Thompson says.

"Maybe, but rye now I don't feel anthinn! So less talk bizzness 'fore tank comes."

"Just give me the keys. I'm going to bleeping see what this wreck can do."

Lloyd hands him the helmet and keys. "Rememmer, it's five speed. One down, four up. The clush is up here. An it's got two brakes. One on rye hannelbar, one down there for your foot. Be sure use both or you'll end up inna bushes."

"Go sit down before you fall down," Thompson says, hopping on the bike. He rolls off the kickstand, guns the engine, but pops the clutch. The bike bucks to a standstill. His second attempt is smooth and fast, leaving Lloyd and Lisa in a cloud of dust.

"I thinn he's going buy it," Lloyd says. "I can see it in his eyes."

"I doubt you can see anything now," Lisa laughs.

"Serious. I thinn he's going buy it — unless he runs inna phone pole or dumps inna lake. He probly rode his sisser's moped once an now thinns he's Misser Evil Neevil."

They sit beneath the tree and watch Thompson cut up and down the nearby dirt trails.

"What was the question you were going to ask me out on the lake?" Lisa asks suddenly.

Lloyd blinks his bleary blue eyes, tries to focus on Lisa — tries to take in her beauty, to love her with his gaze. He grins slyly and reaches for his pocket, but changes his mind. "Better wait until Thompson's gone," he says. He grabs another beer and pops the can open. "Would you look at him? He's going too fass."

"He probably wouldn't drive like that if he couldn't," Lisa says.

"You kidding? He's always living beyon' his brain."

"Like you."

"We're both M'rines."

Moments later, Thompson races back and skids to a stop. The tail pipe belches black smoke.

"What the bleep's wrong with this bomb, Chambers?" he says, jumping off the bike.

Lloyd steps to his side and starts to laugh.

"Well?"

"You dinn push inna choke," he says, fumbling with the knob. "There. See, nothinn to it. Now, you going buy it for Chrissmas or not? Sanna Claus thinns you like it."

"Are you sure it was just the choke?"

"It works fine now," Lloyd says, elbowing Thompson aside. He swings his leg over the seat, "Here, Misser Motorcycle will prove it."

"You're in no bleeping condition to ride," Thompson says, grabbing his arm.

"Get your hand offa me. My connition is fine. One hunner percenn. Well, maybe niney percenn."

"Try forty."

Lloyd laughs, revving the engine into the power band. Thompson hands him the helmet.

"Hang onna helmet," he says, running his hand over his closely cropped hair. The red bristles glimmer in the sun. "I'm juss going up that li'l hill."

"Lloyd!" Lisa screams, running over.

"Be rye back!" he yells above the engine's hornet whine. And then he screams away in a tipsy power wheelie. They both watch, shaking their heads as he blasts down a 200-yard straight and takes a quick left-right-left turn, kicking a rooster tail of dirt at the scrub oak and manzanita. Opening the throttle, he scrambles up a rutted hill, his hungry tires dusting the nearby phone poles. Atop the peak he pauses to survey the lake, the sailboats, the gulls.

"WONNERFUL VIEW!" he shouts down at Lisa and Thompson.

They wave back.

"BIKE WORKS FINE!"

They wave again.

"LISA, I LOVE YOU!" he trumpets from the ridge, blowing her a kiss. And then he guns the bike around and cuts downhill.

He glances back at the exhaust. Holding the throttle open with his right hand, he leans his wiry body over to adjust the choke. His strong fingers fumble among wires, and he looks down for a moment. It is the longest moment of his young life.

The bike suddenly veers right, smashing out of control through a stand of manzanita. Branches grab his legs. The front wheel bucks off a granite boulder and crashes against another. Lloyd flips airborne. His scream hangs in the air.

His piercing voice is echoed by Lisa's screams as she darts up the hill. She paws the dirt wildly, insanely. She trips and falls, clawing the ground like a drowning swimmer. Thompson grabs her from behind.

"Lisa, stop!" he shouts. "Stop!"

He holds her down until her arms stop flailing. "Go for help!" he yells, his face inches from hers. She looks up. Her eyes flood with tears. "Go for help," he repeats, shoving her toward the boat house.

He waits until he is sure she is gone, and then he scrambles through the manzanita and over blood-spattered rocks. A swatch of Lloyd's scalp clings to a nearby telephone pole. He glances suddenly down. His stomach tightens. At its base Lloyd lies twisted, like a broken doll.

Thompson dives to his side. He throws his arms around Lloyd, embracing him and weeping. "No, no, no," he sobs, his tears mingling with blood as he pulls Lloyd's body close to his own. "No, you bleeping Marine, no," he cries, sobbing hard and deep and long. "Don't die, Chambers. Don't die."

When the ambulance arrives at the nearby Naval Regional Medical Center, attendants find a small jewelry box containing a woman's diamond ring in one of Lloyd's pockets. In another they find his brown leather wallet. On the back of his driver's license is a small pink card with the words: "Pursuant to the Uniform Anatomical Gift Act, I hereby give, effective upon my death, the parts or organs listed herein." On a blank line beneath, Lloyd had carefully printed: "I give my heart."

It is his final gift. Two days later at 2:10 P.M. on December 22, 1980, Lloyd Chambers, 19, is pronounced legally dead.

Moments later, hospital officials place an emergency call to the Stanford University Medical Center.

Chapter Fifteen — DAN

ALL-POINTS BULLETIN

At 11:30 the morning of December 22, Dan had picked up the phone and dialed his cardiologist, Dr. Wallwork.

"Hey Doc, got a heart?"

"My own, but no spare. We're still waiting."

"Christmas is three days away, and . . . "

"Yes?"

"I've been locked up on Life Row going on five days now. And I want to get out of here. To be with my friends and family. To sleep in my own bed. To celebrate Christmas at home. And if the heart isn't in by now, chances are it probably won't come before the 25th."

"Well, Dan . . ."

"Please, Doc."

"It is against my better judgment, but go ahead and start packing your bags."

"Serious?"

"You can go home. But I want you back at the Medical Center by noon on the 26th. There are simply too many risks with you flitting around like a butterfly. Understand?"

"God bless you, Doc!"

By 2:10 P.M., the Krainerts have now showered, packed and loaded their car. Just before leaving, they telephone their home in Napa, relaying word to Dan's grandmother, Gaya Gasper, that they are pulling out.

"Perfect!" she bubbles. "We'll be ready. Boy will we ever be ready!"

Five minutes later, their Palo Alto apartment phone rings with news that a donor heart has been located. But there is nobody to answer it. By then, Dan and his parents are merging onto northbound Highway 101 leading toward Napa. Traffic is heavy.

Dan pushes his glasses into place. "The colors," he says, watching the scenery pass by. "It's the colors I notice most. The billboards, the trees, the homes, the clouds, the hills. And the smells! Car exhaust, pollution — it's wonderful!"

His mother, unable to hear Dan above the dashboard music, clicks the radio off. "What did you say, darling?" she asks.

"Just that you forget how colorful everything is when you're locked up in a hospital room that's painted Cream of Wheat white. You honestly forget the importance of little things, of simple pleasures. You grow numb. You think that the whole world smells like Lysol, and everybody wears silly uniforms."

"What's the first thing you're going to do when you get home?" his mother asks.

"Look at my room. And then call Shirley."

"Speaking of Cream of Wheat, anybody hungry?" his father asks.

"Don't stop," says Dan. "Let's just get back to Napa. Home is where my heart's at."

Back at the Stanford Medical Center, Dr. Wallwork slams the phone down. "They've already left," he curses. He glances at the clock, his jaw twitching, and then dials the California Highway Patrol.

"You've got to find them!" he says. "If they're not back here by 4:30, the heart will go to another patient."

"We'll do our best, Sir. Can you describe their car?"

"Their car? I'm a cardiologist, not a mechanic."

"Make and model? Color? Plates?"

"Just a second," he says, covering the mouthpiece of the phone. "Anybody know the Krainert car?" he shouts across the room. "I've got the CHP on the line."

A nurse steps forward and confers with him in muffled tones.

"OK," Dr. Wallwork says, "I've got a nurse here who says it's a two-door Dodge Magnum. Forest green. That's all she knows."

The CHP dispatcher broadcasts an all-points bulletin for the vehicle, and then relays word to several other local police stations between Palo Alto and Napa.

Dr. Wallwork then phones a dozen Palo Alto restaurants and fast food eateries to check if the Krainerts have stopped for lunch. Unbeknown to Wallwork, Dan and his family are 35 minutes away by then, and crossing San Francisco Bay via the San Mateo toll bridge.

After calling all of the restaurants he can think of, he promptly dials every major radio station in the San Francisco Bay Area, asking them to interrupt programming to broadcast a special emergency bulletin for the Krainerts. "I just hope they've got their radio on," he says to anybody who will listen, staring at the clock as precious minutes tick by. He again phones the CHP.

"Every squad car in the area is looking for the vehicle," the dispatcher reports. "But no word yet."

"Call when you hear something," Wallwork snaps, rising to pace the floor. Suddenly he whips around, grabs the phone and calls Dan's home in Napa.

Inside the Krainert home, Dan's older brother George has dragged a large pine tree through the front door and placed it in a stand. His wife is vacuuming the carpets, while Dan's grandmother is racing about, dusting furniture and washing sinks.

"They'll probably be home within the hour," his grandmother says, tackling the living room window with Windex and a rag. "If we hurry, we can whip this home into shape and get it looking like it should for Christmas." She finishes cleaning the window and starts to place a yellow bow around the neck of Dan's dog, when the telephone rings.

"Let it go," she says. "We've got work to do."

The phone continues ringing, on and on, straining her patience. Finally she answers it.

"Has Dan arrived yet?" Dr. Wallwork asks brusquely.

"No, I'm sorry. Can I take a message?"

"This is John Wallwork at Stanford Medical Center. We're trying to — "

"Is something wrong?"

"Not yet, but listen. Listen carefully," the doctor says. "A donor heart for Dan has been found, and is now being flown up from San Diego. It is already past 3 o'clock, and unless he is back at Stanford by 4:30, the heart must go to another patient."

"No," Dan's grandmother says. "No, he's waited too long. You can't just give it away. That heart belongs to Dan."

"There are medical constraints we have to consider. For one, the donor heart cannot be out of the body for extended periods of time. And that's what we're dealing with here. Now, we're doing everything we can to locate them. Radio stations and restaurants have been notified, as well as the CHP and police stations between the bay and the valley. But it seems they have eluded everybody. So, if they get to the house, send them back. Right away! The cutoff time is 4:30!"

At 3:25, the Krainerts turn onto Idlewild Avenue and pull to a stop in their driveway.

"I want to just sit here for a moment and look at the house," Dan says, rolling down the window.

Suddenly the front screen flies open and his grandmother bursts through it, waving her hands. "You've got to go back!" she shouts. "They have your heart! But it will only be yours until 4:30. Another patient is on standby. Hurry! Turn around!"

Dan stares numbly out of the window. His grandmother runs up to the car, panting.

"No, wait!" she says breathlessly. "I almost forgot! The airport! Drive to the airport! We've chartered a plane to fly you back. It's all arranged. Now go! Hurry!"

Dan throws up his hands. "There goes Christmas," he mutters, slumping down into the seat. "Do me a favor, though. Call Shirley. Tell her what's going on. Have her pray."

"Yes. Now go!"

As Dan's father slams the car into reverse, a Highway Patrol car skids to a stop at the curb. "Get in with me!" he shouts. "You want a heart, I'll make sure you get a heart."

Dan and his parents jump into the backseat of the squad car, but his grandmother comes running out to the curb, again waving her hands.

"Wait! The plane only has two passenger seats!"

Dan looks at his parents. "You two go. I'll stay."

"Too late to back out now," Dan's father says, jumping out of the car. "I'll drive back across and meet you there. See who makes it to the hospital first." He slams the door and waves.

"Hang on!" the officer barks. "Unless you've driven in Tijuana or the Indy 500, you're in for the wildest ride of your lives!" He stomps the accelerator and careens around the corner. With siren wailing and lights flashing, he bursts around a line of traffic, and races toward the Napa County Airport.

His cheek bulging with a double wad of Bazooka bubble gum, pilot C.J. Bertagna moves quickly through his pre-flight checkoff, and then reaches for the mike. He is a slight man, with dark curly hair, and a two-day growth of whiskers rising from a purple birthmark on the side of his face.

Cleared for takeoff, he relaxes pressure on the wheel and leans against the throttle of the Cessna Skyhawk. He eases off the brakes, and the plane begins rolling.

"Slowly at first, but then faster and faster," C.J. says as the wheels race down the runway. His voice is smooth and warm, though his words are punctuated by his snapping gum. "And now in a moment, yes *now*! We are free at last," he says as the plane gently skips airborne.

Dan watches the ground and cars drop away, gripping the armrest tightly as the runway and roadways become ribbons in the distance below.

"This is my first time up," he volunteers.

"The first? Then I am honored to usher you skyward through the heavens and to have a small role in your adventure," he says, chomping hard on his gum as he noses the plane toward a cruising altitude of 3,000 feet.

"Just fly fast," says Dan's mother.

"Old C.J.'s going to get you to the big city on time, Ma'am. C.J. and Skyhawk are going to skin the wind. If you want fast, you've come to the right place. This proud bird is sleek and nimble and able to slice through the sky. For you and your ailing son, Skyhawk will skin the wind."

"What is the flight time?" Dan asks, slowly easing his grip and feeling his circulation restored to his knuckles.

"This is a short flight, young man, twenty-two minutes. But your concerns about time are unnecessary baggage while you ride the skies. Turn your watch around. Open your eyes. Look out the window. Enjoy the view. Don't think of what lies behind or what waits ahead. We are, for the moment, timeless as we fly with a full, fair wind at our tail. And we will arrive soon enough for your needs."

Upon landing, C.J. taxis off a branch of the runway where an ambulance is poised with its red light flashing. As the Cessna rolls to a stop, attendants quickly open the plane door, and ease Dan down onto a gurney. Dan looks back at the pilot and waves. C.J. holds his thumb high, and then blows a bubble that obscures his face in the window.

Strapped to the gurney, Dan is whisked into the waiting ambulance. His mother slides into the back seat, reaching to close the door as the vehicle guns across the airport tarmac, through the security gates and races into the street traffic with its siren screaming.

"What time is it?" Dan asks the attendant.

"Ten after four."

"Can we make it to Stanford on time?"

"This run normally takes a half hour. But we'll make it in time. Guaranteed."

"In this traffic?"

"You're probably too young to remember the movie 'French Connection, '" the attendant says. "But there was a chase scene in it. A classic heart-stopper. The guy behind the wheel here handled some of the driving stunts for that part of the flick, so believe me, he can handle this run. If you'd seen it, you'd have no doubts. We'll make it."

"And if we're wrong," the driver shouts back over his shoulder, "you can have my heart."

At 4:26, the ambulance squeals to a halt at the emergency entrance to the Stanford Medical Center. The doors fly open, and the attendants sprint Dan through the halls to the Cardiac Care Unit.

A balding, middle-aged man in a paisley-print bathrobe paces the floor nearby, his eyes glued to the clock. He looks up, startled, when Dan's gurney whips around the corner. Their eyes catch.

"You win," the man says, forcing a smile as Dan rolls by. "And I lose."

Dan twists his head around, watching the man recede behind him. "What was that all about?" he asks one of the nurses.

"He was on standby," she says. "He would have had your heart in just four minutes."

Chapter Sixteen — DAN

THE TRANSPLANT

As Dan is rolled into a side room for pre-surgery prepping, his eyes dart from face to face. Four people hover over him, helping him out of his clothes, but he cannot find the face he most wants to see.

The room is colorless, and bears a biting antiseptic smell — an odor that is too funereal for him to breathe without pondering the thought of fleeing back down the corridor, out the front doors and again filling his lungs with fresh air. But he closets the thought, realizing that hospitals, for whatever the reason, will never smell like strawberry fields, parking lots or ice cream parlors. They will never smell even as good as a city highway. And never will they approximate the friendly fragrance of home. Stanford Medical Center bears a distinctive mortuary odor, an olfactory trademark found nowhere but in other hospitals and in parlors of death.

Standing now in his shorts and socks, Dan watches the door, waiting for the familiar face that doesn't appear.

"Where is Seana?" he asks, taking a hospital gown from a nurse he has never seen before.

"We're wondering the same thing," she says.

"What do you mean? She's supposed to be here. I need her."

"She's off today."

"But she's my primary nurse," he says nervously. She *wants* to be here. Has somebody tried to call her?"

"She always leaves three numbers," the nurse says, "but she can't be reached at any of them. We've tried them all."

"She's probably out Christmas shopping," another nurse offers.

"Christmas shopping," Dan says, repeating the words softly. And then he shakes his head and begins to laugh. "No, she probably just chickened out."

The first nurse turns her back for a moment. She reaches for a Dixie cup on the counter and hands it to Dan. He takes it, eyeing the mixture inside. A pale oily film hangs on the surface, and he sniffs it warily.

Shaking his head, he hands the cup back.

"You first."

"It is mostly milk," the nurse says.

"And what else? Milk isn't greasy."

"Cyclosporin-A. It's the experimental drug Dr. Wallwork told you about — the new immunosuppressant."

"I won't swallow anything I can't spell."

"Come on, Dan, this is history in the making. You're the first person in the world to use it."

"How many chimps and dogs choked before this sucker showed up on the scene?" he asks, smiling.

"Bottom's up, Dan," she says brightly.

With one hand covering his heart, Dan holds the cup in the other and raises it high. "Well, everybody, here's to history in the making, good times and long life," he toasts. "Here's to hope and a healthy new heart. And here's to the Lord, my God, and may His will be done," he says, smiling warmly from face to face. He looks down at his feet, and then raises his head abruptly. "Oh, and here's to hair growing on my body in places where it shouldn't grow," he quickly adds, downing the liquid in a gulp.

"See? That wasn't so bad," the nurse says. Others in the room applaud.

"My heart still feels the same."

"Cyclosporin helps your *new* heart. The doctor probably already explained, but in your body you've got cells and antibodies that identify and destroy viruses and bacteria that cause disease."

"Thanks, prof. But spare me the lecture."

"No, you ought to know this."

"The doc's already been through it. It's all cops and robbers, cowboys and Indians. The antibodies and t-cells wear the white hats, and their job is to fight off the bad guys."

"Exactly."

"But the good guys can be fooled, and will also attack and reject transplanted organs like the heart because its tissue is different from my own."

"Yes, and that's where Cyclosporin-A comes in," the nurse says. "It inhibits the cells and antibodies from recognizing foreign matter."

"I know, I know. But will it turn me into a werewolf?" Dan asks.

"Hairy palms can be very sexy," she says, handing Dan another Dixie cup and pointing him to the bathroom. "One more specimen, and we'll get this show on the road."

When he returns several minutes later, he hears his name on the hospital intercom. He glances at the ceiling speaker, but one of the nurses directs his attention instead to a radio on a nearby counter.

Dan smiles, listening to the news announcer describe his dramatic race back to the Stanford Medical Center and his near miss of a new heart, noting that even as he speaks, Dan is being prepped for surgery.

"What's going on here?" Dan asks. "The guy in the box is talking about me. *Right now!* Is this room bugged or what?"

" . . . particularly his courage and faith in recent months, have greatly affected his home town of Napa and other residents throughout the entire San Francisco Bay Area," the announcer states.

"Who, me?" Dan responds.

" . . . inspiration that has brought a true sense of community to a widespread area. Residents have rallied to his aid in time of need. They have staged bottle drives, can drives, car washes and dances — with all of the proceeds going to the Dan Krainert Trust Fund. They have held benefit basketball and football games, dinners and dances. And in a period of little more than one and a half months, more than $68,000 has been raised to help pay for his operation and expenses."

"Bless them all," Dan says. "Without them, I wouldn't be here now."

" . . . one more thing that residents can do. In cooperation with other area radio and TV stations, the management of this station asks that you observe a minute of silence for Dan, beginning at 6 o'clock. For it is at about that time, according to Stanford officials, that Dan Krainert's transplant surgery will begin."

Dan glances at his watch and swallows. Fifty-five minutes and counting.

Covered on the gurney by a simple white sheet, Dan is rolled into the hallway toward the operating room. His parents, waiting nearby, rise to meet him. Nervous and scared, they both begin talking at once. Dan holds up his thin, frail hand to quiet them.

"No, don't talk," he says. "You've shown me your love for eighteen years, so there's no need to tell me about it now. Please, I just want to look at you."

"Danny, we — "

"Shhh, everything will be fine. Just fine. I have a deep silent comfort about that. God is with me."

"Yes, son," his father says, his eyes glistening, "God is with you."

His mother steps closer to the stretcher, bends down and plants a kiss on his forehead.

Dan quietly reaches out and touches her face. He lays his palm on her soft, powdered flesh, watching the fear in her dark eyes — the fear of a mother who thinks she may be seeing her son for the last time. Dan understands her fears and offers his touch to allay them. He cups the smooth curve of her cheek, plying the warm skin between his fingers and thumb, as their eyes lock.

Before, hers were the eyes that would comfort him as a child when he was in bed with the flu or some other ailment. Or, when the night was dark and the thunder crashed through the heavens, she would come to sit beside his bed, pull the covers tight over his young shoulders, and place her palm against his cheek. It was always a warm familiar touch, and with it came a healing that, while perhaps temporary, allowed him to close his eyes, forget about the storm or sickness, and drift peacefully to sleep. And then she would be at his side the next morning, again stroking his face, while her eyes offered comfort and assurance that the storm had passed in the night.

Now the roles are switched, and he comforts her the way he was taught, the only ways he knows — with his fingers and eyes. Yet he finds silence difficult at this moment. What he really wants to do is tell her that everything will be OK, that the storm will pass, that life and happiness and joyous times will be theirs again, but he cannot find the right words. And so his palm moves gently over her face, conveying what his voice cannot, and rubbing away the tears as they slip from the corner of her eyes.

Without a word, she quietly pulls back the cotton sheet covering his upper body, and lowers her head to his bare skeletal chest. She rests it against him, lightly, her hair spilling over his flesh as her ear finds the place where the thrust of his heart is the strongest.

"I can hear it," she whispers.

"It's not very strong," Dan says, feeling his heart bucking and heaving like a shipwreck. He strokes the top of her head.

"I can hear it," she says again, a smile softly grazing her face.

"Tomorrow it will be a different sound," he says. And then he lowers his hand from her head, slips it beneath the sheet and pulls out a small envelope which he passes to her.

"Should I open it now?" she asks, holding the card against her breast.

"No," he says, squeezing his mother's and father's hands one final time. "After I go."

His father brushes away a tear. "I wish I could go for you," he says, gently squeezing his shoulder.

"I know that," Dan says, smiling up at his father. "But I am not alone. God goes with me."

His father nods.

With tears streaming down her face, his mother slowly, reluctantly eases her grip. Their hands slip away until only their little fingers touch, and then they part as the orderlies roll Dan down the hall and through the double doors into the restricted operating area.

When the doors close behind him, she takes a deep breath and looks at the envelope in her hand. Her fingers shaking, she slowly opens the flap and pulls out a card. It is bare on the inside, except for a Bible verse which Dan has neatly printed:

I will give you a new heart
And put a new spirit in you;
I will remove from you your heart of stone
And give you a heart of flesh.
— Ezekiel 36:26, NIV.

At a basin outside the operating room, Dr. Wallwork and his attending surgeon, Dr. Philip Oyer, painstakingly soap their arms to the elbow, rubbing up and down, up and down in long, luxurious strokes. It is a ceremony of sanctification as they move lower, washing a finger at a time, then the thumb, front and back. With the intensity of stalking hunters, they pry beneath each nail with a pointed stick for stray bits of dirt and bacteria to identify and kill. Tossing the sticks aside, they take up bristled brushes, working the soap deep into the skin — back and forth, and then in ever-increasing circles. When they are finished, they rinse and perform the ceremony all over again.

Dr. Wallwork then nods at a masked scrub nurse standing nearby and she hands him a sterile white towel to dry his hands. He nods again and she sprays his palms with Hexachlorophene foam, which he massages deeply into his skin to disinfect what the soap didn't kill. The scrub nurse then belts him into sterile raiment, and slips a pair of throwaway latex gloves over his hands. He turns, waiting a moment for

Dr. Oyer to finish his prepping, and then together they enter the hallowed operating room.

In the center of the room, Dan lies sedated on a stainless steel table beneath four satellite-dish lights. He wears a narcotic smile as attendants insert IV lines into his neck and wrists, shave his chest and cleanse it with a rust-colored iodine liquid. Beside him, rising from the ground like bare-branched trees in October, stands a forest of IV poles. Other equipment crowds the room: cardiac monitor, heart-lung machine, respirator, ice chests, stainless steel bowls and trays of gauze, towels and glittering instruments.

When he hears Dr. Wallwork, Dan turns his head back and calls for him. The cardiologist steps to his side. Dan looks up with a sedated grin. The initial drugs are working. Dan blinks his heavy eyelids, and his smile turns down.

"Doc, this is important," he says, working to focus the familiar face. Dan's voice is slow and forced. "I have a concern. I don't want the donor to suffer."

Dr. Wallwork nods. His eyes flicker with compassion. "Dan," the doctor says calmly, "the donor is dead."

Dead. The meaning of the word slowly sinks into Dan's head. Somebody, exactly whom he does not know, has died so he could live. He knew it would be this way.

"Yes," he says. "Of course."

The anesthesiologist moves quickly behind Dan, placing a mask over his nose and mouth. "It's oxygen," he lies, placing his arm gently on Dan's arm. "Take deep breaths."

Dan closes his eyes and fills his lungs, feeling for the last time the crimson thump of his own heart. And as the light of his senses begins to fade, Dan breathes a final silent prayer.

Quickly now, Dr. Wallwork steps to Dan's right side and extends his palm. It is a cue, and a nurse quickly places a scalpel in his hand. He holds the handle lightly between his thumb and fingertips, finding the balance. And then he lowers it to Dan's chest, drawing the curved belly of the blade from his collarbone to a point several fingerbreadths above his navel.

Gently easing the long lip of the incision apart, he cauterizes each tiny red artery as if it were a river to be forded or dammed. Here and there, he touches the instrument to Dan's flesh, sending acrid puffs of smoke into the air. When he reaches the sternum, he cocks his head slightly. It is as if he stands on the edge of a forest, listening for the telltale rush of a mountain stream. And hear it he does. There is a faint, far off whisper — of blood coursing through hidden tributaries — and rising above it, there beneath the breast armor, the irregular whoosh of Dan's battered heart.

Back in the waiting room, Dan's parents stare at the walls as the clock moves in slow motion.

"I just wish I could be in there with him — to even take his place," his father says.

"Yes, I know. Dan has suffered more than either of us will ever know," says his mother, clasping his card tightly in her hand. "But he's always been such a strong boy. He'll make it."

"Do you remember back in Little League — how he used to smash homers at practically every game? The kid could really knock the stuffing out of the ball."

"I most remember the little things," she laughs, her eyes wet with tears. "The times he opened the oven door, ruining my bread, or when he'd take the top off a pot of rice. I used to get so mad — chase him out of the kitchen with a spatula! And then I'd feel guilty for hours afterward, and would go into his room and hold him and hug him. He was always so loving, so quick to forgive."

They continue talking about past family vacations, Dan's early grades, his friends, the rousing ovations he always received for his drama performances, when Dr. Wallwork suddenly steps into the room. Mrs. Krainert springs to her feet. Her face goes white.

"It's too soon," she says, drawing her hand to her mouth.

"Your son is in recovery now, doing fine," he smiles. "The operation was performed in record time. We had a perfect match with the new heart. Perfect. I couldn't have asked for a smoother operation."

"His heart? Everything is fine? Danny is in recovery?"

"Yes, your son is fine. His new heart pinked up immediately and began beating without help."

"Oh, thank-you! Thank-you, Doctor!" she says, falling into her husband's arms. Together they bounce and laugh and cry. Mr. Krainert looks at his watch, still surprised.

"How long did the transplant take, Doctor?" he asks.

"A record two hours and twenty-six minutes," he says, beaming brightly.

"We can't tell you how grateful we are to you. You've saved Danny's life. Thank-you so very, very much!"

"No, don't thank me," Dr. Wallwork says, taking their hands in his and shaking his head. "It is not I who saved your son's life. I am a surgeon — a carpenter who simply cuts and saws and patches. Surgeons are servants. I believe that, and I know my place. So please," he says, "please save your commendations for the One greater than I — the One who actually heals." With a wink and a smile, he strides back down the hallway.

Mrs. Krainert runs after him, grabbing him by the corner of his surgical greens. "Doctor, I'm sorry. But I have so many questions. I mean, what happens now?"

"Danny will stay for several weeks in North ICU — monitored, of course, around the clock. His medications, which he must take the rest of his life, have already been started. We place a lot of hope in the new drug, Cyclosporin-A. Though it will likely have strong side-effects, it should greatly improve his quality of life."

"How so?"

"Basically, his risk of infection will be less than others who, until now, have relied on painful injections of rabbit serum — ATG as it's known."

"And after ICU?"

"Once Dan is out of the forest, he'll be assigned a regular room in the ward. And, barring complications or rejection, should be feeling healthy enough to return home within a couple of months."

"*Return home*," beams Libby Krainert. "I can't tell you what that means. Those are such warm words to a parent. Such welcome words!" And then she reaches out and tightly clasps the doctor's hands. "If you're a carpenter, you're the best," she says, "the absolute best. And I want you to know that you did not go unprayed for. I prayed for your wisdom, for your skill. That God would harness your every ability during the operation. And I prayed for these hands," she says, squeezing his palms tightly "I prayed that they would be steady, that they would cut straight and true. These hands, Doctor . . . these hands have been most blessed. Most blessed, indeed."

Two days later, on December 24, Dan rests in North ICU, a bank of four rooms, backing a U-shaped corridor, which have been designed specifically to minimize exposure to germs for transplant patients. Dan's room, identical to the other three, has a positive air pressure system and a glass-walled anteroom where family members and visitors must don sterile hats, masks, gowns and shoe covers before entering his room.

Lying in bed with IVs in both arms and EKG sensors across his chest, Dan is surrounded by hundreds of Christmas and get-well cards, many from strangers. On his nightstand, an open Bible rests beside a cluster of heart medications.

Suddenly the door slides open, and Seana, dressed to the hilt in sterile greens, enters the room.

"A great costume," Dan smiles. "But it's not Halloween."

"I'm stuck with wearing it until you graduate from the unit. So hurry up and get well," she says, sitting on the corner of his bed. "Do you feel as good as you look?"

"There's plenty of pain — especially where the Doc knifed me," he says, lightly fingering his chest. But even lying here feeling awful is better than I felt before. I was just thinking about that — how for the first time in a very, very long time I can't feel my heart beating. I can't feel a thing! When my heart was failing, it beat erratically. It would jump and lurch, skip beats, and always the pain was incredible. But now that I've got a new, improved model, I can't feel a thing."

"That's a good sign," she says, handing him her stethoscope. "Here, try this."

For several minutes, Dan listens in silent awe to the steady throb of his new heart. "You know, Seana, all my life I'll wonder about whose heart I got, what my donor was like, where he lived, whether he liked sports and music, what his name was. Even dumb stuff like his favorite flavor of ice cream, whether he had a girl friend, whether he knew the Lord."

"What have the doctors told you so far?"

"Nothing, really. Just his age — 19; and weight — 180. And that he was a Marine. That's about it."

"Some of these things you will always wonder about. But thank God for him," she says, taking Dan's hands in her own. "The fact that he donated his heart should tell you some things about him: that he was generous, even in death; that he loved life — enough to enable you to continue living. Dan, they say actions speak louder than words, and that's very true. But when it comes to action, it is the level of people's giving that truly and most accurately measures their character. Some people give nothing; others, like your donor, give everything. And the world needs more people as generous and loving as him, whoever he was. Just be grateful you've received the best heart possible — the heart of a Marine."

"Is the donor's name ever released?" Dan asks.

Seana shakes her head.

"How about his family — do they know about me?"

"A donor's family usually knows as little about the recipient as the recipient knows about them. But your case is different. Everybody seems to know about you! The phone on the desk out front has been ringing off the hook. And the news bureau receives calls from the media hourly."

"I'm stumped about it."

"It's odd in a way. You are Stanford's 202nd heart transplant patient, and the media reaction with each new case now is . . . well, just a big yawn. People are used to it. The mystery and miracle are gone."

"It's old news."

"Right. Sure, there might be a paragraph in the *Metro*; maybe a feature profile in the patient's home town paper. But never anything like the hundreds of articles you've generated, plus all of the TV coverage. You're a very special person, Dan."

"All I've done is get sick and nearly die."

"There's more to it than that. You've taught people, perhaps even unknowingly, something about values — that we are here to add what we can to life, not to get what we can from it. For many people, rallying behind you was a chance to do just that."

"I don't follow."

"You were their opportunity to *participate* in life. To care and hope and pray. Don't you see, Dan? Even as you faced the possibility of death, your values didn't change. You still wanted your life to count — to be spent for something that outlasts life. You stirred people. You stirred their slumbering belief in God."

"If that's the case, then I'd gladly go through all of this over again. Seana, if one person now believes who didn't before, my suffering will have been my greatest blessing."

"If you only knew, Dan, what a privilege it is to primary for you. I consider it an honor," she says, placing her hand on his arm.

"You're not too shabby yourself," Dan says, smiling. "Some of the guys back home would die if they knew I had a nurse who looked like you."

"Hmmm!" she laughs, "Won't my husband be jealous!"

"If being married won't stand in the way, I'd like to challenge you to a video baseball game."

"I beat you last time."

"I'm feeling better."

"One game. But then you must rest. Tomorrow is Christmas."

The following morning, Christmas Day, Dan's family crowds into the anteroom outside his North ICU quarters. Each wears the required sterile outfit, and the gathering takes on the rakish looks of a masked ball.

Propped in his bed, Dan opens his Bible to the second chapter of Luke and begins to read aloud the familiar story:

> And it came to pass in those days, that there went out a decree from Caesar Augustus, that all the world should be taxed. And this taxing was first made when Cyrenius was governor of Syria. And all went to be taxed, every

one into his own city. And Joseph also went up from Galilee, out of the city of Nazareth, into Judaea, unto the city of David, which is called Bethlehem; to be taxed with Mary his espoused wife, being great with child.

And so it was, that, while they were there, the days were accomplished that she should be delivered. And she brought forth her firstborn son, and wrapped him in swaddling clothes, and laid him in a manger; because there was no room for them in the inn.

And there were in the same country shepherds abiding in the field, keeping watch over their flock by night. And, lo, the angel of the Lord came upon them, and the glory of the Lord shone round about them; and they were sore afraid.

And the angel said unto them, Fear not; for behold, I bring you good tidings of great joy, which shall be to all people. For unto you is born this day in the city of David a Saviour, which is Christ the Lord. And this shall be a sign unto you; Ye shall find the babe wrapped in swaddling clothes, lying in a manger.

And suddenly there was with the angel a multitude of the heavenly host praising God, and saying, Glory to God in the highest, and on earth peace, good will toward men (Luke 2:1-14, King James Version).

He slowly closes the Bible and looks up. Glancing around the room, he sees tears in everybody's eyes.

"I know what the tears are for," he says. "They are tears of joy. Joy to be together as a family. But there will be no crying over me today. Dry your eyes, please. This is a day meant for celebration!"

"Then celebrate we will!" his father says, turning to his wife. "Libby, I believe this box of presents is for Dan."

"Well, don't stand out there," Dan calls out. "I'm allowed two visitors at a time in this cage. So please, somebody bring the presents here!"

An hour later he is dwarfed amidst a pile of bows and paper and gifts: From Seana, a T-shirt imprinted, "I left my heart at Stanford University"; a baseball cap emblazoned, "HEART THROB" from Shirley; a basketball signed by the Stanford basketball team. There are heart-shaped suckers and balloons, ceramic figurines of rabbits and cartoon characters, each holding a heart and proclaiming their love in verse, and heart-imprinted underwear like that normally found in stores closer to Valentine's Day. From his parents he receives a video cassette recorder, to enable him to keep a broadcast diary of his ongoing TV coverage, and a large scrapbook, filled with all of the newspaper clippings written about him.

"I'm sorry," Dan says after all his gifts have been opened, "but I didn't have a chance to do any shopping! I don't have a single gift for anybody."

"*You* are our gift," his mother says, embracing him. "Just the fact that you are alive today is the biggest, best gift we could have ever hoped for."

Seana enters the room with a large stack of mail and cards. "These all arrived yesterday," she says, placing them in Dan's lap. He opens several, reading them aloud. He starts reading another, from a family in the Midwest whom he doesn't know. Suddenly his hands begin to shake. All at once his lips are stones. He can hardly move them. His voice is dry and dusty.

"What's wrong?" his mother asks.

He begins reading again:

Dear Dan,

Even though we do not know you, my husband and I feel so close to you and your family. Our only son, Lloyd Paul Chambers, was your donor.
Knowing that you have his heart has made our loss so much easier to bear.

With all of our love,

Paul and Barbara Chambers.

Slipping the card beneath his pillow, Dan fights back the tears. His mother pulls him tight to her body.

"Lloyd Paul Chambers," he says, slowly, squeezing his eyes shut. "My donor had a name. He was somebody's son. He was — "

"Now, now," his mother says, stroking his head.

"God bless you, Lloyd!" he cries into her shoulder. "God bless you."

Two weeks later when Seana wheels Dan out of North ICU and into a room in the regular Cardiac Care Unit, Shirley is waiting by the window. The sun glints off her dark chestnut hair, and Dan can't remember when she looked prettier.

"How did you — " he begins, but suddenly the bathroom door bursts open. There is a flash of orange.

"Everybody on the floor and nobody will get hurt!" barks a male voice, pointing a plunger at Seana's head. Somebody pins her arms behind her back.

Dan jumps out of the wheelchair as toilet paper rolls are lobbed at him.

"Kabloom! You're all dead!" the voice snaps.

Dan stumbles toward the chair by the window, laughing. Shirley rises to meet him.

"I would have come alone," she whispers in his ear, "but they were my ride."

"Doesn't matter," he says, giving her a warm embrace. "It seems like years since I've seen you. Talking on the phone is not the same as having you here."

And then he turns back to the orange-clad invaders. "Charlie! Nicole! Everybody! Thanks for coming. But how'd you all fit into one car?"

"We didn't," Charlie says. "We hijacked a bus."

Nicole produces a camera and asks Dan to raise his shirt.

"Smile," she says, snapping a picture. "Ooohh, what a chest! What a scar!"

"What's with the basketball?" Charlie asks, picking it off the floor and hooking a shot toward the trashcan.

"A gift from the Stanford team," Dan says. He suddenly notices that Seana is still pinned in the corner.

"Dan, can you do something about this?" she gasps.

"Hush, Nursey," commands the Jolly Oranger who holds her. "This hospital will be blown into orbit unless our demands are met!"

"How did you all get in here?" she asks, trying to twist free.

"Our demands, Nursey!"

"What demands?"

"That Dan be given a waterbed . . . decent food . . . and a room with a view."

"Dan!" Seana pleads. "Please do something. Now. Please."

Suddenly she wriggles free. "Forget it," her captor says, pulling his ski mask off his head. "Don't let it fool you, man. Being a terrorist is tough work. You get hot. And hungry. By the way, Nursey, where's the cafeteria?"

Seana stands with her back pressed against the wall and points out the door. "That way," she says. "Down. Bottom floor. Please go before Dan dies or I get fired."

Charlie, Nicole and the others file out. Seana waits until their footsteps have receded, and then turns to Dan. "Such nice friends," she says. "Are they on drugs, or what?"

"No, just crazy," Dan laughs, picking up the trashcan. He tosses the ball on the empty bed, and extends his hand for Shirley. "Come on. I'll show you around."

They retreat alone to the solarium, overlooking the Stanford campus and rolling hills beyond Palo Alto. The earth is lush and green. Giant, billowy clouds spill across the sky. Dan fills his lungs and closes his eyes. When he opens them, he fixes his gaze on Shirley.

"You look fantastic," he says.

"You do, too," she whispers, her eyes suddenly misty.

"Come on! What are you crying about?" Dan places his arm around her, drawing her to himself.

"I don't know," she says as tears spill down her cheeks. "I was so afraid for you, Dan. And it's hard to believe that I'm here. That you're here. That we're both here together. I prayed for you every day — every single day for months. And

I always tried to keep you going. Always being a spiritual cheerleader. I tried to be so strong! But deep down I had this fear," she says, crying harder. "This fear that you would die. That I'd said my final goodbye on the telephone and would never see you again."

"Shirley, those feelings are entirely natural. But don't cry now. Not now! I made it! And I've already gained ten pounds back!"

"You don't understand," she weeps. "Having lost my father, my stepfather and my brother, I couldn't bear to lose anybody else close. Dan, you can't imagine what that would have done to me!"

"Is that why you always pushed for us just to be friends?"

"I don't know anymore. I really don't know."

"Well?"

"Well what?" she asks, looking up into his eyes.

"I was just going to ask — "

"If I'd go with you?"

He nods.

She looks at him warmly. "My plans are . . . well, something I haven't talked much about, but I want to go to the mission field someday. Europe maybe. And as for us, the future, I — "

"No problem. We'll get married first and go together."

"Dan, you're dreaming."

"About you." He begins again, "Honestly, Shirley, would you — "

"Oh, Dan," she says, breaking into a new round of sobs, punctuated with laughter, "Don't ask. You can see I'm a basket case. Please don't talk. Just hold me."

"Yes," he says, embracing her and feeling her warmth merge with his own. "Yes, yes."

THE HOMECOMING

Released from the hospital on February 12, 1981, Dan arrives home to find the bushes, trees, telephone poles, car antennas and mailboxes up and down his street clad with thousands of yellow ribbons. The press, with minicams rolling and strobes popping, record his arrival home as he is engulfed by a swarm of relatives, neighbors and friends. His little dog, wearing a yellow bow around its neck, springs into his arms. Dan shakes hands with the crowd of well-wishers, thanks the community via the reporters for its faithful support, and then excuses himself.

"I want to go inside and look at my bedroom," he says simply. "It has been such a long, long time . . . ."

The following week, Dan is invited back to Vintage High School for a special homecoming rally. The entire student body crowds the gymnasium bleachers, with Shirley and members of the Jolly Orange Company sitting in the front row nearest the podium. As the pep band winds down and the cheerleaders pause, the school principal steps to the mike.

"No introduction needs to be given," he booms. "You all know why we are here — to welcome back to Vintage High

one of our own, a very courageous young man . . . DAN
KRAINERT!"

Pandemonium erupts as Dan rises and in a firm steady
gait crosses the gymnasium floor to the podium. Scanning the
mass of chanting, cheering, weeping friends, Dan lifts his
hands for silence. A hush falls over the students as he begins
to speak.

"The last time I stood at this podium, I weighed 117
pounds," he says, clearing his throat. "I was sick, inoperable
and dying. I had a terrible heart disease, end-stage cardiomyopathy. My doctor gave me a year to live.

"I needed a heart transplant then, but I wasn't sure I was
going to get one. I hadn't been accepted by Stanford as a
recipient. As you know, I was eventually accepted. And on
December 22, 1980, I received the best Christmas gift ever — a
new heart. What you may not know is that it's the heart of a
Marine, the heart of Lloyd Paul Chambers. We never knew
each other, but now we are linked together — forever. That's
because he took a moment one day to fill out a small donor
sticker and attach it to his driver's license. He didn't know he
was going to die on December 22. Yet because of that simple
sticker and his gift of life, I now feel better than I have at
any time in the past year."

Dan smiles, feeling the exuberance deep inside. He adjusts
his glasses. "Today I stand before you weighing in at 163
pounds. I am physically active and able to do most anything
I could do before I became ill. And I acknowledge before you
today that every pound I've gained and every breath I take is
by the grace of God.

"As you know, this community raised a large sum of
money to help my family financially. It all started with you,
and I thank God for your love and support. You, my fellow
students, did what many people thought was impossible. I
remember when the Irwin Memorial bloodmobile was here,
parked just outside these gymnasium doors. Many of you stood
in line for three hours in the hot sun, just to ensure I got the
blood I needed. It was you — you at Vintage High who ignited
the spirit of giving and love in this community and surrounding

areas that raised enough money to pay what it took to keep me alive. And believe me, it was some bill! I believe it was Dante who said, 'From a little spark may burst a mighty flame.' You, my friends, were that very spark. And I believe God will bless you for what you have done."

Dan leans forward and gazes intently at the student body. "Finally, I would like to say that there would be no Dan Krainert today were it not for Jesus Christ." Dan's voice is even, well-modulated. No part in a school play ever stirred him more than this moment of just being himself. "It's because of Christ . . . and for Him that I now live and can stand here to say just how very much I love you all. If I could give back to you a gift for what you've done for me, I'd give you the grace, joy, peace and fulfillment that I've found in Jesus Christ. You see, my new heart is still mortal. And like Lloyd Paul Chambers, I too will someday die. It's not something you think too much about in high school, but maybe you've thought a little bit more about your own mortality because of what I've been through. Yes, someday we all will die. Yet because of Jesus, we may experience eternal life. That is the gift I would give you, but it's one which you must personally receive. The gift, you see, is not really from me. It's from God.

"Standing here now, I can't begin to tell you how good it feels to be alive. I will never forget what you've done. Again, from the depths of my brand new heart, I thank you so very, very much! And an especially big thanks to Shirley Simpson, who taught me what a gift of life really means.

"And now, if you don't mind, I will quietly slip away and out the door," Dan says. "I'd like to hang around, because my heart is full of gratitude. But in a moment my eyes will be, too. And I know that watching somebody cry in public is a rather dreadful experience. So, goodbye, my friends. May God bless you all, each and every one of you."

The students spring to their feet, thundering with applause as the band explodes with "For He's a Jolly Good Fellow." Wiping away tears, Dan moves quickly from the podium to the doorway, where he turns to offer a final wave.

Suddenly Shirley — the girl with almond eyes and the 100-watt dimple — is running toward him. The gymnasium roars louder, but he is deaf. He watches her as if in slow motion. Her tawny hair flying, her smile shining, closer and closer. And then in a moment she is in his arms; their embrace silhouetted in the doorway as the band plays on.

EPILOGUE

Dan currently lives in Napa, where he attends college and maintains an active speaking schedule. He remains close friends with Shirley, and plans to become a minister. To contact him, please write:

Dan Krainert
3566 Idlewild Avenue
Napa, CA 94558